THEY CAN

Elliot Vaughn: The billionaire businessman isn't used to failure—and K2 has already beaten him once. This time he plans to be the conqueror, no matter what the cost.

Annie Garrett: She wants to be the climber her father envisioned. On the mountain she can touch his soul.

Tom McLaren: He's leading Vaughn's expedition, but is he really in charge when the tough decisions have to be made?

Peter Garrett: A devastating tragedy made him give up climbing. Now he must lead a treacherous and extraordinary rescue effort to save the only person he loves.

Monique Aubertine: She wants to get away from K2 and her old boyfriend. The rescue mission may be her last climb.

Montgomery Wick: The mountain took what he loved most. Now it's time to settle scores.

VERTICAL LIMIT

At earth's extreme edge, where every breath is a frozen gasp for air and each step takes a lifetime of effort, it's a million miles to redemption

VERTICAL LIMIT

A Novelization by Mel Odom

Story by Robert King • Screenplay by Robert King and Terry Hayes

POCKET BOOKS
New York   London   Toronto   Sydney   Singapore

This book is a work of fiction. Names, characters, places and incidents are products of the author's imagination or are used fictitiously. Any resemblance to actual events or locales or persons, living or dead, is entirely coincidental.

An *Original* Publication of POCKET BOOKS

POCKET BOOKS, a division of Simon & Schuster, Inc.
1230 Avenue of the Americas, New York, NY 10020

Copyright © 2000 by Columbia Pictures Industries, Inc. All Rights Reserved.

ISBN: 0-7434-1874-3

First Pocket Books printing December 2000

10 9 8 7 6 5 4 3 2 1

POCKET and colophon are registered trademarks of Simon & Schuster, Inc.

Printed in the U.S.A.

Prologue

Annie Garrett clung to the mountain's sheer rock face hundreds of feet above the desert floor. Other mountains shot straight up around her, all mesas without shoulders and no foothills to speak of.

Perspiration covered her and soaked the short-sleeved shirt and shorts she wore under the rock-climbing seat harness. But the breeze, even over her drenched body, provided only a little relief from the molten heat of the sun hanging high in the clear blue sky. In the distance, where the red desert terrain rolled up to meet the sky, the clash of colors turned the horizon light purple. The world seemed to go on forever in that direction.

But for Annie, the world ended only a couple hundred more feet straight up. Castle Mesa tabled there, becoming a flat spot she wanted to stand on in victory with her brother and father. Of course, that victory would be short-lived. They all were. Her father would quickly turn his attention toward finding the next mountain, the next climb, and the Garrett family would be off again.

A smile touched Annie's lips at the thought of that victory, though. Climbing felt good. It challenged everything

1

inside her, and she'd met that challenge successfully each and every time.

She was pretty, and she knew it. Even at twenty-one, she was all about confidence. Her father had trained her to be that way. Strenuous hours of rock climbing, which her father insisted on calling "fun, family outings," had served to keep her lean and muscular, but there was no hiding the very feminine curves. She was tanned and fit. She kept her dark hair bound up under the protective helmet she wore. Even though the helmet was hot, there was no way she'd climb without one. At least the "brain bucket" lectures from her father were over.

Movement caught Annie's attention. She turned right to spot the distinctively marked white-and-brown American bald eagle riding thermals. The bird's wingspan was at least six feet. It pulled its wings in briefly and changed direction, coasting closer to the sheer mountain face where the three Garrett family members made their way slowly and carefully to the top.

Even at a distance, Annie could clearly see the eagle's cruelly curved beak and fierce claws. For a moment she felt as if she were eye to eye with the predatory bird.

Freedom, Annie thought, smiling at the eagle. *You always feel it when you're this high up, don't you?*

The eagle banked, catching another thermal, and drifted, yet stayed close. Freedom to the bird meant never having to cling to a rock face.

Showoff, Annie thought. She reached down and took another cam from her belt. At her father's insistence, she carried all eight sizes, and plenty of them. Besides the cams, she also carried an extra fifty-meter coil of kernmantle dynamic rope, extra carabiners—locking and nonlocking—nylon slings and runners to use with her personal belay, and a chalk bag filled with magnesium carbonate to keep her hands dry to improve her grip on rock surfaces.

Annie examined the crack in front of her, searching for another place to position the cam. The spring-loaded de-

2

vice sported a thick center stem flanked by two much smaller rods. The four round gear teeth at the business end of the device sprang out strongly when she tripped it, flaring to maximum flex.

Annie tripped the cam to close it, then rammed it home inside the crack in the mountain. The cam expanded at her touch, locking deep within the wall as the gear teeth smashed tight against the stone.

Then she heard a camera shutter buzzing rapidly above her. She grinned, feeling certain she knew what prompted it. No matter what climb they'd gone on in recent years, no matter how much energy the extra weight of the photography gear drained from him during a climb, Peter, her brother, always took a camera with him.

The shots Peter had gotten over the years had been spectacular. Their father had seen to it that they climbed mountains all around the world. Until lately Peter's pictures had been for them alone, put in scrapbooks they kept at home. Now, however, Peter was selling a few of those pictures to magazines and websites specializing in climbing stories. If the pictures from the Castle climb in Monument Valley turned out well, an editor from *National Geographic* had agreed to purchase some of them.

Annie gazed up at her older brother, watching quietly, admiring his focused intensity.

Peter was twenty-three, with medium brown hair, and stood a little over six feet tall. He was broad-shouldered and rangy, the perfect build for a rock rat climbing in his father's shoes.

Leaning into the harness that held him, trusting the small ledge of rock below his feet, he tracked the eagle with the camera lens, snapping off frame after frame in quick succession. Despite the bloody bandages that covered his fingers from cheese grater slides that had scraped hide from his knees and face as well, he operated the camera smoothly.

Annie lifted her voice and sang a few lines of a golden

3

oldie, challenging Peter to identify it. Her voice was good, strong, and it echoed along the rock face.

" 'Take It to the Limit,' " Peter stated quickly.

"Artist and year?" Annie challenged.

Peter grinned and glanced down at her, snapping off a quick picture of her. She was certain it wouldn't be a flattering shot. "Nineteen seventy-five," Peter answered. "The Eagles, of course." He gazed after the big bird. "Very funny."

Annie thought it was. And a little levity was what the game was all about. When they were both much younger, only a short time after their mother had decided to leave the family, their dad hadn't understood the sibling gameplay. He'd thought they weren't listening. In reality, the game helped them to relax a little so they could concentrate fully on what he was teaching them. Now it was just part of the expected experience, a touchstone they shared.

Above them, their father continued to climb, setting the course they would follow. He sought out handholds and footholds with confidence and an experienced eye. Royce Garrett was a little shorter than Peter, but his body was limber and stout from all the years of climbing.

Annie loved her father with all her heart. After their mother deserted them, her father had become everything to her. And to Peter, she acknowledged.

At the time, she hadn't realized how hard the desertion had been on her father because he was always so together, so calm in the face of anything that went wrong. He loved Peter and her fiercely, she knew, and had brought them into the world of climbing as a means of totally sharing himself and everything he loved.

Peter put away the camera in its special protective case inside his haul bag. He dipped his hands in his chalkbag and covered them in the white powder, drying off any sweat to add an extra layer of friction to his grip. Friction translated immediately into traction, which was a very important component in the constant war against gravity during a climb.

Peter gazed at the overhang above him, then extended

4

his arms, testing his reach. When he gripped the ledge easily, he still waited, turning to Annie and raising his own voice in song, flashing her a taunting smile.

His voice is terrible, Annie thought, grimacing at her brother. "That's not a song—no way that's a song. You're making it up," she protested. Making up songs wasn't allowed in the game.

Lights glinted in Peter's pale blue eyes. Amusement looked good on him. All of Annie's girlfriends had commented on his eyes. He hooked his halter higher up on the climbing rope and prepared to go up the overhang.

"No, no," Peter assured her as he locked his fingers onto the purchase he'd found, "it's definitely a song." He grinned again, knowing something she didn't know, and knowing *that* was going to bother her more than anything else did. "A good song. A *winning* song by the sound of it."

Now he's going mysterious on me. I hate when he does that. Annie smiled stubbornly, enjoying the challenge but irritated all the same. She detested those times when Peter caught her flat-footed.

She stood on the narrow ledge she'd found, her toes locked into position. She was working the belay end of the climb, knowing that her family's safety depended on her. If the climb went wrong, she was the safety valve. "Belay on!" she called, letting Peter know she had the anchor in place. The three cams she had locked down would handle all the emergency weight they'd need.

Almost nonchalantly, Peter pulled himself up the overhang, feet hanging well out over the long drop.

Gazing up past her brother, Annie searched the mountain face for her father, spotting him twenty feet above Peter. Her father scanned the cliff face ahead of them, and the sheer vertical expanse seemed both daunting and exhilarating to Annie. But her father was totally immersed in the mechanics of the climb. He shifted his backpack, resettling the weight distribution. He carried the bulk of their gear as he always had.

Pausing as he easily pulled himself over the ledge, Peter glanced at Annie. "Give up?"

Annie stubbornly didn't let him see her frustration.

Then her father's booming voice came from above. "'MacArthur Park.' Richard Harris. Nineteen sixty-eight."

"Nineteen sixty-eight?" Annie exploded mockingly, laughing because it was one of the few times her father had joined in the game with them. It proved he was having a good day. "You'd have to be a geriatric." She pitched her voice a little lower, knowing full well her father could hear her but wanting him to think she'd spoken only to Peter. "I didn't even know they had recorded music back then."

Royce gave her a heavy sigh, and Annie knew he'd caught on to her ruse. "I heard that! The man was a genius. Way ahead of his time. I've got a signed album."

Annie exchanged knowing grins with Peter and wisely refrained from saying anything further.

"Peter," their father called down, "check your sister's belay." He couldn't see the setup she'd rigged from where he stood.

Sighing, Annie shook her head and swapped looks with Peter.

"You want to tell him we're not fifteen anymore?" Peter asked.

"Why bother?" Annie asked, meaning it. "We'll always be fifteen."

Peter glanced at the three cams thrust into cracks in the wall. He laughed quietly, then spoke. "She needs a second cam, Dad—it won't hold in a fall."

Shaking her head, Annie leaned back against the wall, preparing for the inevitable lecture.

"I don't care how experienced you are, Annie," Royce called down sternly, "a smart climber always wears a belt *and* suspenders."

"Dad," Annie protested, glaring at her brother.

Peter laughed softly and pulled himself up the overhang. "See ya."

6

"Listen to me, Annie," her father continued, really on a roll now. "Two cams are safe. Three's even better."

He had always been the consummate father and teacher, Annie knew, which had worked out well because he was also the consummate stickler for detail. "Dad—"

Peter was getting a great chuckle out of the whole situation. He kept his back to her, though, knowing better than to look at her while the lecture was going on. They'd both end up laughing, and then they'd *both* end up getting lectured about safety.

"Nobody's going anywhere," her father stated with an air of finality, "until—"

"Dad!" Annie shouted up. "I've got *three* cams! He's winding you up again."

Her father quieted at once. He didn't enjoy the little digs his children took at each other nearly as much as they did.

Annie continued feeding out rope as her father and Peter climbed steadily higher. Without warning, a dusting of scree—the loose rocks and stones that covered slopes beneath cliffs—peppered Annie's face and rattled off her helmet, falling from somewhere above. Anger and fear warred instantly within her. Falling scree was an accepted by-product of climbing, but it was also an indicator of trouble.

Once the worst of the scree had washed over her, she glanced up, searching for the cause. Peter and her father had taken cover as well, hugging the cliff face.

Another forty feet above her father, two young men climbed recklessly in tandem, coming around the side of the mountain, obviously seeking a new path to the top. Each of them would advance a few feet, digging wildly at the unforgiving stone with fingers, knees, elbows, and toes, then lock in and belay the other to attack the climb in the same savage fashion. A thirty-foot length of rope connected them.

They're out for the adrenaline rush, Annie realized. During the time she'd spent climbing, she'd come into contact with all kinds of climbers. Most of them climbed for the

7

sheer joy of the experience, for knowing they were skilled enough and clever enough to challenge the mountain and win. Then there were the rock cowboys, guys that took their lives in their hands on every climb just for the thrill of it, always pushing their limits, their equipment's limits, and the thin envelope of safety that only got thinner with every vertical foot.

The two climbers wore grunge clothing that had seen better days. Their arms and legs worked madly, expending energy in frantic bursts instead of conserving it in case things turned ugly. One of them carried a red bag across his back.

"Amateurs—twelve o'clock!" Peter warned. "Check your safety lines—Annie, Dad!"

Annie clung to the rock face, pressing against it for protection, but she heard her father's climbing whistle bleat shrilly. It was designed to warn climbers that other climbers were in the area. She glanced up cautiously, hoping the two rock cowboys had heard it.

The two radical climbers held onto the rock above, positioned on either side of the three Garretts, the rope tether between them bowing slightly as it went slack. Then one of the climbers moved again, obviously not happy about where his ascent had led him.

Oh my God, Annie thought as a chill of understanding filled her. *They haven't even planned this climb.*

The climber released his hold in a wild man maneuver and swung across the cliff face, depending on his buddy to anchor him. He scrambled into position at the swing's deadpoint, just before the fall back down started. His fingers slipped, and his body jerked as he fought to stay locked.

Even belaying each other, Annie knew the two climbers were just one short piece of rope away from going free solo. Free solo was a climber's term and had only one translation for the layman: you fall, you die. Only amateurs and cowboys did something like that—or someone in truly dire straits.

As the guy struggled to find a secure position on the rock and battled gravity, the red bag on his back tumbled free and dropped.

"Rock!" Peter called out in warning, pulling into the cliff face.

Annie also jammed in tight against the stone as the rolled-up sleeping bag whizzed by. Her heart hammered ninety-to-nothing inside her chest. Harsh edges bit into her fingers as she gripped the stone tightly. The rock surface scratched at her cheek.

Then a scream of fear and disbelief filled the air above her.

Glancing up, Annie watched as the struggling climber lost his grip and plummeted. The tether line brought him around in an arc, swinging him again to the other side so that the two young climbers higher up framed the Garretts. For a moment it looked as if the guy's buddy would be able to hold them. Then that belay broke free as well.

In the next heartbeat, the two climbers were in freefall, plummeting down the cliff face, the tether rope between them rubberbanding them, drawing them toward each other. They screamed, clawing the air, reaching desperately back for the rock face. But their hands found only empty air.

Annie stood in frozen disbelief, watching in helpless horror. She'd known people who had died from falls, but she'd never watched someone fall to his or her death. She silently prayed for some kind of miracle, anything that would halt that long plummet. Only death waited below for the two climbers unless a miracle occurred.

Then the whipping loop in the rope between the two climbers caught the back of her father's pack. He'd tucked himself in against the cliff face, but the pack stuck out just a few inches. The rope clung to the pack, yanking on it, yanking her father from the cliff.

He didn't have his anchor set! Annie realized. She wanted to scream, but there wasn't time because her father was falling past her, almost close enough to reach out and

9

touch. Annie grabbed for him, but by then he was already gone, the tether rope paying out behind him. Seeing the rope tighten, tears slightly blurring her vision, she suddenly knew that more than her father's life was at risk. She glanced upward, spotting Peter just as the line went taut.

Fear filled Peter's features, too; then he was yanked free of the cliff face, dragged into freefall as well.

Annie screamed, but she reacted the way she'd been trained, holding fast to the belay rope and locking it into the three cams. The cams were positioned a few feet apart, partly by design, but partly because that was where the cracks were.

The belay rigging has to hold! Annie screamed inside her own mind. *It has to hold! I won't let them fall! I won't allow—* Then she was yanked from her position as well. The rock scraped her fingers, and one of her trimmed nails ripped loose as she fought to maintain her grip. She fell.

The kernmantle climbing rope stretched as it took all their weight. It brought Annie to a halt, pulling at the seat harness wrapped around her waist and thighs. Constructed around a braided core, the kernmantle rope had a supple nylon sheath allowing it to snap taut and designed to stretch and relieve stress on safety systems during an emergency.

Incredibly, Annie and Peter and their dad and the two climbers stopped falling. In dazed disbelief, Annie hung from the rope, her feet out over open space. Her fingers still touched the rock, curled over a ledge she'd somehow instinctively found.

The wind whistled around her, but she could still hear her own frightened breathing and the breathing of the people below her. Heart beating frantically, she slowly craned her head downward and looked. *Don't give up on a situation,* her father had always told her. *As long as you're alive, there's always a way out.*

Peter hung twenty feet below her, looking back up at her. Their father hung another twenty feet down, his face wracked by pain. The tether, still holding the two young

10

climbers who had fallen from above, hung from her father's pack, making the shoulder straps cut into his flesh. Both of the rock cowboys hung from the tether like pendulum weights, and her father was taking all the strain. The two climbers weren't moving; it was impossible to tell if they were alive or dead.

Annie wanted to move, but everything in her screamed a warning not to. The fear yammering maniacally in the back of her head assured her that the slightest move would lead to the long fall. And if they fell, death would take them all.

A shrill, grating squeak sounded above. Then the line dropped a few inches.

Clinging tightly, Annie forced herself to breathe and hold onto the ledge. She glanced up at the three cams she'd placed so carefully. *They weren't set for this,* she told herself. *Nothing could have been set for this.*

They were lucky, she realized, that they weren't dead already.

Suddenly, the first cam shifted again, sliding free of the crack. The motion was called *skating*. The cam skated again, almost out of the crack now.

Annie yelled down to her father. "There's too much weight!"

Her dad looked up. She met his eyes briefly, then the grating scream of metal against rock sounded even louder. In the next instant, the first cam popped completely out of the crack and all five of them dropped another four feet. Annie couldn't maintain her grip on the small ledge. She watched helplessly as she fell below the ledge, out of reach now. She dangled free from the other two cams that had somehow managed to hold.

Annie screamed, unable to hold it back.

"Anchor, Annie!" Peter yelled up at her desperately. "Another anchor! The cam—"

For a moment everything got confused, both of them trying to talk at the same time. Then her father's stern, calm voice cut through, bringing them both to attention.

"Hold it together, you two!" her father demanded. "We're getting out of this!"

Annie calmed slightly. Over the years, her father had gotten them all out of dangerous situations. There had never been a situation like this, but if anyone could get out of it, she trusted her father to be the one. Shaking but able to stop the screaming, she looked at her father.

One of the young climbers shifted slowly at the end of the tether looped over her father's pack. He shook his head, then froze, suddenly aware of where he was. He started yelling and scrambling, pulling desperately at the rope hanging from the pack in an effort to climb up.

Another grating screech yanked Annie's attention upward. She watched as the second cam started to skate.

"No!" her father commanded below, yelling at the guy trying to climb up the rope. "Don't move. Stop!"

Frustrated and scared, Annie watched helplessly. Pain wracked her father's face as the straps cut into his shoulders.

The climber continued trying to grab hold of the line to pull himself up. All thought of an adrenaline rush was over, leaving only panic behind.

Annie listened to her father scream in pain as the backpack straps tore at his shoulders more deeply. Then the nylon bag ripped and the rope slid down, perilously close to the pack's edge.

"Stop!" her father commanded.

Scree from the second cam's skating rained down over Annie. Sucking air, unable to catch her breath, she screamed silently as she saw the cam shifting treacherously in the crack. *It's not going to stay! It can't hold us!*

"Dad!" she yelled down.

He gave her a short nod as he fisted the rope above his head. He pulled, trying to take the strain from the line so he could allow for the jerking motion created by the desperate climber flailing at the tether.

Then the rope slid completely free of her father's nylon backpack. The two climbers fell, only one of them screaming as he streaked toward the ground. Both of them slammed against the hard, sun-baked red earth far below. Neither of them moved again, their bodies twisted and bent, limbs broken and turned in unnatural directions.

Sickness roiled in Annie's stomach, painting the back of her throat sour with bile. Before she had a chance to be sick, though, the second cam popped free of the crack, dropping them another few feet.

All of them screamed. Even her father.

Peter yelled at her, clinging desperately to the rope, too far away from the mountain to do anything. "Anchor us back in! Use your cams!" His blue eyes focused on her. "Try it, Annie."

Controlling her fear as best as she could, Annie glanced down at her tool belt and selected one of the medium cams. She tried to hold it steady as she leaned out from the rope, but the geared head shook dramatically. Even when she leaned out as far as she could, she wasn't able to reach the cliff face. Before she could stop herself, she glanced down, seeing the ground and the broken bodies below. *We aren't going to make it! That's too far!* Unshed tears burned her eyes, but she refused to let them fall.

The last cam slipped again, screeching.

"Annie!" her father called up.

She glanced down at him.

"The *other* one," her father said, and she knew he didn't want to call it the *last* one, "the cam! Is it skating?"

Annie peered up but couldn't see over the ledge. *Is it better to know or not know?* She shifted on the rope. "I don't know—I can't see!"

Her father's face worked, and she knew that even for him keeping calm at this time was almost impossible. Annie couldn't bear to watch him hanging there so helpless.

She turned back to the wall, so close but still just out of reach. She swung toward the cliff again, thinking somehow her desperation and the unfairness of the whole situation would allow her to succeed. *This isn't right,* she told

13

herself frantically. *We've always been careful climbers. Dad has seen to that. This isn't our fault! We're not supposed to die for someone else's mistake!* She pushed the cam toward the cliff face but somehow still kept missing it.

"Peter."

Annie glanced down at her father and brother, hearing a tone in her father's voice that she'd never before heard. She waited desperately, terrified, hoping their father had come up with a plan based on something he'd done or something someone had told him. He was good at that.

"There's a knife in the top of my pack," her father stated calmly. His words carried easily in the thin air. "Can you reach it?"

"What?" Peter asked.

Her father's voice hardened, as resolute as the mesas jutting up from the desert floor around them. "Just get it!"

Twisting his body, Peter turned upside down and hung from the line. He released the D-ring carabiner that held him latched in place on the rope, but kept his harness secure. He crept down the line by inches, trying his best not to put any undue stress on the last cam. He stopped when his fingers reached the top of their father's pack.

Annie waited in frustrated helplessness. Gravity pulled at her eagerly, but maybe that was just her imagination, triggered by knowing there was nothing under her to stop the long fall. A sudden rush of small rock rained down on her helmet and shoulders. Dust collected on her perspiration-dampened skin.

The cam slipped just a fraction of an inch, putting slack in the rope for just an instant.

"It's skating!" Annie called, even though she knew her brother and father were well aware of it.

The movement stopped, turning into just a nerve-rattling tremor that passed. Annie looked up but still couldn't see the cam. *Maybe it will hold this time. It has to hold!*

Below, Peter ripped open the Velcro closure on their father's pack. He pulled out the thick utility knife. Annie had no clue what her father intended to do with it. She watched, almost hypnotized by the distant ground revolving slowly beneath them.

Then her father gazed at Peter, and Annie could see the love and fear in his eyes. "We don't have much time, Peter," her father said gently. His voice sounded distant and hoarse. "You have to do something for me."

Annie watched, guessing what her father was thinking.

Peter gazed at their father helplessly, shaking his head, not understanding at all or rejecting what he guessed his father would ask.

"Cut me loose," Annie heard her father say.

Peter hung there, not moving, his hand suddenly trembling.

"No!" Annie shouted hoarsely, the sound ripping through her throat.

Her father ignored her, concentrating on Peter. "There's still too much weight," her father said calmly. "One cam will never hold us!"

Peter's voice came out then, dry and strangled. "No, Dad!"

Her father kept his voice level and calm but put authority in his words. "I'll pull you both down!"

Annie protested, looking at the fear and guilt filling her brother. *Oh, God! How could Dad even ask something like that?* "He can't! He—"

"Shut up, Annie!" Her father's voice cracked like thunder. He kept his attention riveted on his son. "Think, Peter. One dead, or three?"

Trapped and scared, seeking some kind of salvation, Peter looked up at the last cam. Tears made the blue of his eyes more vibrant.

Annie felt another wave of scree trickle over her. She kept focused on her brother, willing him to focus on her. "Don't listen to him, Peter!"

Peter hesitated, torn, tears tracking the dust on his face and turning it to mud. The knife was open in his hand, a thin edge that balanced life and death.

15

"You're killing your sister," his father shouted up at him. "She'll die if you don't. Now cut it!"

Peter broke eye contact with Annie and glanced at their father. He held the knife tightly in one shaking fist.

"No!" Annie screamed.

"Yes!" her father ordered.

Peter looked up. Maybe he was looking toward the heavens, Annie thought, hoping for some kind of divine intervention or an answer there. But his eyes, Annie knew, were focused on the skating cam.

"Do it," their father ordered. "Quick! Now! Now!"

"No!" Annie pleaded. "No!"

Peter wavered, tears in his eyes, scared and confused. Annie saw the boy in him as well as the man, and both of them were suffering. She kept screaming, her voice warring with her father's. She'd never argued so vehemently with her father in all her life, but she'd never thought she'd have to argue with him for his life.

A new onslaught of dust and debris rained down across Annie's head and shoulders, trickling down her collar and turning her back gritty.

Then the knife in Peter's hand flashed as it caught the light.

In the next instant, Annie watched her father fall, growing smaller and smaller as he plummeted toward the ground. *No, no, nooooooo!*

The hard red earth took her father into its stony, bone-breaking embrace. His body lay still under the pall of dust that gusted up, and the nearby flowers waved in the slight breeze that sighed over the land.

Annie cried, gut-wrenching sobs that left her weak and empty. But the last cam held. Even though it held, she knew it hadn't really saved them. Nothing would ever be the same again.

16

Chapter 1

Foothills of the Himalayas, Pakistan, 14,500 feet
Three Years Later

Peter Garrett remained stationary inside the blind, staring at his subject on the mountainside through the zoom lens of the camera mounted on the tripod. He kept the cross hairs centered but moved through the zoom magnification at the touch of a button. He took a few shots of the whole meadow and the high mountains beyond, then closed in till only the brown hare filled the lens.

The hare sat beside a clump of vegetation, cautiously eating tender shoots of grass. Its ears twitched nervously, searching for any sound of warning.

The hare didn't hear the snow leopard padding cautiously and patiently through the grass behind it. The big cat crept along, flowing like a river of muscle and reflex. She was long and lean, a study in grace and economy as she moved. Her gold, white, and black pelt had shed its winter coat and now looked sleek and shiny. The pictures, Peter knew, were going to be great, just one step short of savage.

The leopard stayed low to the ground as she moved. Peter shot carefully, bringing the focus in tighter as predator closed on prey.

Then the big cat settled down on her haunches, ears flattened back on her massive head. Her tail stiffened, then

17

twitched once, twice, and she sprang between heartbeats.

Peter captured frame after frame as the auto-advance whirred to keep up with him. Some sixth sense must have warned the hare that death was upon it, because it broke and ran while the leopard was in the air. Skittering crazily, the hare tried broken-field running, but its speed was no match for that of the leopard.

The big cat landed where the hare had been, then dug her claws into the ground and took off in pursuit. In three long strides, muscles bunching and flaring explosively, she snatched the hare up by the back of its neck. The hare's eyes dilated, knowing death was upon it.

Peter watched the hare's eyes, captivated for a moment. *It knows,* he couldn't help thinking, and a chill dawned at the base of his spine that had nothing to do with being inside the blind.

Death came too quickly for the hare to contemplate, but the animal looked surprised. *It's worse,* Peter reconciled himself, *if you know death is coming. Worse if you actually see death coming.* His father's eyes still haunted his dreams, still kept him up nights.

Peter knew what his father's eyes had looked like when he'd accepted death. But the thing that bothered Peter most was wondering what his father had seen in his own eyes. There had been no words; there couldn't have been. His vision blurred for a moment, and he suddenly realized he'd lost sight of the snow leopard.

Forcing his mind out of the past, he concentrated on the meadow, regretting again how limiting the blind could be. The low-ceilinged structure that had been half home and half workspace during the last few months had a view that stared out over the harsh, broken foothills of the Himalayas. A small heater in the corner of the lean-to raised the temperature only to barely tolerable. Empty supply boxes served as meager furniture.

After only a moment of searching, Peter spotted the leopard slinking through the brush. The bloodied hare hung limply from her maw. Peter heaved a relieved sigh through the slit in the wall that overlooked the meadows that he'd come to know intimately, and his breath turned to a gentle, eddying white-gray fog. He'd spent months watching the big cat, and today was going to be one of the payoffs. *National Geographic* was generous with the funding for the photo spread he had going.

The leopard continued on her way, twisting and turning her head to either side. She was at the top of the food chain in the area, and she'd laid claim to a large amount of territory. There wasn't much she had to worry about and she knew it. However, the hare was also a valuable commodity and hard to replace.

Peter continued following the leopard, finishing off the roll of film. He took another roll from one of the loops on his jacket and opened the camera. He flipped the exposed film back to Aziz, his Balti porter. The porter caught the film deftly and put it into a bag with the others.

Peter reloaded the camera and looked through the viewfinder again. *C'mon,* he thought tensely. *It's a nice day. Let the kids come out to play.*

The snow leopard kept moving sedately. Peter knew there were less than six thousand of the big cats left in the wild. Scientists kept track of the snow leopard numbers also because they were considered to be an indicator species—one that gave information about a particular environment's general health. *National Geographic* had sent Peter to the Himalayas partly for research and partly to capture the beauty of the animal.

Spring had come to the mountain foothills, melting the snows into rivers of near-freezing water. Barren rocks and boulders jutted up like miniature islands from the newly greened land, and white frost clung to some of the boulders because the chill had not quite given in to the seasonal change. A riot of colorful flowers spread across the meadow, yellows and reds and whites that Peter's film captured perfectly.

Himalaya translated as "Land of Snow." In the beginning months of Peter's stay in Pakistan deep in the foothills of the Himalayan Mountains, the name had been appropriate. The nights in the great Asian mountain system had been long and freezing, and the days hadn't been much better. He'd been told about the beauty of the coming spring season, but he hadn't believed it until he'd seen it for himself.

The snow leopard started down the slope away from Peter.

Don't do that, Peter silently entreated. *It's a nice day. And there's nobody here to threaten you. Just one photographer looking for a way to earn a bonus check.* He shifted the camera carefully, aware that the sun was behind him now; there was no chance that the sun would ruin a shot or reflect off the lens and spook the big cat.

Aziz breathed behind Peter, moving quietly as he shifted so he could peer through the slit as well. The porter was there for the bonus as well. Despite their long months together, Peter still didn't know much about the man. Part of it was due to the language barrier. Peter spoke hardly any Urdu, and Aziz spoke very little conversational English. That suited Peter, though. These days he wasn't much of a conversationalist anyway.

The snow leopard paused along the ridgeline, the massive snow-covered mountains far in the distance serving as a spectacular backdrop. Peter didn't hesitate to burn film, snapping off frame after frame. Photography was skill; every photojournalist knew that. But grabbing a prize-winning picture required a lot of luck as well.

Then the snow leopard hunkered down, laying her prize before her. In the next instant, three cubs came charging into the clearing. One of them had a very distinctive ring around its eye, giving it a swashbuckler appearance.

Peter smiled, warming to the work. He manipulated the zoom automatically, as if it were a part of him. He took a few shots of all three cubs streaking across the clearing, then closed in, photographing each in turn. He had names for them all, but they weren't going into the article.

He extracted the finished roll and flipped it back. Aziz caught it even as Peter slid another roll into the camera. Peter shot the cubs eating the hare till they had their fill. *National Geographic* might pass on the shots, but Peter never tried to outguess them. He captured everything with the lens.

After their meal, the cubs turned to play. Under their mother's watchful eyes, the three cubs pursued and wrestled one another. They instinctively worked on perfecting the stalking techniques their mother had used to bring down the hare.

Finished with another roll of film, Peter removed the exposed roll from the camera and tossed it back. While he was loading fresh film, watching the cubs jump and nip at one another, the sound of ringing metal filled the blind and carried out into the meadow.

The sound was alien to the mother snow leopard. She moved instantly, chasing her cubs to cover with a growling, spitting snarl. All four of them vanished into the brush in an eyeblink.

No! Peter stared in disbelief at the empty meadow for a moment. Then he glanced back at Aziz.

One of the heavy-duty metal canisters they used to protect the film lay on the cold stone floor between the porter's feet. Aziz looked apologetic, but Peter waved the incident away and blew out a sigh of resignation.

They'd try again tomorrow. He had nothing but time on his hands these days.

Peter settled the weight of his pack across his shoulders as he crested the ridge above the campsite. Aziz led the way, obviously uncomfortable with his pack as well. Every time they made the trip back and forth to the blind, Peter became aware again of how heavy the cameras and film were. *And why is it the packs always seem heavier on the way back?*

He gazed up at the mountains ringing the area. The Himalayan Mountains formed a broad fifteen-hundred-mile half-moon through northern Pakistan, northern India, southern Tibet, Nepal, Sikkim, and Bhutan. North of the mountains lay the high plateau of Central Asia, and to the south were the fertile Indian plains.

There were fourteen mountain peaks in the world that were more than twenty-six thousand feet high, and nine of them were in the Himalayas. Mount Everest at 29,035 feet was the tallest, but K2, the second tallest mountain in the world, was the nearest to the campsite.

Not once did Peter ever think about climbing the mountains. Those days were over. A lot of things were over.

He turned his eyes down, watching his step on the treacherous ice-covered rocks. Here on the north side of the slope, the winds sometimes froze the smaller streams trickling down from the upper mountains.

He glanced ahead at the three tents that made up the campsite. They were tucked between a bubbling stream that served as their fresh water supply and a boulder as big as a school bus. The boulder knocked most of the wind off when it was headed in the right direction.

One of the tents served as a darkroom for shots Peter wanted to develop himself before sending them to the magazine editors. The other two were private quarters for Aziz and himself. The small satellite dish was inside Peter's tent, but the mast stood up tall in the circle of tents. The latrine was farther downstream. There were no neighbors.

It wasn't home, and Peter never intended for it to feel like home. He trudged down the slope, still filled with dark thoughts and painful memories. He concentrated on the fact that hot stew warmed on a tiny butane stove would take away most of the chill that had ached within him all day. Then, as if to spite him, the wind picked up suddenly, gusting wildly as it sometimes did this high up.

Raising an arm to ward off the vicious wind, Aziz slipped on an ice-covered boulder and went down in a tangle of flailing arms and legs, sliding a few feet to the bottom of the slope. He hit hard, crying out in pain. Bone snapped with a brittle pop.

Peter trotted forward immediately but took care with his own steps. When he saw the angle of Aziz's lower leg, he knew it had been broken.

Aziz screamed hoarsely, but there was no one around to hear but Peter.

Dropping his pack, Peter reached into it and took out the emergency medical kit. "Hey, take it easy," he said as calmly as he could. "We're going to be okay here." He removed a morphine ampoule from the medical kit, filled a sterile hypodermic needle with the drug, and jabbed the needle into Aziz's thigh.

The porter held his leg, his breath coughing from him in great, gray gusts.

Peter stayed beside the man, waiting for the painkiller to kick in. He glanced at the northern ridge, at the unforgiving mountains, and knew that under normal circumstances Aziz would probably die there, unable to make it back to any kind of civilization. At the very least, he'd lose his foot, maybe his leg to frostbite. The icy mountains weren't gentle to interlopers. But for now help was only a phone call away.

Yammering helicopter rotors woke Peter the next day. He blinked sleep out of his eyes as he rolled out of the sleeping bag on the tent floor. A glance at his watch told him it was after twelve. He automatically checked the fuel reservoir on the tent's heater. Frostbite was a real killer at these heights and sometimes didn't get noticed until gangrene set in.

Still dressed in the clothes he'd put on the night before so he'd be ready to move at a moment's notice, Peter stood and checked on Aziz as the helicopter came closer. The porter was still asleep on Peter's cot, heavily drugged by the painkillers. His injured foot was encased in an inflatable cast and elevated by pillows.

23

Aziz hadn't been lucky at all. The fracture was a greenstick break, an irregular crack that ran diagonally through the bone. The jagged end had pierced the flesh near his ankle. The heat of the leg above the cast told Peter that infection had started setting in despite the antibiotics.

When he'd called the Pakistani military rescue base camp for assistance, the dispatch officer had told him they couldn't send the helicopter till the morning due to the high winds and availability of craft. The night had been long for Peter. Even though Aziz had been on painkillers, he'd needed water at regular intervals to help keep the fever down. Peter hadn't slept well.

He pulled on his coat and went out to meet the helicopter. The rotor wash picked up snow and loose bits of debris, pushing them back over him and the tents.

The Augusta-Bell AB 205 multipurpose utility helicopter bore the familiar gray-green coloration of the Pakistani army and the green-and-white moon and star flag on the tail fuselage. The pilot expertly dropped the skids to the ground and left the rotors turning, then went to the rear of the helicopter and opened the cargo door.

Peter moved toward the pilot, ducking below the rotors. "Hey, Rasul. Thanks for coming."

"No problem," Major Kamal Rasul answered. He was in his early thirties, with neatly cropped black hair, compact and lean in his flying suit. He was smiling as he shoved aside cargo boxes, making room for Aziz. Rasul was Peter's usual aerial transport. "How bad is he?"

"I think he's going to keep everything," Peter replied. It was a fair enough answer.

"Excellent. He's a good man."

Peter nodded in agreement.

Rasul leaped from the helicopter and strode toward the tent. "You packed and ready to go?"

"Yeah."

"I could take him by myself," Rasul offered.

Peter shook his head. "I want to make sure he's okay." He followed Rasul into the tent.

The helicopter pilot checked Aziz over quickly, then looked up at Peter. "If we tie him to the cot, he'll be safe enough and comfortable enough for the trip up the mountain. That way we won't have to move him from the bed."

"Sounds good," Peter replied. He helped Rasul make the restraints from the bedclothes. Aziz groaned as they shifted him, but he didn't wake.

Peter took a final look around the tent, making sure he'd turned off the stove. The rotor wash whipped inside the open tent flap, covering the vinyl floor with snow and debris that would have to be cleaned when he got back. It also riffled through the papers and magazines on the desk he'd made out of empty camera and supply boxes. The *Sports Illustrated* cover taped to the wall behind the desk almost tore loose.

The magazine cover showed his sister, Annie, a big smile on her face, standing on a snow-covered mountaintop. The title read, "At the Top of Her Game. Annie Garrett—Fastest Female Ascent on the Eiger." It was, Peter thought, a good picture of her.

Peter caught Rasul looking at him when he turned back from the cover. Rasul seemed to want to say something but didn't. After making sure Aziz was covered against the cold, Peter grabbed one side of the cot and Rasul grabbed the other. Together, they marched from the tent with Aziz between them.

"We're cleared for Siachen Glacier," Rasul shouted to be heard outside. "The army's got a doctor on standby."

Surprised, Peter glanced at the major. Siachen Glacier housed the Pakistani military base, and their doors didn't open to just anyone. Things between the Pakistanis and the Indians had heated up again lately, and the bitter struggle over Kashmir and other border areas had resulted in recent attacks on both sides of the disputed territory.

"I was heading there anyway," Rasul went on. "Milk

run—mail and supplies. I can drop you back here on my way down to K2 base camp. How's that?"

"Sounds good," Peter answered.

Rasul guided Aziz and the cot into the helicopter's cargo section. Peter closed the cargo door once they were inside and walked forward, following Rasul. The major dropped into the pilot's seat and strapped in.

Peter sat in the co-pilot's seat, strapping in as well and pulling on the headset so he could communicate with Rasul over the throbbing rotor motors.

After glancing at Peter, Rasul took the yoke in his hand and powered the rotors. They lifted into the thin air with a small leap. In seconds the campsite was far below.

Peter gazed at the tents, hating to leave. The campsite was a cocoon, and the mother snow leopard and her cubs were a reason to get up every day. That was all he needed. Going into Siachen and K2 base camp to get another porter meant bumping into too many people. He preferred social visits in small doses, grateful for his privacy.

He glanced at the back of the helicopter, checking to make sure Aziz was okay. The porter was still out, deep under the effects of the morphine, and his broken leg was elevated. For the first time, Peter noticed how much cargo was aboard the helicopter. *This is no ordinary milk run.* A large portion of the cargo was medical supplies.

"I tried to get up to see you last week," Rasul said, expertly handling the high-altitude modified helicopter, "but the weather closed in. How are the kids?"

Grinning, Peter handed the major five prints from the rolls he'd shot in recent weeks. Most of them were of the snow leopard cub with the peculiar ring around his eye.

"Good grief," Rasul said, "look at Pirate. You'd hardly know he was the runt."

Peter smiled, looking at the pictures again. "The mother lets him feed first. Made his life a misery—his sisters gang up on him."

Rasul laughed and passed the pictures back to Peter.

A friendship with the major had been unexpected, but Peter had managed it. He'd been slow to respond at first, but felt more comfortable once he'd realized it could only be transitory at best. Rasul was into a lot of people's lives; it was the nature of his assignment. *And he doesn't press,* Peter thought, which was one of the best reasons to like him.

Looking through the Plexiglas nose, Peter watched as the earth seemed to fall away on the other side of a high ridge. The area here was called Concordia, and it was the meeting place of the Himalayan giants. K2 loomed ahead, but a number of other tall peaks lay around it. Blankets of white snow swaddled the mountains, covering all of the massive shoulders and most of the foothills.

It's clean up here, Peter thought, *peaceful.* And so far he'd been lucky enough to find reasons for *National Geographic* to keep him in the area. He felt Rasul's eyes on him and turned toward the man.

Rasul glanced away nervously, raking his gaze over the instrument panel.

Peter kept quiet. Rasul was more talkative than he, but if Rasul wasn't ready to talk about something, he didn't.

Rasul was, however, ready to talk now. "There's another reason I tried to get up to see you."

Peter waited, not even wondering. Thinking too far ahead led to thinking too far back as well.

"Your sister's at base camp. Arrived last week." Rasul didn't look at him.

Shocked, Peter tried to get his mind around the news. He turned his gaze back to the view. *If Annie was coming up here to see me, she would have called.* His editor had his satellite phone link-up, as well as strict instructions to put through any messages from Annie.

There hadn't been any messages from his sister—not for a very long time now. But he couldn't blame her. He hadn't called either, and most of the time he didn't know where she was. He'd followed her through magazine articles and television coverage. *Or, maybe, followed her career would be more correct,* he admitted to himself. He had no clue what Annie had been doing with her personal life.

So what is she doing at K2 base camp now? he wondered. He focused on the huge mountain ahead.

Situated on the border between China and Kashmir, K2 was presently occupied by the Pakistanis. The Pakistani military base on Siachen Glacier was there to support the Pakistani claims on the Kashmir area as well as the mountain itself against India's efforts to reclaim it.

The name *K2* derived from the mountain's designation as the second highest in the Karakorum Range of the western Himalayas. K2 stood 28,250 feet high and remained covered in snow above sixteen thousand feet the whole year around. The temperature barely rose above freezing at fifteen thousand feet and above. In the winter months, the snow line started at four thousand feet. K2 was a jagged dreadnought of ice and limestone mounted on a granite base.

Between 1892 to 1954, eight expeditions had made assaults on K2. The summit had finally been conquered on July 31, 1954, by an Italian team. Most climbers considered K2 harder to scale than Everest. Weather conditions on the mountain changed drastically within minutes, going from warm and sunny to arctic chill, high winds, and snowstorms.

A sudden gust of wind caught the helicopter and knocked it sideways. Calmly, Rasul worked the yoke and the tail rotor pedals, bringing the aircraft smoothly back under control. Then they were over the last ridge and Siachen Glacier stretched out below them.

Peter spotted figures moving across the level expanse of snow, but his thoughts centered on Annie and the growing dread he had about the real reason she was there. Only one thing brought climbers to K2.

Chapter 2

Siachen Glacier, 18,000 feet

The figures atop the Siachen Glacier ridge were Pakistani Rangers assigned to repel any attempts to invade the area by the Indian Border Security Force. The Pakistani military personnel wore high-altitude camouflage fatigues and were set up in opposing teams, playing cricket.

The bowler lined up on the circular field and threw the ball toward the batsman. The ball hit at the bottom of the batting area, spinning viciously. From the occasional times Peter had played, he recognized the throw as a yorker, designed to strike the ground so the batsman had to dig the ball up, giving the eleven-man team in the field an opportunity to catch it if he did hit it.

The batsman didn't hesitate, getting the flat bat off his shoulder in a tight turn and hammering the ball onto the pitch. *That was a good hit,* Peter thought, watching the field players scramble to cover the ball while the batsman ran to the other end of the pitch to score points.

Rasul blew by over the cricket players, heading for the bull's-eye-marked helipad. The rotor wash disrupted play and drew a number of curses and angrily waving arms. The soldiers, Peter knew, took their cricket very seriously. A good match could take days to finish.

Huts spread across the snow-covered terrain made up the military base camp. Although they were temporary structures, they were considered permanent due to the war. Hostilities between Pakistan and India blew hot and cold over the disputed territory of Kashmir and K2, but they never completely went away. Stone storage bunkers were over to the right, opposite the three 80mm guns that could deliver a high-explosive round deep into India.

Peter figured it had to be one of the most remote military base in the world. When the war efforts between the two countries weren't taking lives, the mountain and the cold were.

Siachen Glacier was important to Pakistan because it was part of the Karakorum Highway, Pakistan's most strategic route into China. India wanted to cut that route off but hadn't been able to do so yet.

Siachen Glacier was forty-four miles long, the biggest glacier in the world outside of the North and South Poles. It was also the highest glacier, and was often referred to as the Third Pole.

Both India and Pakistan wanted the Siachen Glacier area for strategic military and economic reasons, but Pakistan had managed to hang onto it. In the helicopter at different times, Rasul had shown Peter old battle sites as high as 22,000 feet up the mountain, where the air was so thin that just being there was life-threatening enough before bullets and mortar shells were taken into consideration.

Rasul guided the helicopter down gently, not even disturbing Aziz still sleeping on the cot in the back.

Even before Peter could unstrap himself from the co-pilot's seat, two men rushed from the hospital hut carrying a stretcher between them. The hospital orderlies unlocked the cargo door and hauled the cot out, quickly shifting Aziz to the stretcher.

Peter followed the major out of the helicopter, stepping into the freezing winds. *Only a difference of thirty-five hundred feet,* Peter thought, closing his coat and tugging his gloves on again, *but man, what a difference*. His hiking boots crunched across the frozen snow layer. His breath came out in gray clouds that were quickly sucked away in the wind.

The hospital hut wasn't much warmer. When he followed the men and the stretcher through the door, the roaring wind came after them like a ravenous beast. Hospital personnel standing near the doors wrapped their arms around themselves and cursed.

Peter gazed around at the interior of the hospital hut in dismay. Cots lined the walls on both sides of the long hut, and sick men lay on them, under threadbare blankets. Two charcoal heaters labored unsuccessfully to chase away the cold. *And this is as good as it gets,* Peter thought bitterly. Aziz would do well if he got out of the hospital with a temporary limp.

Some of the men were accident victims or victims of frostbite. Most of them, Peter realized when he noticed the lack of bandages, were suffering from altitude sickness and hypothermia.

Hypothermia was a decrease in core body temperature that prevented normal muscular and cerebral functions. The greatest cause of hypothermia was cold temperatures, which the military outpost on Siachen Glacier experienced year-round. Wetness, fatigue, and improper clothing and equipment could intensify the effect of the cold.

Acute Mountain Sickness (AMS) resulted from the body's inability to adjust to a rapid gain in altitude. Even climbing a mountain slowly could trigger AMS. Most climbers in cold territories suffered through at least a mild bout of AMS. But it could become worse, turning into full-fledged pulmonary and cerebral edema. The quickest and easiest route to recovery was rest and lots of fluids. However, neither of those was readily available to a climber working his or her way up a mountainside.

A doctor stepped over to Aziz's stretcher and began taking his vital signs, quickly motioning the stretcher carriers over to one of the few empty beds.

Rasul crossed over to the nearest charcoal heater and lifted the battered steel urn siting on top. "Tea, Peter?" he offered.

"No thanks," Peter responded, joining him at the heater and trying not to feel guilty about being able to stand so close to the warmth while the patients couldn't. He rubbed his hands together and blew on them. "Any coffee?"

Rasul shook his head. "Sorry. The tea's very good, mind you. Indian, of course." He filled a cup, then replaced the urn on the charcoal heater. "We may be at war with them, but there's no point in overreacting. Their tea's the best." He blew on the dark liquid and sipped carefully.

The strong smell of the tea made Peter's stomach growl, reminding him that he hadn't eaten. Poor food intake also led to hypothermia, he reminded himself.

Doors at the other end of the hospital hut suddenly burst open and a Pakistani colonel in full military dress strode into the room. He was in his fifties and, judging from his erect carriage and overall attitude, had spent most of those years in the military. Peter had never met Colonel Amir Salim, but he'd heard Rasul speak of the man. Salim had been educated at Sandhurst, the British military college, and he was the commanding officer of the Siachen Glacier outpost.

Anger colored the colonel's pinched features as he surveyed the cots containing sick men. He exchanged meaningful looks with the doctors, who quickly returned their attention to their patients. Orderlies quickly got out of the colonel's way.

Rasul put down his cup quickly and saluted immediately.

Salim ignored the salute and began talking quickly and harshly in Urdu. Though Peter was able to identify the language, he couldn't follow the conversation. Salim slapped papers on the clipboard he carried. Then the colonel's eyes met Peter's and the argument abruptly broke off.

"Forgive me," Salim said in a British accent. "Mr. Garrett, isn't it?"

Peter nodded a little uncertainly. Whatever the colonel was unhappy about, he was positive he didn't want to be considered part of the reason.

"*National Geographic* is always welcome," the colonel stated. "They're the only Westerners who ever come to Pakistan without trying to conquer something. How do you do?" He offered his hand.

Peter accepted the man's hand and shook it, feeling the steely strength and the hard calluses. "I'm fine, thanks."

Rasul, never one to balk at a chance to turn a bad situation around, stepped into the conversation, speaking to Peter. "The colonel's angry that only twenty-five percent of his medical supplies are on board the helicopter."

Salim gave the major a hard glance. "And three days late." He gestured toward the hospital hut and the nearly filled cots. "Look at this place. I've been here for six years and lost over eight hundred men. Not one of them to the enemy. I need dex for altitude edema, chlorsep for hypothermia—"

Peter interrupted, feeling somewhat confused. Dex was short for Diamox, a drug that could be used to help or prevent AMS. And if a person already had AMS, dex could reduce the severity of the sickness. "The chopper's full of dex—"

"Not for soldiers on the frontier, Mr. Garrett," Salim stated angrily. "It's for wealthy Americans who can pay two or three million dollars for climbing permits."

Anxiety rattled inside Peter, constricting his chest. *Annie?* But she didn't have two or three million to squander on climbing permits. It had to be someone else. It *needed* to be someone else. "What American?"

"Elliot Vaughn, the entrepreneur," Rasul answered. "He's brought about forty people in with him. He's taking a crack at K2." He paused. "I've been seconded to his team."

Forty people? Peter glanced at Rasul, knowing now what the major had left out of his story. Annie was one

33

of those forty people, probably one of the few that was going to try to summit the mountain. A sick, twisted knot slid greasily through Peter's stomach and bile rose to the back of his throat. *Annie doesn't know what she's getting into. Doesn't know what Elliot Vaughn and all his money is getting her into. That mountain is a killer and has been for years.*

Salim glanced at Rasul. "Seconded or sold? That's probably a question only a general in Islamabad can answer." He turned and glanced at the clock on the wall. "Three o'clock. Time to wake up the Indians." He nodded to Peter and left the hospital hut through the main door, walking out into the blustering wind.

Rasul picked up his tea and started drinking again, cupping his hands around it to take full advantage of the warmth the liquid provided. "I'll let the base camp know you need a new porter and get your supply list turned in. Give me ten minutes and I'll take you back to your camp."

Peter hesitated, thinking about Annie being on the mountain. *I can't just walk away and pretend I don't know that she's going to try that climb.* But there was no guarantee that she'd listen to him, either. *We haven't been very good at talking for a long time.* He looked at Rasul. "If it's okay with you, I'll go down to base camp."

Rasul met Peter's gaze, held it for just a moment, then nodded.

Right after that the 80mm guns opened up in quick succession, filling the air with thunder. Before the echoing din could fade away, they fired again.

Twenty-first–century saber rattling, Peter thought, but he knew the shuddering sensation in his stomach wasn't from the cacophony created by the 80mm guns. He didn't know which scared him more: the thought of Annie attempting to climb K2 or going to talk to her about it.

Chapter 3

Base Camp, 16,700 feet

Peter sat in the helicopter's co-pilot seat as Rasul sent the chopper screaming through a chasm leading to the foothills of the mountain. Base camp was nestled at the end of Siachen Glacier at just under seventeen thousand feet.

He craned his head and glanced up at the towering might of K2. Anyone climbing the mountain still had more than eleven thousand feet to go, and those feet were all harsh and dangerous. *Annie still has more than eleven thousand feet to go.* Peter turned back to Rasul. Both of them had been silent since they'd left the military outpost.

"I guess Annie's come in with the Elliot Vaughn team?" Peter asked.

Rasul nodded but kept his attention riveted on his flying. The chasm kept most of the bitterly cold winds from buffeting them, but occasional slipstreams could throw the wasp-shaped craft out of control. "She's leading a WNN documentary crew. They're going up the mountain with him."

"WNN," Peter said, impressed. "That's a break." He paused, unable to look at the pilot. "Have you met her?"

"Not yet," Rasul answered. "One of the guides told me."

A crosswind caught the helicopter, knocking it sideways and causing it to lose altitude. Peter grabbed for something to hold on to, but Rasul handled the dramatic shift nonchalantly, pulling the chopper back to an even keel.

"What about Vaughn?" Peter asked. "What's he like?"

Rasul shrugged. "Pretty much what you'd expect. Sensitive, kind, modest. You know, your typical billionaire businessman."

Peter smiled.

"People say he buys the summit," Rasul said. "That's not true. Four years ago he was part of an American team that took on the south face. Got within eight hundred feet of the top when the weather closed in. Twenty-four hours in the Death Zone, but the next morning he walked down." The major glanced at Peter as if to reassure him. "I don't care what anybody says. He's a good climber."

Good to know, Peter thought, but it didn't make him feel any better. He glanced through the helicopter's Plexiglas nose and spotted the base camp at the end of Siachen Glacier.

The base camp was still two thousand feet below, but already he could see that it was a small city of tents and structures designed to be erected quickly and efficiently— and replaced the same way if necessary.

People in winter gear moved through the snow-covered trails that served as streets. Snowmobiles hauled freight from newly arrived cargo helicopters, dragging the sleds toward warehouses.

As Rasul cut the helicopter's speed and dropped toward the waiting helipad, Peter's pulse quickened and his stomach turned acidic. *Annie's down there somewhere,* he mused. Then he tried to tell himself that it was a good thing, an event whose time had come. The problem was that he just wasn't completely convinced.

Tom McLaren turned away from the gusting wind made by the latest helicopter descending from the blue sky. Loose snow and tiny ice chunks stung his face. Once the rotor wash had died down to a tolerable level, he urged the waiting porters forward to handle the supplies. Like them, he wore a green parka with the logo of Summit Expeditions on a patch over the left breast. It was his company and he was proud of it, and he'd never been one to leave even the grunt work to other people.

Vaughn may not be here, McLaren reminded himself, *but his people are, and they're probably waiting, ready to report about how his shipments were handled.*

McLaren strode into the midst of the porters, calling out orders in Urdu, making sure every man knew how important the gear and supplies were—as if he hadn't already told them that for months since his entire guide business had been hired out by Vaughn for the whole season for this one climb.

Tall and well built, McLaren kept himself in shape for climbing. He'd been born in the U.S. Midwest, where the land was hilly, not mountainous, but he'd fallen in love with mountain country when he'd first seen it. Then he'd learned to climb, and he'd been as close to the top of the world as people ever got on their own two feet. There was, in his opinion, nothing like climbing.

When he'd put together enough money to form a company, McLaren had come to Asia, to the Himalayas, to become a mountain guide. He'd made money so far, but his existence had been a lot like Skip Taylor's, another local guide—strictly hand-to-mouth. But there was going to be a feast this year, thanks to Elliot Vaughn's business. And with the WNN coverage he was getting from Annie Garrett's media team, the Vaughn expedition looked like only the tip of the iceberg.

McLaren signed the cargo manifest the pilot, Major Rasul, presented to him, then tucked his copy away inside his parka. He noted the brown-haired young man with the Pakistani major and thought he looked familiar but couldn't quite place him. *Another climber?* McLaren

37

thought. The guy had the build for it and didn't seem to be overly impressed with the mountains ringing them.

He turned his attention back to the cargo. It was important to get some of it in out of the wind immediately. Unconsciously, he glanced at the blue sky. Thankfully, the horizon remained clear. He hoped the weather would hold the way Vaughn had said it would. Once they were on the mountain, the weather determined a lot of whether they lived or died.

Annie Garrett scanned the banks of computers and sophisticated hardware carefully arranged inside the hut that housed the Vaughn command center. *I'll bet if anyone needed to launch a moon shot or take over a foreign country from Siachen Glacier that this is the team and the hardware that could do it,* she thought.

Maybe it was an overstatement but not by much, she believed. Elliot Vaughn hadn't stinted on the budget for his own personal mission control. Besides the radios and video equipment, there was Doppler radar weather imaging and satellite links for the sat-radio they'd take along on the climb.

Annie paced through the tables, feeling tense and antsy. But she knew it didn't have to do with the coming climb. At least the coming climb wasn't the complete source of her anxiety. *Peter is here,* she reminded herself.

Although she didn't stay in constant communication with her brother, several of the material handlers and porters knew of Peter. They'd asked if she knew him since their last names were the same. Thankfully she hadn't had to endure many questions, but she hadn't gotten very much information about her brother, either.

Annie crossed the room to study the Doppler radar image. She saw nothing alarming in the electronic feedback registering on the big screen. Up-to-the-minute information came from geosynchronous satellites Vaughn had purchased time on during the key phases of the mission. Months ago they'd needed access only every now and again to build up weather information in archives. These days they remained online with the Doppler imaging twenty-four hours a day.

Satisfied with the radar reports, Annie turned her attention to her own packs. The camera crew carried the main units that were going to be used to record Vaughn's historic journey, but she had some backup gear herself.

She glanced up and looked through the window in front of her, noticing the Pakistani military helicopter. Tom McLaren and the Summit Expedition crew were already unloading the cargo. Annie felt good that McLaren had been available for the climb. He was one of the most experienced climbers in the area.

A quiet voice came from behind her. "Hello, Annie."

Surprised, Annie turned around quickly, her heart suddenly pounding as if she'd just run a marathon. Her brother stood only a few feet away from her inside Vaughn's command tent. "Peter."

He looked the same as she remembered for the most part. His eyes were the same intense blue, but a shadow seemed to be lying over them. His smile wasn't as easy as she remembered.

"I heard WNN hired you," Peter said, having trouble meeting her gaze. "Hosting Vaughn's special, too. Congratulations."

Annie shrugged, passing off the praise, not sure at all how she was supposed to take it. Praise wasn't something each of them expected from the other since . . . over the last three years. "They wanted someone who could climb K2 and look presentable. There wasn't exactly a rush."

Peter smiled and shook his head. "C'mon, that's not true. You're the best. Read about you on the Eiger—fastest female ascent." He paused and his eyes gleamed with wetness. "Dad would have been proud."

For a moment Annie almost let go the old hurt and

anger, but she held back. Peter didn't deserve that. Her throat constricted too tightly for her to speak for a moment. She covered by checking cameras. Then, a moment later, the constriction passed and she was able to face him. "What are you doing here? Heard you were a photographer. I didn't think you climbed anymore."

"Just visiting."

Lights stirred in Peter's eyes, and Annie knew her statement had hurt him. She felt guilty about that, but there was nothing she could do. There was nothing either of them could do.

Peter tried to smile but couldn't quite manage to. "Got a family of snow leopards at fourteen thousand. Been shooting for *National Geographic*. I'm more or less on staff now."

"Great." Annie tried to mean it, but she knew she didn't. She was still hurting, and Peter deserved to hurt, too. "You were always good at that."

"Annie—" Peter's voice was softer.

She knew what he wanted to bring up, but she couldn't go back there. Utah lived with her every day, and she didn't want to relive it with anyone. "No, Peter." Her voice came out harsh and ragged.

Peter's mouth closed, and his blue eyes glistened with moisture. After a while, he managed to say, "When do you leave?"

Annie hugged her arms to her chest, letting out none of her emotions. If Peter saw anything, she knew, it was the anger inside her. That would never go away. "Early tomorrow. We need to be summiting two o'clock Wednesday."

"What does the mountain say about that?" Peter asked with a trace of accusation in his voice. "I thought you laid siege to it, took a run at it when you could."

Annie recognized those words as their father's. That had been his thinking about climbing. The mountain ran everything. It was up to the climber to find a weakness that could be exploited.

"I didn't know you could schedule a summiting," Peter stated.

"It's a plan, Peter," she replied, "that's all. Vaughn's aggressive but he knows the mountain. Drill down, he says, lay a strategy, think about winning." *And back off. Give me some breathing room here. I wasn't prepared to see you here and now, especially with all of this going on in my life. And I don't think you're any more ready for this than I am.*

More helicopter engines throbbed in the distance, growing closer as the old hurts and new insecurities widened the chasm between brother and sister. Annie felt confused. She wanted to cry and she wanted to yell at Peter at the same time. Neither was professional, and if she was going to be anything on this expedition, on this climb, it was going to be professional.

"How long have you known him?" Peter asked quietly.

The accusation in his words stung Annie as sharply as a slap in the face. *How could you even think such a thing?* She turned her heated gaze on him and struggled to keep her words measured and polite, soft enough that they didn't carry to everyone in the command post. "Even if I was personally involved with him, it wouldn't affect my judgment. Three years is a long time, but I haven't changed that much."

Peter's eyes searched hers, but she could see the lights dim and the fight go out of him. He gazed away and nodded.

How much of you is left, Peter? Annie wanted to ask. But she didn't because she wasn't ready to deal with that either. Climbing K2 was struggle enough at the moment. "Anyway," she said in a quieter voice, "I've got to go." She was certain the arriving helicopters would be Vaughn's. The man was ruthlessly punctual—especially when he was playing to a crowd. She turned from Peter and walked out of the tent.

Chapter 4

Helplessly, Peter watched Annie go, knowing from her long strides that she was about as angry as she got before she totally exploded. *Maybe it would have been better if she had exploded,* he thought. *Maybe we could have gotten everything out.*

But even as he thought that, Peter wasn't at all sure that was what he wanted. *Three years. She said three years is a long time, but she said it as if three years wasn't anything.* A bubble of pain swelled up inside his chest almost to the bursting point. Somehow, he managed to push it back down.

Numbly, he stepped from the tent and moved toward the helipad. Two large white helicopters sped toward the base camp. Their rotor blades beat the air, thundering loudly in the enclosed space made by the mountains ringing Siachen Glacier.

Peter watched as Annie worked her way into the gathering crowd waiting on the aircraft. She looked good, healthy. She looked like she'd finally made it through to the other side of their loss. The anger she felt toward him, Peter told himself, was natural. And deserved.

He thrust his hands into his coat pockets to warm them. Paper crinkled in one of the pockets, reminding him of the list of supplies he needed to check on. *Go,* he

42

told himself. *You've got things to take care of. She's doing fine. Definitely doesn't need you hanging around telling her what to do.*

But his feet wouldn't move. He watched Annie. And like most of base camp, he waited on Elliot Vaughn's arrival.

Montgomery Wick sat on his bed inside his small tent. He leaned forward and massaged oil into his callused, toeless foot. He concentrated on the work, grateful to have it. Work, especially something with his hands that took concentration, was a blessing these days. It kept his mind off other things, sometimes even kept the pain of his loss from him.

He dipped his fingers into the oil again and shifted feet. His other foot was just as toeless. He'd lost the toes years ago to frostbite while climbing K2. He wiped his fingers across the end of his foot, smoothing the oil on, then started working it into the rough skin and scar tissue. Feet were important in climbing. They had to be limber and strong, able to take a lot of weight and strain without cramping. A foot cramp could kill a man hanging onto the side of a mountain.

Wick wore only thermal underwear bottoms, leaving his chest and arms bare despite the chill that filled his small, battered tent. An oil lamp rolled gold light over him, revealing the scars that marked his body. They were from long falls down mountains, places where the cold touch of ice had left burns, and spider-tracked scars where broken bones had come through the flesh or ice had sliced into him.

His long gray hair caused his back to itch and his long beard dug into his chest and upper belly. Although he was in his fifties, he kept himself lean and taut. His muscles played under the lamp's glow, and he took a little selfish pride in them.

Unbidden, his eyes turned to the small Buddhist shrine against one of the tent's canvas walls. Finished with the foot massage, he left the bed and knelt on the thin, frayed brown mat in front of the short puja table. The lamplight gleamed against the rubbed walnut surfaces, and Wick

43

could almost see himself reflected in the wood. The puja table was designed to be collapsible, making it transportable inside a pack.

Wick changed the seven-bowl water offering on the lowest level of the shrine, pouring out the old and replenishing it from a canteen. Clean water was precious at this altitude, and he knew it was a cherished offering, generously given.

Candles burned behind the seven bowls, and between them lay a clutch of wildflowers he'd searched for and found. They'd grown stubbornly less than a mile away in the protection offered by an overhang, getting just enough sun and warmth to bloom beautiful purple and white blossoms. They were wilted and dying in the dry cold now, but their beauty had been greatly enjoyed and offered up.

Behind the candles was the small locket that contained the picture of his dead wife. He gazed at her and felt the sense of loss wash over him again. He missed her. He missed her warmth and her laughter and the way she sometimes looked at him when she'd become convinced once again that he was crazy.

But most of all he missed the way she listened to him when he talked about whatever he wanted to talk about. Nobody had ever listened like that.

Tenderly, he reached out and touched her face in the picture. The mountain had her now, though. K2 was a savage, primeval force that demanded its offerings and sacrifices.

He arranged the two hand-carved plinths on the top shelf. His wife had carved the statues herself—a Buddha and a four-armed Avalokitesvara, the bodhisattva of compassion—and presented them to him shortly after he'd accepted her faith.

Using the control and self-discipline he'd learned from his wife, Wick breathed out, forcing himself to relax, reaching for the meditative state that had helped him remain sane these past years.

There were two types of meditation in Buddhism. Samatha was the beginning of the journey. A practitioner learned to develop a serene, clear, one-pointed mind, which led to the further development of virtue and compassion and made the mind ready for vipassana meditation. Vipassana meditation was the true path of insight and enlightenment.

Wick had never achieved vipassana, but he lived in samatha. It allowed him to keep his grief and rage in a box in the back of his mind.

He was just starting to relax, perhaps even to be tired enough to sleep. He couldn't remember the last time that he'd slept well. But just as the rest of the world started to go away and leave him at peace within himself and with the memories of his wife, the thundering slap of helicopter rotors roared over him.

Agitated again in spite of his best efforts, Wick heaved himself to his bare feet and walked toward the tent flap. Base camp hadn't enjoyed this much activity in a long time, and this many helicopters flying into the area could mean only that an expedition was gathering for another assault on K2.

He stood out in the dry cold, ankle-deep in the snow, and watched the two white helicopters cruise by overhead. He read the name on their sides—Majestic Airlines.

Wick knew that name, and he knew the man behind that name.

Elliot Vaughn had returned to K2.

Wick watched the helicopters grow small again, knowing the serenity he'd reached for only moments ago was now torn from his grasp. He wouldn't be sleeping now. Nor would he be sitting idly by as Vaughn stepped back out to challenge the mountain.

Malcolm Bench, dark-haired and broad-shouldered and wearing absolutely nothing except a pair of cucumber slices over his eyes, lay on the lawn chair. The air was cold, sure enough, but at this high altitude less than sixty percent of the ultraviolet rays in sunlight was filtered out by the thin atmosphere. It provided a hell of a tan.

He peeked out from under one cucumber slice at his brother, Cyril, making sure neither of them was getting burned. Having a sunburn and having to wear a coat as well as thermal underwear totally sucked. "How are you doing over there, bro?"

"Me, I'm doing nothing but absolutely chillin'." Cyril Bench was blond and bearded, more slightly built than his brother. Right now was siesta time. The brothers would walk down to base camp later in the evening, stir up the locals, drink, then crawl back up to their tent before morning caught them.

"Okay, just checking." Malcolm plopped the cucumber slice back over his eye. Both of them were in their late twenties and hadn't held a steady job since they'd discovered the Asian mountains and deserted Sydney, Australia, years ago.

They'd fallen in with mountain climbers, and mountain climbers took care of their own. They'd learned everything there was to know about climbing and saved up money from infrequent expedition work with Skip Taylor to keep themselves living in the style to which they'd become accustomed. They worked when they had to at whatever there was to be done, but they hadn't needed much since they'd paid off the tent.

Malcolm sighed happily, sinking back into the lawn chair again. Their campsite was just up the mountain from the base camp, off the beaten path, so to speak. Of course, there were a few young sheilas down in the base camp that had binoculars and waited with bated breath for these sunbathing periods. Malcolm knew none of them would admit it, but upon occasion some of them had knowingly remarked on the location of tattoos.

The wind changed, and the strong smell of alcohol cooking washed over Malcolm. He glanced from under a cucumber slice again, checking the tent behind Cyril where they kept their homemade still. The still had been the second of their major investments. They brewed steadily, and after a while were making so much that they couldn't drink it all and had to sell some of it to the bars in base camp.

Satisfied that the still was in fine shape, Malcolm lay back and reached down for the bottle he and Cyril were currently sharing. His hand found it unerringly, fingers slipping knowingly around the narrow neck.

Then the sound of helicopters hammered overhead.

Yanking the cucumber slices from his eyes, Malcolm peered up into the bright sky, having to squint for a moment against the unaccustomed glare. He thought he saw two helicopters limned against the sun but wasn't sure. He took a pull from the bottle of homebrew, feeling it burn all the way down. "How many are there, Cyril? Is it two, or is this stuff better than we thought?"

Peter stared up at the sky as the two arriving aircraft got close enough for him to observe in detail.

The helicopters sported brand-new paint jobs, and both were emblazoned with huge, stylized red *M*'s that headed up the title Majestic Airlines. The pilots handled the aircraft expertly, kicking the tail rotors around in tandem, like synchronized swimmers. An explosion of whirling snow blasted over the gathering crowd, causing them to pull their heads into their coats.

The man definitely likes to make an entrance, Peter thought.

By the time the swirling cloud of snow had settled, the lead helicopter's door swung open. Peter easily identified the journalists who stepped from the big helicopter first, followed by a dozen other people. None of them looked like what he expected Elliot Vaughn to look like.

Then, after a moment more, Elliot Vaughn stepped into the helicopter doorway and peered out at the waiting crowd as if he couldn't believe they'd all bothered to show up. Slowly, a big grin formed.

Vaughn dropped from the door onto the helipad. He

was big and rangy, wearing a cowboy-cut Western coat and a short-cropped beard. He stood at least three or four inches over six feet. Although he had to be in his early forties, Vaughn came across as boldly and brashly as a confident teenager, swaggering a little. Peter could swear there was even a little twinkle in the guy's eyes.

Reaching back into the helicopter, Vaughn started helping unload the cargo. He hoisted his own pack across his shoulders, then turned and shouted, "Howdy," to Annie. In three long strides he was at Annie's side, swooping her up in a one-armed hug and kissing her on the cheek.

Annie looked embarrassed and a little flustered.

As if it was something that didn't happen all the time, Peter told himself, trying to take comfort in that thought. Despite the situation and the fact that Vaughn seemed to be in his sister's good graces when he himself wasn't, Peter found that he couldn't immediately dislike the billionaire.

Vaughn was a showman, and even though he acted like a country boy surprised by all the attention, he was definitely playing to the audience. Peter couldn't fault the guy for that, either, because big business generally meant big public relations.

In the middle of greeting his staff, Vaughn suddenly looked up at one of the older men in the crowd around the helipad. The billionaire dropped his pack to the ground and strode over to the other man. Vaughn shoved a hand out. "Ed Viesturs?"

Peter recognized the man now, too. Ed Viesturs was a mountaineering legend.

Viesturs took Vaughn's hand and shook it.

Still holding onto Viesturs's hand, Vaughn turned around to his crew, pointing at the other man. "Five times up Everest. One of the only men to climb twelve of the world's highest mountains. All without oxygen." The billionaire turned his attention back to Viesturs, who looked uncomfortable sharing Vaughn's limelight. "By comparison, all of us are amateurs. It's an honor to meet you, Mr. Viesturs—a real honor."

Peter watched from the outside as the crowd closed in around Vaughn and Viesturs. Annie was caught up in the mass of people somewhere, lost to view. Maybe Vaughn had arrived as an ostentatious outsider, but he was leaving the helipad as one of the members of the base camp.

Slick, Peter thought. *That couldn't have turned out any better if Vaughn had hired Viesturs to be there.* But he knew that wouldn't have been the case. Viesturs was a stand-up guy, a mountaineer who had enjoyed successes but knew all about tragedy as well.

Peter shifted his hands inside his coat and heard the supply list crinkle again. He glanced at Annie, barely able to make her out in the crowd. There was nothing more to be said at the moment, and Peter knew it. Maybe there was nothing to be said ever again. He turned and got his bearings, remembering the directions Rasul had given him to Snowline Adventures, where he could get his supplies and a new porter.

Still, he couldn't help glancing up the mountain, seeing the savage face of it in the distance. *She hasn't gone yet,* he told himself. *Maybe something will change.* But he knew Annie, and he knew that she would go if there was any way possible.

Chapter 5

Base Camp, 16,700 feet

Monique Aubertine sat morosely at the desk inside the small office. Calling the cramped space an office was a joke that she no longer saw the humor in. The desk, which had seen the last of its good days, was placed between two old filing cabinets. Boxes of climbing supplies were stacked all around her. Faded articles about Snowline Adventures flapped listlessly on the wall in front of her, as if they didn't even have the strength to mock her anymore.

Sighing, Monique leaned back in the rickety office chair and tried to work the kinks out of her back. There was nothing enjoyable about the mail these days. Major Rasul's mail pouch had brought only more bad news. She'd sorted the mails into two piles: sales brochures and bills. Lately the bills stack was definitely winning.

She glared at the articles on the wall, wondering how she could ever have thought Skip Taylor was that attractive or actually had a clue about how to run an expedition business. Well, actually the attractiveness was something Skip still had. He was rugged and manly—and Australian, which may have been a redundancy now that she thought about it. The problem was that the attractiveness didn't work on her anymore.

Which had run out of luck first? she wondered. *The relationship or the business?* At least Skip had a chance of salvaging his business. With Tom McLaren's crew busy servicing only Elliot Vaughn's group, everyone else needing a guide or supplies would have to turn to Snowline Adventures.

The hut had once been a storage shed. Skip Taylor had emptied it just before she'd gone ballistic about not having a place to work. The plywood floors still held, but they showed stains and creaked.

They creaked now, letting her know someone had stepped into the hut. Fully expecting it to be Skip, without turning around, she said, "*Outdoors* magazine wants to do an interview with you—'Bankruptcy at High Altitude.'"

There was no answer.

Thinking she'd somehow finally gotten through Skip's macho bravado and wasn't about to get another of those patented Everything's-gonna-be-okay lectures, Monique turned around and found a stranger standing in the office doorway. He was about her age, with brown hair and the bluest eyes she'd ever seen. Embarrassment turned her face red.

The stranger grinned and pointed toward the door, speaking softly. "I could go back out and come in again."

Monique shook her head. This was turning out to be a really bad day. "Looking for Skip? Try the command tent."

He nodded and smiled again, and those blue eyes held hers for a heartbeat too long to be casual. But she saw the pain in them, too. *Who hurt you?* she wondered.

Then he waved, turned, and walked back outside.

Monique sighed and turned her attention back to the bills. They weren't her problem, she tried to remind herself. She only worked at Snowline Adventures; she wasn't indentured there. She was a few years short of thirty, blonde, and trim. She still had a lot of living ahead of her. All she had to do was find a new place to live it in. Leaving Canada might not have been the smartest thing she could have done.

As Monique sorted through the mail one more time, she remembered the guy's blue eyes. Maybe she could ask around and find out who he was. Base camp wasn't that big. Everyone who lived there more or less knew everyone else's business.

And maybe she wouldn't ask around, Monique decided. At one time she'd asked around about Skip Taylor, and look how that had worked out. She blew out a short, angry breath.

Peter followed the rutted snow that served as a street between tents and huts that looked as though they had been in place for months, if not years. Many of them looked like permanent structures, weathered and scarred and faded from the sun. He thought briefly of the blonde, remembering how pretty she was, but quickly put her out of his mind. He tried to keep his life simple, and adding people to it only complicated it.

He walked past a community campfire burning in a fifty-five-gallon barrel where mechanics, cargo handlers, and porters clustered for small breaks to warm themselves and exchange gossip. It was easy to figure that most of the gossip now would center on Elliot Vaughn and the timed assault on K2.

Thinking about attempting to climb a mountain, especially one as fierce as K2, to some kind of timetable irritated Peter. His father had never been one to think of climbing a mountain as a timed event. Climbing was an experience, something to be treasured.

Peter continued walking until he found three large tents near one another that had Snowline Adventures placards hanging above the main flaps. Peering through an open flap, he spotted a man sitting on the canvas floor and working on a rappelling rig. Rope was spread all around him like an overturned plate of spaghetti.

The man looked to be in his late thirties, with a smooth-shaven face and sandy hair. He wore a long-sleeved shirt instead of a coat. As if sensing Peter's eyes on him, the man glanced up and smiled.

"Skip?" Peter asked.

The man nodded.

"I'm Peter Garrett."

If the name meant anything to Skip Taylor, he didn't show it. When he spoke, it was with a thick Australian accent. "Rasul passed on your message. Bad luck about the porter." He attached a plate to the rappelling rig, then tightened the screws. "You can meet four new ones tomorrow. The other supplies, no trouble."

Peter smiled. "Thanks."

Effortlessly and gracefully, Skip rose to his feet. He wiped his right hand on his pants and stuck it out. "Anyway, no shortage of entertainment. I take it you saw Vaughn fly in."

The irritation still rattled in Peter's skull. "What's this about him climbing to a deadline?"

Skip hesitated for a moment, watching Peter carefully. "A friend of yours, is he?"

Sarcasm, Peter thought. *You have to love sarcasm when you're in no mood for it.* "Our companies went public on the same day."

Skip smiled broadly and retreated far enough into the tent to grab a coffeepot from the charcoal heater. He poured a cup and held it up.

Peter nodded and took the cup of coffee. "My sister's climbing with him."

Skip's eyes widened as understanding dawned on him. "*Annie* Garrett. Of course."

Peter knew that Skip had put together more than that family relationship, though. He was certain Skip knew about Utah as well. All the climbers did. They were a close-knit bunch, and any news about them traveled quickly through their circles. Bad news traveled fastest of all.

"Vaughn's got some publicity stunt," Skip went on. "He's launching a new airline." He posed with a big sappy

53

grin on his face. "He stands on top of K2 and everyone waves as the 777 goes over. Get it?"

Peter couldn't believe it. Vaughn was tying up that much money and risking that many lives to make a commercial? *Annie's life is one of those he's risking.*

"I'm not kidding," Skip said in response to the look. "Don't worry about your sister. Tom McLaren's heading up the expedition, and he's solid." Skip shrugged. "Tom probably told Vaughn he can get him there in that time frame. Who wouldn't for a million bucks?"

"That's what Vaughn's spending?"

Skip nodded. "And that's just for Tom. Vaughn bought his company out for the entire season. Not that I'm pissed or anything. Look what I've got to drag to the top." He jerked a thumb toward an older man sprinting across the tent at the back, making for the outhouse with a roll of toilet paper desperately clutched in one hand. "A sixty-eight-year-old movie producer with dysfunctional bowel syndrome. He's got the runs, mate—permanently."

The man disappeared into the outhouse and slammed the door shut.

"Don't laugh," Skip advised. "The Bench brothers are taking bets that he won't make it past eighteen thousand."

Peter couldn't help himself and burst out laughing in spite of his best efforts. "Will he?"

Skip shrugged. "Depends on the odds. I'm so broke I might have to push him into a crevasse myself."

Peter laughed again and Skip joined in, but all traces of humor left the big man's face. Peter turned, spotting the blonde he'd talked to in the small office only moments ago. She approached Skip with a pile of papers in one fist.

"Monique's our base camp manager and medic," Skip said. "Monique, Peter."

"We've met," Monique replied, not looking at Peter.

Skip reached back to the coffeepot and dug up another cup.

Monique put the pile of papers into one of Skip's hands.

"You should really look at these." Without another word, she turned and left the tent.

Peter watched her go, thinking that the cold tent was actually warming now that she was gone. *Wow! Now, that was a major cold front.*

"Don't mind her," Skip advised nonchalantly. "She's French-Canadian. Some days she's Canadian. Can be quite pleasant." He paused, looking at the woman's retreating back. "Today she's obviously French."

Now, this, mate, this is a party, Malcolm Bench thought as he walked through the thronging crowd to the free bar where Cyril stood with a Spanish woman climber he'd been getting to know. Trust Cyril to try to horn in on his action.

Since there was no structure at base camp big enough to accommodate the party, Elliot Vaughn and his people had decided to throw the barbecue outside. The heavily laden tables stayed brimming with food and drink even though everyone in base camp must have turned out for the party.

Country music twanged from mega-speakers strung on poles and tents, so loud that it was hard to hear people speaking even nearby. The strings of colored lights that hung around the party eclipsed the stars against the velvet black of the sky.

Malcolm sidestepped one of the charcoal grills that had mountains of thick, marbled steaks sizzling on them. The Majestic Airlines banner, complete with the stylized red *M*, waved overhead, the flag that everyone rallied around.

Sliding past his brother, Malcolm stepped up to the bar and ordered another vodka on the rocks. It was a lot smoother than their own homebrew. He turned to the woman, letting her get the full effect of his eyes.

The woman looked at him a little nervously.

"Hi," Cyril said to the woman. "I'm Cyril. I'm not much, but I'm all I think about."

The woman grinned at the brothers and shook her head. Malcolm guessed that her English probably wasn't that good and she wasn't quite keeping up with the conversation. "Watch him," he advised, pointing at his brother. "Cyril's a dog." He paused and caught Cyril's eye. "It's easy to tell us apart—"

"I'm the shy one," Malcolm and Cyril announced together. Then they broke out laughing, slapping each other on the back.

With a perplexed look on her face, the Spanish woman leaned back against the bar and lifted a cigarette to her lips. She had a lighter in her other hand.

Before she could light her cigarette, Malcolm plucked the lighter from her hand and offered to light the cigarette for her. Tentatively, she gave him the cigarette as well. Malcolm took a big gulp of vodka. He flicked the lighter, holding it inches from the cigarette. Then he spit.

The gleaming ball of alcohol hit the lighter flame and turned into a snarling, fist-size fireball that sent people nearby diving for cover. The fireball spread, quickly consuming itself, but the outer fringes caught the cigarette and lit it.

Malcolm offered the woman the lit cigarette. She peered at it in disbelief.

Cyril and Malcolm broke up.

"If you like that," Cyril crowed, "feed him some beans and see how he does it."

Malcolm moved in closer to the woman, dropping a heavy arm across her shoulders. She peered up at him, but she didn't push him away. He grinned. *Mate, now, this is a party.*

Peter felt lost in the maze of people gathered at the barbecue. He walked past media people shooting video and gathering sound bites from attendees. *I should have grabbed a cot somewhere,* he thought ruefully. But he hadn't because he wanted to see Annie one more time before she started the climb tomorrow.

He didn't know if he had the courage to try to talk to

her again, but he wanted to see her once more, and he didn't know when—or if—he'd get the chance. At least, in person. With the kind of life Annie was choosing to lead, he felt certain he'd see her again in magazines or television.

He circled the perimeter of the party, partially deafened by the country music and not able to see clearly because of the bright lights and the sheer number of people.

Tom McLaren and Ed Viesturs stood only a few feet ahead, involved in an animated conversation. Even Rasul was there, talking with a group of New Zealanders, judging from their accents. The Pakistani pilot was demonstrating how to throw a sweeping cricket shot.

Before Peter knew it, he bumped into someone. He turned, finding himself briefly face-to-face with the beautiful blonde woman he'd met earlier. He excused his clumsiness, and she smiled at him. Before she could say anything, he excused himself and hurried on.

He kept peering through the crowd, beginning to wonder if Annie had even attended. Maybe she was getting some sleep, getting ready to begin the assault on K2. In all the noise and confusion, Elliot Vaughn might not have even noticed she was missing.

But Vaughn, Peter realized, was also the kind of guy who would make sure Annie had an assigned place. She was part of the PR of the whole package, a trophy. It made Peter angry to believe that Vaughn would think that way, but he also knew it was true.

A moment later Peter saw Vaughn step away from a group, shaking hands but never breaking stride. *A man on a mission,* Peter thought. *Probably has a timetable for whom he's going to talk to and how long he's going to talk to them.*

Annie stepped away from the group as well, immediately following Vaughn.

Peter stopped his pursuit, knowing his sister wouldn't welcome his attention at that moment. He watched silently as Vaughn led Annie through the crowd. Tom

McLaren fell into step with them a moment later, joined by two other men Peter had seen earlier but didn't know.

"Hey, Peter," someone called.

Turning, Peter spotted Skip Taylor nearby, in a crowd of young women at one of the bars. The Australian excused himself and came over to Peter, carrying an extra drink.

Skip handed the drink to Peter, "Compliments of Mr. Vaughn."

Peter took the drink and looked around at the party as balloons and confetti soared into the sky and drifted back down over the crowd. "What time is the laser show?"

Skip grinned and shrugged.

The music stopped abruptly, drawing protests from the celebrants. The hollow thump of a finger on a live microphone echoed over the crowd, causing everyone to quieten down and look toward the impromptu stage area that suddenly lighted up.

When every head was turned toward the stage, the man passed the microphone over to Elliot Vaughn. Baby spotlights kicked on, lighting him up for the crowd. He met the attention with that broad, winning smile of his.

Annie stood near the billionaire, quiet and composed, and Peter could glean no indication from her of what was about to happen.

Peter waited, wondering if there was a new announcement in the works. Maybe Vaughn had even upped his own timetable.

Chapter 6

Base Camp, 16,700 feet

"Can you hear me at the back?" Elliot Vaughn asked. The microphone carried his voice to all the speakers. Peter believed that if anyone had stayed home in base camp they still would have heard the billionaire speaking.

"No!" people screamed.

"Well," Vaughn promised, never losing his Texas-size grin, "you're the lucky ones."

The celebrants laughed out loud.

"While some of us have been acclimating in Nepal," Vaughn continued, "all the real work here at base camp for the climb has been done by two people." He turned and waved at an athletic-looking man in his fifties standing at his side. "Frank 'Chainsaw' Williams, chief executive of three of my companies."

Williams stepped forward and raised a hand in greeting to the crowd. Applause thundered, and a few shrill whistles joined the response.

"And Brian Maki," Vaughn announced, waving to a thirtyish guy in neat dress and wearing a plastic nametag. "Wonk to his friends. He's been the weather officer on twenty-two high-altitude assaults."

Maki stepped forward and waved energetically, obviously enjoying the limelight.

"Yo, Wonk!" a deep voice with an Australian accent cried out.

"Go, Wonkie!" another Australian accent called.

"The Bench brothers," Skip told Peter quietly. "Have you had the chance to meet them yet?"

"I don't think so," Peter answered.

"Unforgettable," Skip promised. "If you'd met them, you'd remember."

Vaughn waited till the applause died away before speaking again. "Four years ago I came here with a dream: To climb K2, the toughest mountain in the world."

Peter listened to the silence that followed the announcement. Every climber in the area had heard about that ill-fated attempt, and Rasul had filled him in about it on the way to base camp.

"The weather closed in on that mission," Vaughn went on, "and I failed. On Wednesday, with the help of Tom McLaren, I intend to fulfill that dream." He smiled, waving to McLaren, who nodded toward the crowd in response to the cheering and applause.

Peter took the opportunity to study McLaren again, wondering how the expedition guide had allowed himself to more or less guarantee the summit of K2 on a timetable. Expedition guides didn't do that. They hired out for an attempt, and if the attempt lasted two hours or two months, they were paid. *A million bucks,* Peter reminded himself, *is plenty of reason to promise someone nearly anything.*

"And while I'm at it," Vaughn went on, still smiling broadly, "I'm going to do a little business. At two P.M., the inaugural flight of Majestic Airlines will pass over the summit. We'll be there to meet it. To all the other teams, I just want to say—travel well and good luck!" He raised his glass to the audience.

The applause that followed was deafening.

Peter had to admit that the guy had style. Maybe if

60

Vaughn hadn't been responsible for Annie trying to make the climb as well, he could have cheered him on. But he didn't.

Vaughn turned and started to hand the microphone back to Frank "Chainsaw" Williams.

Then a hard voice out of the crowd demanded, "What about the weather, Mr. Vaughn?"

Peter turned, looking for the speaker. Dozens of heads around him turned as well. Then he spotted the man. Peter didn't recognize him at first. It had been years since he'd seen the pictures his father had had of the man, and those years hadn't been kind to him. The long gray hair and beard threw easy identification off as well.

"Montgomery Wick," Peter said quietly, wondering what had brought the man down out of the mountains. From what Peter had heard, Wick had very nearly turned hermit. But what was the man doing here, and why was he challenging Elliot Vaughn?

Montgomery Wick strode forward, stopping just short of the line drawn by Elliot Vaughn's personal security people. Most of the other celebrants hadn't even noticed the men moving through the crowd and weren't paying them any attention at all.

Vaughn peered at him, looking more closely.

Wick stood, letting the light hit him full in the face. He should have realized Vaughn would have trouble recognizing him with the long hair and beard. That wasn't the face that the billionaire would have known.

But Vaughn did know, Wick saw in satisfaction. The billionaire's eyes widened slightly, but he was skilled enough to hide his reaction.

Wick spoke again, giving Vaughn less time to put a positive spin on things. "The weather closes in and people die up there. You know that, Mr. Vaughn." The words almost caught in Wick's throat, mired in all the pain and anger that lived within him, but he forced them out and kept going. "Or don't you have to worry about that?"

The words were an accusation, as brutal as a slap in the face.

There was only a brief hesitation, then Vaughn smiled again, treating the encounter as if it were some part of the entertainment. "It's a good question," the billionaire said. "Of course we have to worry about that. Brian did a high atmosphere analysis of the last four decades. We've planned for this. Brian." He waved up his weather specialist and passed the microphone to him.

Maki took the microphone reluctantly, obviously not enchanted by the prospect of suddenly being grilled in front of so many people. "Most years there's a nine- to twelve-day lull before the fall storms start. On August second, we calculate we have an eighty-two percent chance of fine weather." He passed the microphone back to Vaughn.

"Give me odds like that," the billionaire said when he took control of the microphone again, "and I'd be a wealthy man."

The audience laughed appreciatively, enjoying the way Vaughn thought so quickly on his feet.

Wick ignored the response. There was a greater truth here, one that could expose Vaughn for what he truly was, and he went for that instead. "Who's the leader, Mr. Vaughn? Who makes decisions on the mountain that mean other people live or die?" He paused, knowing his words had an impact on the climbers.

If this had been an inexperienced crowd, they probably wouldn't have thought twice about his question. But these were climbers like him, men and women who had been forced to think on their feet to survive.

"Who plays God, so to speak?" Wick demanded. Lights flashed in the sky from the direction of the Pakistani military outpost.

Vaughn returned Wick's gaze, managing to meet it and hold it. "There can be only one leader," he answered. "In every properly organized expedition, it's always the best climber. I've made it clear to everyone that Tom McLaren's in charge."

The crowd gave an enthusiastic response to the announcement. Catcalls and whistles joined in the applause. Almost on the heels of the congratulatory wishes, the Pakistani 80mm guns on the other side of Siachen Glacier went off, their booming echoes rolling over the barbecue.

"Even the Pakistanis agree," Vaughn said, grinning, seizing the moment. He turned and clapped McLaren on the back. "They're giving you a twenty-one–gun salute, Tom!"

The applause and laughter drowned out any response Wick might have made. He watched in cold frustration as Vaughn took that moment to pass the microphone to one of the men standing there.

Knowing that the moment was lost, and maybe the battle as well, Wick stepped back into the crowd even as Vaughn turned around and stared after him. Vaughn had recognized him, Wick thought as he strode through the crowd. Vaughn had recognized him, and Wick had seen the guilt in him. For now that was enough.

Wick left the party, stepping into the night's shadows just beyond the farthest reaches of the lights. He stared up at cold and distant K2. *The mountain has marked him,* he told himself. *Whether Vaughn knows it or not, the mountain has marked him.*

Now it only remained to be seen who was the stronger, the man or the mountain? One of them would be conquered this time. Wick was certain of that.

Wick sat silently with his hands on his folded knees in the middle of his tent, staring into the blue flame of the butane stove. He heated water in a small pan on the burner, noticing the small bubbles gathering along the bottom.

The only light in the tent came from the butane flame. The weak yellow illumination barely made a dent in the shadows that filled the tent. Wick kept Elliot Vaughn as far from his mind as he could, but he couldn't keep the pain and fury inside him from turning over and over.

Satisfied that the water was hot enough and now purified enough, Wick picked up the small wooden box lying beside him. The wood felt cold and slick beneath his fingertips.

When he opened the box, he stared down at the straight razor lying on red velvet inside. Gently, he took the straight razor from the box and tested the edge with his thumb. It was clean, sharp, and free of blemish, as precise as surgical steel.

He tilted his head back and placed the razor's edge against his throat, almost hard enough to break the skin. Then he drew the razor carefully up, shaving through the beard, leaving only clean skin behind. He washed the blade clean in the near-boiling water, then returned it to his neck and scraped at his whiskers again.

He moved at a controlled pace, shaving his face entirely by touch even though it had been years since he'd looked at his own features. The blade dropped into the water for a moment, then he lifted it to his throat again.

An hour later Wick stepped from the tent. His shaven cheeks felt the bitter cold of the night wind more than they had in years. He'd cut his hair, too, and now the wind ran long fingers down his neck, raising goosebumps.

He'd dressed to travel warmly, in thick boots and gloves, and a thick woolen watch cap to keep his head warm and body temperature in. After facing Vaughn, he'd known he wouldn't be able to sleep. Not until he'd climbed himself to exhaustion.

Glancing up at K2, he was barely aware of the crystal-clear stars above him. Only one thing mattered; only one quest. Maybe he wouldn't find peace on that savage mountain, but he'd lost other things on it.

And if he was able to beat Vaughn to the summit, even though the billionaire would be using a helicopter until the air got too thin to support the aircraft, he'd see about finding what he had lost. After Vaughn's last climb, there had been no opportunity to talk about what had gone wrong and who was responsible.

Now they were going to talk.

Then Wick would figure out what he needed to do.

With grim determination, Wick turned his steps toward the mountain and began climbing, leaving behind the big tent he'd shared with his wife. For now he'd live in the small one he carried on his back when it came time to rest.

He started up the mountain, knowing his heart was colder than anything K2 had ever experienced before. And despite that, despite the hurt, it had managed to keep him alive this long. He leaned into the steep incline, pushing himself. Or maybe he was being pulled. He was no longer sure.

Chapter 7

Base Camp, 16,700 feet

Annie sat in her tent at the folding table she used as a desk and studied the screen of the laptop computer in front of her. The display held graphics of the routes and staging camps she'd chosen for the climb up K2.

Tiredly, she reached for the cup of coffee well to the side of the laptop and tried to stifle a yawn. She needed to get more sleep, but there were so many things to prepare for. So many unforeseen things happened during a climb.

She thought of Peter, the way he'd just quietly stepped back into her life. *There are a lot of unforeseen things that happen* before *a climb, too,* she told herself. She had no idea how she was supposed to prepare for those. But then, she supposed, he hadn't been very prepared either.

She tapped the laptop's keys, scrolling through the different notes, maps, and courses she'd reviewed hundreds of times. None of them had changed.

A shadow fell on the tent's screen door, catching her eye. She reached for the coffee and deliberately sipped again, feeling certain she knew to whom the shadow belonged. Then she heard the screen zipper open and someone step into the tent. She still didn't turn around. *Please don't do this now,* she thought.

"Do you know who the old guy was asking the questions at the barbecue?" Peter asked.

Annie didn't turn from the computer. The pain and resentment she'd carried since Utah flared to renewed life within her. She tried to keep it back. Peter didn't need to deal with that.

"It was Montgomery Wick," Peter went on. "Remember? Dad used to talk about him."

I remember, Annie thought. *Please, Peter, go away.*

"They were in the service together," Peter said. "Wick was the Army Ranger—"

No, Annie thought, *I don't want to go through one of Dad's stories with you. That was all a long time ago.* "Of course I remember."

Peter hesitated, and his voice turned even softer. "I miss him, Annie, miss him just as much as—"

Annie turned so abruptly that Peter stopped talking. As evenly as she could, she said, "I don't want to talk about it."

"You never have. That's why I came. We're going to talk about it now."

No! You're not going to arbitrarily choose some moment when you're comfortable about it. Annie cut him off. "There's nothing to say. He was our father, Peter."

Tears welled in Peter's blue eyes. It was almost more than Annie could stand. She knew he was hurting, but they couldn't help each other. They hadn't been able to since their father died.

"Blame me, sure," Peter said in a choked voice, "but the last cam would have failed."

"It held the two of us," Annie told him, growing angrier. "You want to do this? Okay. Let's do it." She looked at him full measure. "You didn't give that cam a chance."

"Dad didn't think it would hold either."

"Of course he didn't!" Annie exploded. "We were his life, Peter! He'd rather have died than take a chance anything might have happened to us! We were family—we owed him the same."

"I'd have taken any risk for him," Peter argued. "Of course I would! But you were up there, too. I didn't want to lose you either."

"Oh no," Annie said, her voice rising, "no! Don't put it on me! I was begging you!" She forced herself to breathe out. "It was your decision!"

"I know that!" Tears ran down Peter's face. "I did what I thought was best—"

"If you were so right, how come you've never climbed again? How come you haven't even been to his grave?" Annie paused, unable to stop beating him down now that she had started. "I'm not going up there for a TV program. I'm going for him. I want to be the climber, the person he always wanted me to be."

Peter couldn't hold her gaze and looked away.

"And you know something?" Annie asked. "I feel close to him. On a mountain, I touch his soul." She paused. "What have you done?"

Shaking his head, Peter looked at her but said nothing.

"Taking pictures is fine, Peter. But always in the wilderness? Always alone?" Annie told it to him straight out, making him face the things he knew but probably didn't admit even to himself. "The only way you can live with yourself is by yourself."

Weakly, Peter pushed himself to his feet and started toward the door. "Take care up there tomorrow." Then he turned and left.

Annie almost went after him, but she stopped herself when she realized that she had nothing to say. She'd already said it all, and she'd only prolong their shared agony.

His footsteps took him away from her tent. They grew fainter and fainter, then in a short while she couldn't hear them at all. For one insane moment, she felt that she and Peter were still falling from that mountain in Utah—still falling and just hadn't hit the ground yet.

* * *

With dawn just breaking to the east, Annie shifted her pack across her shoulders as she walked with the rest of the assault team. The Majestic Airlines helicopters sat on the helipad, rotors whirling and warming up. Vaughn walked beside Annie, firming up last-minute details on deals he'd put together that morning.

Vaughn laughed and joked with the people at the other end of the sat-radio connection, acting as though he was pacing in his office or in the executive boardroom where she'd first met him. He didn't act at all like a person about to take his life into his own hands.

Annie envied him his cockiness to a degree. Confidence was a necessity for a climber. It allowed him or her to weigh options and make decisions with a degree of faith when facts and figures were completely out of the picture. But confidence was a two-edged sword. Too much confidence could land a climber in a lot of trouble.

Ali, the porter they'd hired to help with the WNN team, stood waiting by the lead helicopter's cargo hold. He quietly took Annie's pack and stowed it aboard. She stopped outside the helicopter, watching Vaughn work the phone.

"Hey, man," Vaughn said easily, "it's been really good talking to you. And I'm glad we could iron out those deal points. I promise you, soon as I get back Stateside, I'll treat you to one of the best ribeye steaks you'll ever have in your life. I'll even grill it for you myself." He said good-bye, switched off the radio, and tucked it away in his coat. He took a last look around the base camp, then swung himself into the co-pilot's seat.

Glancing back through the side cabin windows, Annie watched Tom McLaren and his crew board the second helicopter. In minutes they were ready to lift off.

The porter, Ali, stood nearby talking to his cousin, Kareem. When the rotors kicked into a higher rotation, Ali said his final good-bye and boarded the aircraft.

Annie hesitated, glancing up at the fierce mountain towering above them. Then she looked around, wondering if Peter was there somewhere. So many people from base camp had shown up to watch them take off.

Then she spotted Peter in the distance, recognizing him by his stance and the coat that he wore. He stood alone near some monuments that she hadn't noticed yesterday. She wondered if he'd slept last night. She'd finally fallen asleep early that morning, too keyed up about the climb and her conversation with Peter. She wished things hadn't gone down the way they had, but she really didn't know how it could have been otherwise.

She thought about waving to him, but he would have mistaken that for encouragement. And then there was the possibility that he wouldn't wave back, which would undermine her confidence. Not knowing what else to do, Annie stepped up into the helicopter and took one of the bucket seats behind Vaughn. She buckled in, thinking about the lone figure by the monuments but not looking back. It would have been too hard.

"Okay," Vaughn declared. "Let's get this show on the road!"

Immediately, the helicopter pilot powered up, and the big chopper seemed to leap into the air like a powerful bird taking flight. The pilot brought the aircraft around the outer perimeter of the base camp, followed by the other helicopter.

Then they turned and headed up into the mountains. Annie watched as the peaks grew closer. The plan was to set up one of the staging camps and climb as far as they could today, then reach the summit by two o'clock the next day. If everything went according to Vaughn's plan, they'd summit in less than thirty hours.

Peter stood at the memorial to those who had died trying to climb K2. He gazed up at the helicopters as they raced by overhead. In minutes they were gone, streaking up the mountain as high as their high-altitude equipment could take them.

He watched for a time even after the fat-bodied wasp shapes had disappeared. He hadn't slept last night at all and felt worn to the bone. His eyes felt grainy, and they hurt every time he blinked.

He wasn't sure how the conversation with Annie had gotten out of control last night, but he wished it hadn't. Things had been said that had hurt them both, and he knew it. He'd been certain that Annie was attacking him, blaming him for their father's death as she'd wanted to three years ago but just never had the strength or anger to do.

Neither one of those was lacking last night. She was a lot stronger than he remembered. Looking at the mountain, though, he hoped she was strong enough.

Now that the helicopters were out of sight, the rest of base camp returned to its normal routine.

Peter rubbed at his eyes tiredly, hoping he could sleep. Skip had volunteered the use of a cot, and Peter intended to take him up on his offer.

He glanced back at the memorial to those who had died fighting to get to the top of K2. The wooden crosses, tin plates, and oxygen cartridges were all marked with a person's name and sometimes a date. Some of the names he knew, but he'd never really looked at the memorial before.

In memory of John Smolich 1986.

Dr. Norbert Wolf 1951–1982.

Early morning sunlight glinted on a brass circle with the picture of a middle-aged Indian woman in profile. The inscription read, Myama Wick 1952–1996.

Wick? Peter wondered. But the name was too uncommon to be mistaken for anything else.

Feeling hollow, Peter turned from the memorial and trudged back toward base camp. Skip had said he wouldn't be able to fill the supply order or come up with another porter until the next day. Peter had considered having Rasul drop him back at his own camp on a flyby later that afternoon when the major had to return to the military outpost, but had decided against it.

Spending another day at base camp would give the snow leopards more of a chance to get comfortable again with the blind he had set up. And if he hung around late enough tomorrow, maybe he'd hear that Annie and Vaughn had summited before he left. He told himself that nothing could go wrong, then willed himself to believe it. That was the only way he was going to get any sleep.

Chapter 8

Base Camp, 16,700 feet

Two days after he arrived at base camp, Peter felt almost human again. Despite worrying about Annie, he'd slept and rested and eaten. Skip Taylor had proven to be good company, seeming to know when Peter felt like talking and talking only about what Peter felt comfortable with.

Base camp was still very attentive to the Vaughn expedition. Media from a dozen different countries had gathered in base camp to cover the billionaire's assault on K2. The cameramen and anchor people clustered in groups generated by past friendships, stories they'd covered, and language. All of them talked animatedly as they stood in strategic areas around base camp. From those vantage points, they could shoot pictures and video of the expedition as it marched up the mountain.

Peter helped carry the last of the supplies Skip had arranged for him to Rasul's waiting helicopter. Once Peter lifted off from base camp, he wouldn't be back for a month or more.

He couldn't honestly say if the prospect of being alone again was any less grim than staying at base camp for a few more days. His schedule would permit it, and his editor at *National Geographic* wouldn't have a problem with it.

The young snow leopards were growing quickly now, but sometimes days passed before he saw them anyway.

Talking with Annie—

Peter stopped himself. Talking wasn't what they'd been doing, but he didn't know what else to call it. The confrontation with Annie had opened up thoughts and feelings inside him that he'd believed safely put away so they couldn't hurt or confuse him anymore.

Now Peter knew that wasn't true. The cocoon he'd wrapped himself in had been only a false sense of security. There were still too many things left unanswered.

He remembered his father's face again the way it had been in Utah. He could still hear his father's words.

We don't have much time, Peter. You have to do something for me. Cut me loose.

Annie screamed in Peter's mind again, telling him, *No!* over and over again.

You're killing your sister! She'll die if you don't!

Peter felt as if steel bands were closing around his chest, so tight he couldn't breathe. Mechanically, he added the crate he was carrying to the stack Skip and the new porter had stored in the back of Rasul's helicopter. Then he glanced back up at K2, staring at it, wondering where Annie was. If anything had gone wrong, all of base camp would have known about it. Vaughn maintained regular radio contact with the weather station.

Spindrift whirled up over the north face of the mountain. The whipping winds lifted loose snow high into the air, signaling a change in direction. Weather conditions changed very rapidly on the mountain. Peter knew that drastic alterations in weather patterns could take only minutes.

People had been killed on that mountain as a result.

"What is it?" Skip asked. The big Australian stepped up beside him and looked toward the mountain as well.

Peter pointed toward the northern peaks where he'd seen the activity. "The two peaks at three o'clock. Spindrift coming off the top."

Skip followed his pointing finger, squinting against the harsh glare of the sun-kissed snow. He spoke calmly. "Relax. Your sister's fine. The spindrift is local. If something was coming in, the other peaks would be showing it."

Still not totally convinced, Peter turned his attention to securing the cargo. There was nothing else he could do.

Annie hung upside down by her hands and feet from a rope stretched across the chasm. She didn't know how deep the chasm was and didn't even want to think about it. They were at twenty-five thousand feet, with only a little more than three thousand to go to summit.

The expedition was going to make Elliot Vaughn's timetable after all.

Maybe if she hadn't seen Peter she would have felt happier about that. As it was, this climb was another success in a line of them. But there was never anyone to really share those successes with. Vaughn would have his parties and launch another corporate business venture in his own inimitable style.

Annie chased her thoughts from those areas and concentrated on the task at hand. The traverse along the taut rope was made harder because there was a slight ascent. She slid the jumar—a ratcheting device—forward and gripped the rope, then pulled herself forward another foot. The ascending device was only a little larger than her hand and allowed her to clamp securely to the rope without risking injury to her hands or wearing out her grip. Straps buckled her harness to the rope.

Elliot Vaughn and Tom McLaren stood on the other side of the chasm and watched her as she slid confidently along the rope. Ali and the cameraman waited for their turns at the other end of the line.

Once she reached the other side of the chasm, Annie unbuckled her harness and lowered herself to the ground. Her boots crunched through the frozen snow.

Vaughn nodded to her, then turned and started up the next ascent, following McLaren.

Annie marched behind them, noticing the change in the atmosphere. The air was thinner here. Another thousand feet and the expedition would enter what climbers called the Death Zone. At twenty-six thousand feet, the human body was challenged to find oxygen in the thin air, and every breath was labored. Little more than two thousand feet of the climb would remain after that, but every foot of it could turn deadly at any time.

Lack of oxygen affected climbers in different ways. Annie had heard some of them talk about being above twenty-six thousand feet as a mystical experience, a climber's equivalent of a runner's high, when the body was using up oxygen faster than the lungs could filter it into the bloodstream. Pain went away during those times, and with it went fear—and sometimes, common sense. Climbers were more apt to make mistakes, believing they were indestructible or that they were dreaming and nothing was real around them.

Annie continued up the incline, forcing herself not to think of Peter. At the top of the next rise, she found McLaren and Vaughn anxiously listening to the weather information on the radio. She caught only the end of the transmission, but the techs were talking about masses building to the north.

Annie scanned the skyline to the north, spotting the spindrift whirling along the peaks there. She saw only five peaks from this vantage point, but they all had spindrift creating clouds of snow on them.

"Thanks, base," McLaren said. "Over." He turned to them and looked grim. "You heard 'em? The computer model shows it's building."

Vaughn nodded but didn't appear upset. Annie was surprised because the billionaire had not only spent money, but put his pride on the line as well. Majestic Airlines wasn't the only business deal that was influenced by Vaughn's success at K2.

"We're an hour from the Bottleneck," Vaughn said. "Let's go on. It gets any worse, we'll shelter under the ice cliff, bivouac until it passes."

The Bottleneck on K2 wasn't as safe as Vaughn made it sound, and Annie knew it. It had an exposed, icy traverse with cliffs above and below.

McLaren shook his head doubtfully. "Say a storm comes in really fast. We're too high on the mountain, totally exposed."

Annie could see the logic in Vaughn's strategy, though. If they reached the Bottleneck, they would have some cover, maybe some time to make a real decision based on all the facts.

"They said it's slow moving, Tom. There's a seventy percent chance it'll turn east and miss us," Vaughn countered.

"We can't risk a storm," McLaren argued. "Not at twenty-six thousand."

"Of course we can't," Vaughn agreed. "Nobody's saying we do something stupid. I'm talking about probability, a tolerance for risk."

McLaren looked back at the mountain. His forehead wrinkled in indecision.

He's not sure either, Annie realized. And suddenly she realized that she wanted the summit, too. She wanted it for herself and for her father. Vaughn's plan was safe enough.

"Five hours from the peak," Vaughn said softly. "Tom, we're that close." He put his forefinger and thumb only a fraction of an inch apart. "Pull back now, we lose too much time. There's a lot riding on this."

"I know that." Tom met the billionaire's gaze fully. "But it's my responsibility. I can't let a marketing campaign—"

"It's not about that," Vaughn argued. "I've never been this close before."

Annie looked at Vaughn, seeing the hunger in him to summit. She'd seen it in the faces of a lot of climbers but never so naked.

"I don't want to turn back," Vaughn said, "not without

a compelling reason. Faint heart never climbed any mountain."

McLaren blew out his breath angrily. He glanced at Annie, looking for reassurance.

Annie knew an expedition guide's first responsibility was to the safety of his team and the people he was taking up. A guide was paid for his or her experience, not for the willingness to risk life and limb of every person in the expedition. But McLaren expected an answer from her, and she gave one that she knew he wouldn't fully agree with. Vaughn's conclusion made sense.

"I'm comfortable with going on," Annie said. "The Bottleneck's only another five hundred fifty feet. I think Elliot's right."

Vaughn smiled at her.

McLaren blew out another breath and finally nodded. He adjusted his pack, set his shoulders, and looked more confident. "Let's go."

Peter climbed into the military helicopter and dropped into the co-pilot's seat. The main rotor whipped around above him, but it was nowhere near as wound up as he was. He forced himself to breathe, trying to relax.

He concentrated on the snow leopard and her cubs. They would change in days now, growing bigger and losing some of their kittenish features as they became adults.

There were a number of additional pictures he wanted before he ended the assignment. Maybe he'd even stay on for a while after his contract had been fulfilled, take a chance on getting some more shots for his portfolio that he might be able to sell later.

Annie is up on the mountain.

The thought wouldn't leave Peter. He had to remember that she didn't want him there. She'd as much as told him that last night. Remembering the accusing way she'd looked at him, he knew he never wanted to go through that again.

Rasul powered up the rotors, getting ready to lift. He wasn't talking this morning, leaving Peter alone with his thoughts and personal demons.

Annie is up on the mountain.

Peter looked at K2, staring at the peaks towering high above the rest of the world, stretching another twelve thousand feet above base camp. He wondered how far the group was now.

There was more spindrift around the peaks now, and it was flurrying around *all* of the peaks, filling the air with flying snow.

That's not just spindrift, Peter realized, growing cold and frantic inside. "Wait!" he shouted at Rasul as he threw open the helicopter door and vaulted outside. He hit the helipad tarmac running, barely able to keep his balance because he was throwing himself forward so hard.

A storm in the thin air of the mountains was unstoppable, a primitive fury that could obliterate everything in its path. And Vaughn's conceit and ego had put Annie directly in that storm's path.

Peter ran faster, hoping he wasn't too late. That high up with nothing to stop it or slow it, a storm moved suddenly and quickly. By the time someone on the mountain saw the danger, the storm could already be on him or her.

Chapter 9

Vaughn Compound, Command Tent, 16,700 feet

Brian Maki pulled the last of the printout pages from the laser printer and shoved himself up from his chair. The three other computer wizards working under him fell in line behind him. He felt as if he was heading up his own small army, and considering the enemy he was taking on, that felt pretty good.

Elliot Vaughn had hired Maki because he was good at what he did. Vaughn's misjudgment was that he thought he owned Maki. But the weather officer only rented out his time, and someone's paying for that time didn't check his self-reliant streak. A number of employers had made that mistake, and that was why Maki had moved on each time. He'd never hesitated to step across corporate chains of command and onto a few toes once he was convinced of the rightness of his actions.

Maki was definitely convinced now, and angry because his expertise was being questioned. *No,* the weather officer corrected himself, *it's not being questioned. It's flat-out being thrown out the window.*

With the three computer men at his back, Maki crossed the command post and skirted the rows of high-tech computers, to confront Frank Williams. "We need to talk," Maki said.

"Later." Williams didn't even turn from the meeting he was having with the Vaughn aides who constantly flocked around him.

"Now," Maki declared, raising his voice.

Williams turned slowly to face Maki, and the deadly steel in his gaze reminded the younger man why they called him Chainsaw.

"I've just spoken to Tom," Williams said in a flat, measured voice. "They're going on."

Maki slapped the printout in his hand, shaking his head. "You've seen the projection! A weather system like this, you get off the mountain."

Williams's face hardened. "You've made your case. Everyone listened. That's the decision!"

Maki glanced at the men behind Williams, seeking support, but they all nodded. Vaughn had them well trained and well bought. They weren't going to rock the Vaughn boat even if there were icebergs all around them.

"It's a forecast," Maki said, trying to get the older man to realize getting a printout from a computer and satellite system as complicated as the one they were using wasn't like reading tea leaves or pulling a card from a Tarot deck. "Thirty percent is too high a risk! If you're not bothering about analysis, why did we come?"

"We'll assess the risk, thank you very much," Williams stated coldly. "As for why you came, if you're not on the team, I'm asking myself the same question." His head turned suddenly and his eyes narrowed.

Maki turned as well, spotting the young man who had spoken with Annie Garrett briefly the day before yesterday. He hadn't gotten the story of exactly who the guy was and he didn't know Annie all that well, but Maki had gotten the definite impression that they shared a history.

The guy looked at Maki and Williams, his blue eyes alert, sizing up the situation. He spoke calmly, politely even, but with a sense of urgency. "I'm Peter Garrett, Annie's brother."

The damn cavalry, that's who he is, Maki thought.

Peter glanced at the two men in front of him, barely re-membering their names from the introduction Elliot Vaughn had made at the barbecue two nights ago. He didn't know what Maki and Williams were arguing about, but it looked serious. "I want to check that McLaren's pulling the expedition back," Peter said.

Williams faced him, shoulders squared like a general's. "They're on target. They're going to make it."

Peter looked at the two men again, wondering how they could be so nonchalant about the weather after what he'd seen. Maybe they didn't realize how quickly things could change up there. "The wind's hit a dozen peaks to the north. Haven't you seen it?" He glanced past them to the computer equipment and the Doppler radar screen. "What does the satellite show?"

"We've assessed all the data—" Williams insisted.

"Sure," Maki spoke up, cutting the other man off abruptly, "we've seen it. It's bad air coming in from India."

Williams glared at Maki.

Watching them, Peter suddenly understood what they'd been arguing about, and the defensive posture Williams took let him know the Vaughn corporate execu-tive knew the stakes as well.

"What the hell are you guys doing?" Peter demanded. He roughly pushed past Williams and through the other Vaughn yes-men and stopped in front of the computer screens, scanning the satellite feeds.

The storm front showed on the computer screens in dark, angry red. The mass swirled, feeding on itself, grow-ing larger. *My God, it's big!* Peter realized.

He turned to Maki. "How high are they?"

The weather officer didn't hesitate. "Twenty-six thou-sand."

The Death Zone, Peter thought. He moved over two steps and seized the radio microphone at the communications system. He tapped the Send key, trying to get a response.

"What are you doing?" Williams demanded, striding across the room immediately.

"Warning my sister," Peter replied.

Williams moved faster than Peter thought the man could and snatched the microphone from his hand. "We've made the decision! You can't just come in—"

Peter struck without warning, using his weight and quickness in an effort to overpower the man. But Williams responded immediately with a forearm shiver that almost knocked Peter's breath from him. Peter balled up a fist, reaching for Williams with his other hand. Before he could strike, two of Williams's associates grabbed him and restrained him, but not before Peter was able to grab the microphone. He tried to wrest it from Williams's grip, but the older man hung onto it with grim determination.

Williams swung a fist back, and Peter knew he couldn't stop the man from hitting him in the face. The other Vaughn men were holding him too tightly.

Then a big calloused hand reached in quickly and plucked the microphone from Williams's grip as a child would pluck a daisy. The men turned on the newcomer, then stepped aside when they realized it was Skip Taylor.

Skip's face and eyes were hard-set and flinty. Peter doubted much forgiveness would be found in that stone-cold expression when Skip figured he was right. And Skip obviously figured he was right now.

Williams reached for the microphone, opening his mouth as if to protest.

"Leave it!" Skip barked.

Williams pulled his hand back.

Stepping up beside Peter, forcing back the men who had held him, Skip handed the microphone over.

Peter keyed the microphone up at once and started calling for Tom McLaren. He gazed at the angry red mass surging across the computer screens. The storm was getting bigger and meaner. He called for McLaren again, knowing there was a chance the expedition might be out of radio range even with the satellite relays.

God, please let Annie be safe.

Tom McLaren took a deep breath, already aware of how different the air was. He could breathe it in the same as always, fill his lungs completely, but he still felt that he needed more air. And that was exactly the case, he knew. They were in the Death Zone, just out of reach of the oxygen-rich atmosphere where life was easier and safer.

Summiting with oxygen supplements was still a hot topic among climbers. Many felt that getting to the top with artificial aid was cheating and that it robbed a climber of the full experience of summiting above twenty-six thousand feet. Some said that carrying oxygen was no different than carrying food, that it was just another fuel the body demanded to get the job done. Others felt that carrying oxygen along was simply too much of a burden for an expedition when they were already transporting so much equipment up the mountain.

Vaughn had chosen to summit the old-fashioned way, and McLaren was sure some of that decision was based on the Texas-size pride and ego the billionaire had. McLaren believed in summiting unaided, too, but he'd brought others up who had used oxygen. He preferred oxygen for his clients because it was safer that way.

The expedition leader glanced up Bowie Ridge and watched as Annie Garrett climbed the steep ice slope in front of them. Once they got over the ridge, the Shoulder wasn't far away. K2's Shoulder was an easy, gentle climb, as close to effortless as it got. He knew he'd feel better once they got that far.

The radio crackled under his coat. McLaren reached a hand through a special pocket and took the radio from its holder. He switched the volume up, aware that Vaughn had stopped and was looking at him. Radio contact wasn't scheduled at this time.

"Tom McLaren," a voice McLaren didn't recognize called out. "This is base camp. Come in, Tom." There was no mistaking the frenzy in the voice.

Vaughn came closer, irritation showing on his face.

"Come in, base," McLaren said.

"This is Peter Garrett speaking."

McLaren recognized the name at once. When he'd found out Annie Garrett had been coming along on Vaughn's expedition up K2, he'd checked on her. He'd already been familiar with the name but wanted to confirm what he remembered. He remembered Peter Garrett, too— and what had happened three years earlier in Utah.

"You've got a major storm coming in from the north," Peter said. "You've got to start down now."

The irritation on Vaughn's face deepened into an unhappy scowl.

"Who did you say this was?" McLaren demanded. The talk of a storm moving in was scary, but there was also the possibility that the radio transmission was a hoax. Elliot Vaughn had a lot of enemies in the business world who could arrange a radio call. The expedition leader turned and gazed north, but he couldn't see a monster storm building out there.

"Peter Garrett!" the voice insisted frantically. "Did you copy about the storm?"

Suddenly, McLaren felt as if he was on shaky ground again. His first instinct when he'd seen the spindrift had been to call it a day. As leader, the most important thing he could do on an expedition was keep everyone safe. If the radio contact was legitimate, it was possible that he wasn't doing that. "Where's Frank Williams?" McLaren asked.

Skip Taylor glanced at Peter Garrett and gestured for the microphone. McLaren didn't know Peter, but he knew Skip, and there wasn't any time for introductions and winning trust. The big Australian dropped a hand on Peter's shoulder reassuringly. Together, the two of them formed an island against Frank Williams and the other Vaughn men in the command post.

"Tom," Skip said gently, "Skip here. We're looking at the weather screens." He still couldn't believe the storm mass had gotten that huge and the expedition team couldn't see it. "If this thing doesn't—"

"—turn, you are gonna be in a load of trouble. I suggest you turn back now."

The words, delivered so matter-of-factly by Skip, weighed heavily on McLaren. He tried not to meet Elliot Vaughn's worried gaze. Gazing to the north, McLaren struggled to spot some warning indicator of the storm but couldn't. The sky looked blue.

"Tom," Skip called over the radio, "are you there?"

"Yeah," McLaren said. "Copy that. Thanks, Tom. Out." Then he turned back to Vaughn, knowing the fight for who really led the expedition was about to begin all over again. He braced himself, remembering that safety first was the most important thing.

Peter looked at the microphone in Skip Taylor's hand, then at the big Australian. He felt his heart hammering inside his chest. Worriedly, thinking the storm could possibly overtake Annie and the others before they got down, he checked the computer monitor again. The Doppler radar feed showed the angry boil of crimson hovering near K2.

"It's okay, mate," Skip said. "Tom heard me. He's a smart man. He'll nip on down the mountain now. You'll see."

Silently, Peter hoped so. He glanced at Frank Williams, who glared at Skip and him. *We didn't make any friends here,* Peter thought.

"Let's go," Skip suggested. "If my credit's still good at the base camp bar, I'll stand you to a beer."

Peter nodded, knowing he wasn't leaving base camp

now until Annie was safe again. After that, he had no clue. He and Skip walked from the command post without another word being spoken.

Elliot Vaughn watched Tom McLaren. The billionaire had gotten to know the expedition leader well over the past few weeks. McLaren was a good man, Vaughn knew, and good men always had their faults and weak points—just like a mountain. Men, however, never came as big or as strong or as fierce as a mountain. Most men buckled and broke before him.

Vaughn hadn't lost an argument or a business deal in years. When he went to the table to negotiate, he never settled for less than he wanted or more than he was willing to give. It was a way of life for him, and he'd turned that way of life into a successful business strategy.

The only thing that had ever beaten Vaughn was K2. That had been four years ago. Now he stood on the brink of conquering it, of bringing that mountain to its knees.

He wasn't going to back away now. It just wasn't in him.

"I think we should go back," McLaren stated, but his words lacked any real force.

"You do?" Vaughn asked with a little edge in his words. He bared the steel verbally, putting McLaren on notice. No one else in the group was close enough to hear them.

"I'm sorry," McLaren apologized.

Apologies, Vaughn knew from experience, were primary signs of weakness and uncertainty.

"You pay me to make decisions like this," McLaren went on.

"Actually," Vaughn said coldly, "you've been paid to get me to the top."

McLaren exploded. "You said *I* was in charge up here."

"That was when I had confidence in you."

Anger darkened McLaren's features. "Then I'll tell the others. I'll go down alone if I have to."

"Sure," Vaughn said casually, driving home to McLaren

how much control he had, going for blood now, "sit it out. The storm will turn east as forecast, and you can live it down the rest of your life."

Despite the challenge in Vaughn's words, McLaren seemed stubborn enough to handle it.

Vaughn dove in for the kill, keeping his voice light but his words heavy. "I'd say that should do wonders for your business."

McLaren's eyes swiveled up to meet Vaughn's.

He hadn't thought about that, Vaughn knew from the expedition leader's expression. *Once you get people past thinking about the present, the idea of a bad future scares the hell out of them.* The billionaire met McLaren's gaze directly, watching the man weaken and come apart right before him.

Outside Elliot Vaughn's command post, Peter trotted through base camp toward the rocky outcrop just beyond the perimeter. The outcrop had been an observation deck for years as men had climbed K2 in the hopes of summiting.

With Skip running easily at his heels, Peter made his way through the media photographers, climbers, and base camp managers, finally locating a pair of binoculars mounted on a tripod that weren't being used. He bent and focused the binoculars, sharpening the view as he panned up the mountain.

He'd heard a few stories about the Shoulder and the Bottleneck and Bowie Ridge, all the places that made up the mountain. Then there were dozens of pictures he'd taken of the mountain during the infrequent trips to base camp with Rasul. He knew the mountain the way his father had trained him to know a climb, but he'd never been up it.

He tilted the binoculars too far too quickly and found himself staring at the roiling clouds blowing the storm in. The storm had reached the summit now, wrapping greedy fingers around the mountain and preparing its assault.

Tensely, Peter shifted the binoculars back down, finding the Shoulder, then looking below for Bowie Ridge. A moment more and he found the expedition group, recognizing Annie's red coat. Then the sudden realization of what they were doing slammed into him and took his breath away.

McLaren hadn't turned the group back. They were still climbing, still aiming for the summit—where the storm lay waiting.

mortant more and sad around the expedition group doing
running. Annie's reference. Then the soldier realization of
what they were doing slammed into Jim, and took his
breath away.

McLaren started running for great Laila. They were still
several hundred yards from the complex where the storm
was raging.

Chapter 10

K2, the Shoulder, 26,500 feet

Gasping, Annie drove her ice ax into the slope and forced
herself toward the top. The Shoulder was a gentle slope, but
still not an easy one to climb for someone without oxygen.

She stopped for a moment, knowing the others behind
her would appreciate the rest. She sucked in air as if she
were drowning, trying desperately to get enough of it into
her body. Her arms and legs felt like lead. All she wanted
to do was lie down and go to sleep, but she knew that was
dangerous. With the lack of oxygen, she wasn't noticing
things around her as much now. The cold was still there,
but it didn't bite anymore, just occasionally nipped.

Glancing back, she saw Tom McLaren lift his arms over
his head to broaden his chest to take in more air. Vaughn
was next in line, followed by her cameraman and Ali.

At the top of the next ridge, Annie promised herself, *I'll
make sure he hasn't forgotten to shoot footage.* She turned her
gaze back up the slope and started going forward again.

A few minutes later, she stood at the top of the ridge.
Even though her senses and emotions were dulled by the
lack of oxygen, the horrific sight that greeted her left her
frightened, reaching down to a very primitive level.

The sky had turned black on the north side of the ridge,

and the huge storm front seemed to stretch all the way to India. The huge black clouds scudded and twisted in the sky, and the headwinds lifted spindrift and scree high into the air. As Annie watched, the spindrifts danced wildly up the other ridge, coming at her quickly.

McLaren cursed out loud beside her. His face was pinched and tight from the cold, but also from the fear that suddenly dawned within him.

At that moment Vaughn, the cameraman, and Ali crested the ridge. All of them stopped and stared in slack-jawed amazement. Even Vaughn seemed appalled.

The black clouds scudded closer, whipping and whirling, seeming to swallow themselves and explode back out again, like snakes eating their own tails, then purging them immediately in a twisted tangle of coils.

McLaren turned to the billionaire. "We're going back."

Annie watched Vaughn, expecting some kind of outburst. The man had been defeated in an assault on K2 twice now, and Elliot Vaughn wasn't a man who took defeat well.

Slowly, Vaughn twisted his head and gazed up the mountain. The summit was less than a thousand feet above them. A determined glint showed in his eye, and his jaw was firm.

He's still thinking of trying for it, Annie realized, even more amazed at his attitude than at the storm that awaited them.

"We don't have a choice!" McLaren growled, stepping into the billionaire's face, shouting so he could be heard over the roaring winds. "We're dead on the ridge! Now let's go!" He turned and headed back down the Shoulder, moving as quickly as he dared, setting a pace for the others to follow.

Insane anger replaced the disbelief on Vaughn's face. He screamed up at the mountain, shaking his fist.

Annie followed McLaren, the cameraman, and Ali. Vaughn knew the way, and if he stayed up on the mountain to die, it was his choice. She hurried down the mountain, hoping they could find safety before the storm caught up to them.

The roar of the storm grew louder, taking away all hearing. Annie continued, almost running even though a fatal misstep and a long, uncontrolled slide could send her plunging to her death. The storm wasn't going to be any more merciful.

Annie knew they'd descended five hundred feet before the storm overtook them. By the reading on her wrist altimeter, they were back at twenty-six thousand feet.

The sky around them grew blinding white, then the swirling wind filled the air with debris. Annie managed to remain upright for a time through skill, strength, and luck.

The group followed the lines of rope they'd left over the shoulder. McLaren had known they would be worn out and lethargic from the climb. He'd ordered the lines left up for support as they worked their way below twenty-six thousand.

Without warning, the storm lashed out with a ferocity that Annie had never experienced. The gusting winds knocked her flat, pressing her facedown into the snow. The line between her and Vaughn grew taut and yanked the billionaire from his feet, dragging him after her.

Annie skidded for a short distance, propelled by the howling wind, then managed to stop her forward momentum by hammering her ice ax into the frozen ground. The keen edge bit into the ground, and she gripped the handle tightly, locking down. She glanced over her shoulder and saw Vaughn scrambling behind her, flailing with his own ax now.

Squinting against the snow and scree whipping around her, Annie tried to spot a safe place. She felt the tether tighten between her and Vaughn, and thought for a moment the billionaire was going to break her loose from her hold. But he had his ice ax dug in as well.

To the left, she spotted Ali tethered to the cameraman.

They crawled along the ground away from Annie, but if there was safety in that direction, she didn't see it. Still, she knew they couldn't stay out in the open. If the wind didn't tear them from the Shoulder, the freezing temperature would induce hypothermia and kill them.

Seeing that Vaughn was anchored in, Annie pried her ice ax from the ground and stretched out her arms, bringing the ax down again. The blade bit into the ground and held. She pulled herself forward, not knowing for certain where she was headed but hoping to get lucky.

The third time she drove the ice ax home, the blade chopped through the ice, sinking much deeper than before. She raised her head, looking at the spot, a frenzy already building in the back of her mind. Just when she saw the clear ice under her and realized that she was lying on a sheet of ice crust instead of solid ground, the ice gave way with a crunch loud enough to be heard over the howling wind.

Annie fell, screaming, but she couldn't even hear herself over the storm.

Elliot Vaughn watched in astonishment as Annie disappeared into the ground ahead of him. For a moment he thought what he'd seen was an optical illusion created by the whirling snow. Then the tether between Annie and him drew taut again, yanking him forward and dragging him effortlessly across the snow-covered ground.

Vaughn tried to dig his crampons in, but the spikes only chipped away the ice because he wasn't standing and couldn't put enough weight on them to drive them deeply. He yelled hoarsely, but he knew no one could hear him. He couldn't hear himself. He turned, finding Tom McLaren behind him as the tether between them grew taut.

McLaren gazed at the place where Annie had fallen through as well. His eyes were wide. As Vaughn was pulled away, he saw McLaren shift and drive his ice ax down, sending ice chips flying.

Vaughn's safety harness tightened and jerked as Annie fought at the other end of the tether. "Stop! Stop moving!" he yelled as her efforts dragged him toward the jagged edge of the dropoff. He twisted and brought his ice ax down again, struggling to drive it deeply into the frozen earth. But the blade skidded across the icy crust as he was pulled three feet closer to the edge. He rolled over, watching as McLaren was yanked free of his own position, both of them sliding across the ice now.

The drop-off waited ahead.

At the end of the tether, Annie swung like a pendulum. Three times she crashed with bruising force into a wall of ice. Trying to protect herself, she whipped her head around, using the helmet light she'd turned on right before the worst of the storm had hit. The yellow beam seemed too weak for the cold dark that surrounded her.

She glanced up at the drop-off, knowing she was dragging Vaughn and McLaren after her. She didn't know what lay beneath her, and she didn't know how far down it was. Ice crusts like the one she'd fallen through were a typical danger for climbers.

Spotting a protrusion on the wall that looked as if it could support her, she grabbed for it, missing by only inches. Before she could draw another breath, she suddenly dropped, free-falling, knowing from the sensation that the sharp edges of the ice crust above had sheared through the kernmantle rope.

Annie plunged through the darkness, screaming incoherently. She was still screaming when she hit a ledge face-first. The impact drove all the air from her lungs, and for a moment she thought she was going to pass out. The snow and ice pressing against her face revived her.

Struggling, she forced herself to relax a little so her breath could return to her lungs. She got her arms under her and pushed herself onto her back. She peered up at the cavern roof at least thirty feet above. If the snow on the ledge hadn't been so deep, she knew the fall would have killed her.

Elliot Vaughn's head suddenly appeared above her, over the side of the ice crust. He looked panic-stricken. "Annie!" he shouted.

Carefully, checking for broken bones, Annie sat up. She turned her head, playing her helmet light in all directions. She was in a very large cave, and a tunnel extended farther into the mountain behind her. The helmet light penetrated the darkness only a little. To her right was the chasm. When she peered into it, knocking snow and ice over the edge, it looked as though it went on forever. Her stomach twisted sickeningly.

She looked back up at Vaughn. "Ice cave!" she shouted. Then she started looking for a way up.

Vaughn lay on the ground near the edge of the drop-off and tried to breathe. Even though he filled his lungs, there wasn't enough oxygen to satisfy him. The storm continued unabated, as strong and as fierce as it had been when it had first overtaken them.

He cursed the storm with every bit of anger and fear in him. But the verbal onslaught didn't last long. He didn't have enough oxygen, and that frustrated him further. So close to his objective and beaten by a force he couldn't even compete with; it was almost more than he could stand. But when he survived the storm—and, by God, he would—he planned to come back again. K2 had tried to kill him twice. *You haven't yet!* he thought fiercely. *This may be your day, but you haven't killed me yet!*

"Elliot!" McLaren called out. "Are you okay?"

"I'm fine," Vaughn said. "I'm okay." He glanced up at the expedition leader, watching the man stumble toward him, pummeled by the lashing wind.

For a moment, when Vaughn saw the storm clear above them, giving him a view of the mountain's higher peaks, he thought the storm was breaking up. Hope started to rise in him.

Then he watched numbly as a huge section of a mountain overhang was torn loose. Almost impossibly, the wind caught the school-bus–size piece of rock and ice and sent it skidding down the Shoulder. As the rock slid forward, digging deeply from its weight, it threw up a huge wave of powdery snow that rose at least two or three stories high into the air and moved like a speed-modified bulldozer driven by a suicidal pilot.

The wave of white death, followed the gentle slope of the Shoulder as though it was on a slot racing track. The only place it could go was straight for Vaughn and McLaren.

Annie felt the mountain shudder and heard the muffled thump of impact inside the ice cave. For a moment she thought a bomb had gone off overhead. She clung to the crevasse wall, halfway up to the hole through the ice crust.

Dull roaring reached her ears, filling the ice cave with basso thunder that rolled and rolled, gaining speed and intensity. Then the wall Annie was climbing started to shake as if it had developed palsy. Ice cracked around her, joining the cacophony of destruction. Rocks fell, and bigger sections of the ice crust rained down on her.

She pulled her head against her shoulder and jammed herself to the rock face as more debris fell. "Oh, God," she whispered.

Vaughn continued staring at the immense white wall of flying snow that closed on their position. He couldn't believe what was happening. The falling rock had continued to gather speed and push even more snow ahead of it. The white snow wave had to be at least four stories tall now. Anything in its path would be torn up, plowed over, or destroyed.

"Avalanche!" Ali, the porter, screamed. He and the cam-

eraman were hunkered down nearly fifty yards in front of Vaughn and McLaren.

Vaughn looked south, toward the end of the Shoulder, nearly eighty yards away. Even if they could make it that far before the avalanche overtook them, there was no way to negotiate the steep climb down safely. If the avalanche didn't tear their rappelling lines loose, provided they had time to set them, the debris would tear them free of the lines and the long fall would kill them.

McLaren, knocked about by the wind, stumbled toward the hole in the ice crust.

Understanding dawned on Vaughn. The ice cave Annie had fallen into might be the only chance they had for safety. The billionaire threw a leg over the edge of the hole, fumbling for a toehold as the snow wave thundered down on top of him and McLaren.

Chapter 11

K2, the Shoulder, 26,500 feet

Jammed into the side of the cavern wall, Annie looked up and spotted Vaughn scrambling down toward her. Thinking he might be checking to see if she was all right, she yelled, trying to tell him that it wouldn't be easy to get out of the ice cave. The walls were steep and slick, completely iced over.

Suddenly, Vaughn's grip on an outcrop slipped. He plummeted, arms and legs pinwheeling, missing Annie by inches.

Annie jammed herself harder into the wall. *He'll be okay,* she told herself. *I survived the fall.*

Then Vaughn's tether to McLaren snapped taut, slowing his fall. Annie realized that McLaren was still above. She glanced up and saw the roiling mass of powdered white snow billowing around the expedition leader. The growling rumble grew louder and closer.

Avalanche! Annie realized. She turned back toward Vaughn and leaped back down to the ledge, hoping it wasn't simply a thicker ice crust that would give way. She landed hard, shivers of pain thrilling up through her ankles and legs. She ran, feeling the ice cave shake around her, trying to stay away from the bottomless chasm to one side.

Vaughn ran ahead of her, going as far as the slack in the rope linking him and Annie would allow.

The snow wave exploded down the Shoulder. Short, gnarled trees and boulders were ripped from the ground as it passed.

Ali stood up, pulling at the cameraman, realizing that they couldn't stay where they were. He'd seen Annie Garrett plunge into the ice hole and watched Elliot Vaughn crawl in after her once the avalanche had started.

Allah willing, they would find shelter there. He tugged at the cameraman, unwilling to leave him. The avalanche was coming much faster than Ali realized, though. He managed only one short step, then the gale force winds from the air displacement caused by the tons of falling snow, ice, and rock slammed into him.

He sucked in one cold, last breath before the force lifted him off his feet. The cameraman was blown off his feet as well. Before the next heartbeat, the snow wave hit, swallowing them whole as it rolled on toward the hole in the ice crust. There was one intense moment of freezing cold, then blackness filled Ali's mind.

Inside the ice cave, the thundering roar of the avalanche filled Annie's senses. She couldn't hear anything over the noise, and the vibration rattled her body.

She tried to run, but the ground twisted and heaved beneath her. Then, just when she thought the way was clear, more debris would drop from overhead. She twisted her ankle on an ice chunk and went down, catching herself on her hands.

Unable to stop herself, she looked over her shoulder and watched as a snarling maelstrom dropped through the hole at the top of the chasm. The frozen crust that covered the chasm tore like tissue paper, giving way as a mountain of snow and ice crushed inward.

Tom, Annie remembered, looking back at the tether

that connected Vaughn to McLaren. It disappeared somewhere inside the snow.

The storm hammered down again, forcing more snow
and ice into the cave. The snow spilled over toward Annie,
mounding up and spreading outward, devouring everything in its path.

Annie pushed herself to her feet and ran. A wall of dis-
placed air caught up with her, shoving her forward off her
feet, driving her against Vaughn like a huge fist. They
both went down, tangling with each other and skidding
dangerously close to the chasm. Annie's head hit something hard and unyielding. Pain exploded inside her skull.
She felt her arms and legs go rubbery and struggled desperately to remain conscious. She was still moving, propelled by the debris, when she blacked out.

Breath burning the back of his throat, Peter ran back to
the Vaughn command center. No one tried to keep him
from entering, and he wouldn't have let anyone stop him if
they'd tried. He'd seen the storm slam into the top of K2 and
didn't know for sure what had happened to the climbers.

Williams, Maki, the other computer operators, and
Williams's team stood in front of the computer monitors.
Other than the equipment noises, there wasn't a sound in
the room.

Peter sucked in air greedily as he moved forward into
the group. He stared at the monitors, knowing the devas-
tation he was looking at was from a live video feed from a
satellite link Vaughn had arranged.

Onscreen, the cloud of powdery white snow continued
across the Shoulder, leaping off into space at the end of
the ridge the expedition team had gone up earlier. A huge
chunk of rock sailed out and dropped, pinwheeling, onto
the side of the mountain below.

Then it was over, and everything near the top of K2 was
still again.

Peter looked more closely at the computer screens,

searching desperately. Skip was at his back now. There was nothing left on the Shoulder to show that anything human had been there in years. The snow layer was pristine and looked undisturbed.

Williams turned around and spotted Peter. Immediately, the corporate man backed away, holding his hands up defensively.

Peter didn't really register the man's movement. He stepped in close enough to seize the microphone. "Come in," he called desperately. "Tom McLaren, come in! This is base camp. Tom. Annie!"

Only static and white noise came from the speaker.

"Summit team," Peter tried again, "this is base! Come in, Annie. This is base! Come in."

Annie felt as though she'd been laid to rest in a bitter cold grave. She opened her eyes slowly, remembering where she was. *I'm alive.* However, she was buried in a pile of snow and ice and a long way from help.

Bracing herself, she shifted her body. Luckily, she wasn't buried too deeply and easily slid out from under the loose debris. Her helmet light lanced the darkness of the ice cave. She was only a few feet from the chasm.

Annie spotted a thick chunk of ice lying across the chasm. It must have fallen through the crust, and it now formed a narrow, fragile bridge. However, there was nowhere to go on the other side, which was piled with snow and ice that had tumbled into the chasm.

Greenish ice gleamed on the walls around her, and from the ceiling above. Ice and snow continued to shift, dropping down in clumps. The cave came to an abrupt end at a chasm only a little farther ahead and the ceiling was uncertain, looking like a haphazard logjam of rock and ice. Occasionally the jumbled mess creaked, as if it all might suddenly come tumbling down.

Annie ran her hands over her arms and legs automatically, checking for breaks or unusual swellings. Satisfied that she was intact enough to begin searching for the others, she pushed herself into a standing position.

A moaning sound drew her attention. She traced it to the closest helmet lamp and found Tom McLaren lying half-covered by debris.

McLaren looked pale, but Annie didn't know if that was from injuries or the dimness of her helmet light. She worked quickly to clear away the debris to assess the damage he'd suffered. If it wasn't life threatening, however, she didn't want to take off his parka. Body heat was going to be hard to conserve in the freezing ice cave.

McLaren held his left hand against his ribs and groaned every time she touched that area or he had to shift. Annie took her pack off and rummaged through one of the outer pockets for her medical kit. At least she could try to make him more comfortable.

Vaughn joined them, glancing at McLaren. Annie studied the billionaire's face, looking for some sign that he wasn't going to be able to handle what had happened to them. But he looked fine physically and emotionally.

Moving carefully, Vaughn reached inside McLaren's jacket pocket and took out the radio. He didn't ask about McLaren and that bothered Annie. Was Vaughn that selfish, or did McLaren's situation look so bad that he didn't want to ask?

Vaughn pressed the Send button on the radio and spoke more calmly than Annie thought she could have at the moment. "Come in, base. This is summit team. Do you read me? Come in, base."

No one answered Vaughn's call, though, and Annie tried not to let that bother her. She occupied her mind with taking care of McLaren.

"Anyone," Vaughn tried again, "do you read me? This is the Vaughn summit team. Come in!" His voice sounded a little more strained now. "Come in, base."

Annie kept working, but she listened to the silence, too. No one could hear them, and she had no idea how they were going to get down from the mountain.

Vaughn didn't give up, though. He kept clicking the Send button on the radio and repeating his message.

Peter sat quietly in a chair at the communications equipment. None of Vaughn's people even tried to move him. He held the microphone in his hand and listened to the meaningless blur of white noise coming over the radio channel.

Annie is up on the mountain.

He studied the live satellite feed coming through the monitors. Nothing moved on K2's Shoulder; maybe nothing up there was left living.

It hurt him to think that. And it brought Utah to the forefront of his mind all over again.

More base camp personnel and visitors had made their way into the Vaughn command center. Most of them, when they talked at all, talked in whispers that carried only a few feet. Life had slowed down to a dirge.

Peter adjusted the volume on the radio, turning it up. But all he got was an increased broadcast of white noise and the infrequent clicks.

Coffee flowed constantly now as everyone settled in for a long wait, not knowing what else to do.

Ed Viesturs stayed in the back, talking to a few of the other men who had summited K2, and Peter knew they were probably comparing their own close calls. Viesturs had lost a friend on Everest, Peter recalled. Monique, who worked for Skip, was there as well, though she kept to herself mostly.

Peter lowered the volume on the radio, listening intently. He ignored the bursts of static and rush of white noise. He listened only for the clicks. Why were they spaced so far apart? Why did they transmit so clearly? He glanced around the room, thinking desperately.

Kareem, the slimly built porter Peter had hired to work with him at the snow leopard shoot, stood near the doorway talking to other men. Peter had discovered that Ali, the porter who had gone with Annie, was Kareem's cousin. He kept watch over the monitor and Peter.

Click. Click. Click-click.

The clicks came through distinctly, through the white noise and the static.

Peter stood, growing excited. He tapped the microphone's Send button repeatedly, remembering the rhythm, surprised at how easily it came back to him.

The clicking Send button echoed over the command center. People stopped talking, and every eye in the room turned to him. Peter knew they were thinking he'd lost it completely, but he knew what he was doing. His dad had taught him the skill, and somehow he'd never forgotten. He kept clicking.

C'mon, Peter thought anxiously. *Be there, Annie!*

At first Elliot Vaughn thought the radio was busted. It had clicked only every now and again earlier, but now there was a machine-gun staccato coming over the radio. He glared at the device, thinking, *Cutting edge, huh? Top of the line?* He shook his head, listening to the infuriating clicking. *End of the line is more like it.*

Annie snatched the radio from him unexpectedly.

Vaughn started to react. This was his expedition, his command. Whoever lived and died here was going to do it on his say-so. He started to speak, then he noticed what Annie was doing.

The clicks she made had a rhythm, and they filled the ice cave.

Sudden understanding dawned in Vaughn. "Morse code?"

Annie nodded, smiling at the radio as though it was the greatest thing she'd ever seen. "My father took us caving when we were kids. He always said a real adventurer left a margin for escape. If you got lost down there, knowing Morse code could save your life."

"Smart man, your father," McLaren said weakly. He tried to smile but instead grimaced in pain.

"He sure was," Annie agreed, continuing to click.

Vaughn studied McLaren, trying to figure out how

much the man had left in him. So far they didn't know the extent of his injuries, but Vaughn felt they had to be fairly major. McLaren was the weak link in their survival. If McLaren couldn't help himself down the mountain, their chances of rescuing themselves grew even slimmer.

And one thing Elliot Vaughn had always prided himself on was knowing when to cut his losses. He was absolutely ruthless when it came to that.

"Are they all right?" asked one of the reporters who had slipped into the Vaughn command center.

Peter ignored the question, concentrating on translating the clicks that sounded from the other end of the radio frequency. More people asked questions as well, crowding closer.

Brian Maki strode up beside Peter, listening intently and waving the others back, keeping Peter's working space clear.

Peter appreciated it. He'd learned Morse code years ago, and it wasn't coming back as quickly as he'd hoped.

"There's three of them," Maki announced suddenly.

Peter sighed with relief, grateful that someone else in the room knew Morse code. There would be less chance that he'd make a mistake.

"Vaughn," Maki said.

Williams cheered suddenly, the noise loud and almost frightening in the packed command center. The computer techs and other Vaughn people joined in. They crowded around Maki, congratulating him, disrupting his concentration.

Maki held up a hand as the second name came through. "Tom."

Viesturs and the other base camp personnel joined in the celebration, yelling and hugging each other.

"Annie," Peter said with relief, not waiting on Maki to get all of it. Brian patted him on the back. Peter glanced up and saw Kareem standing nearby, patiently waiting. Peter stepped forward, feeling guilty all of a sudden for not thinking of the others in the command center waiting for news. "I'm sorry, Kareem."

Kareem nodded stoically. "Three survived. Maybe the others did, too."

Peter didn't have the heart to take the thin hope away. From the little that Annie had sent through and the way the storm had looked, Peter doubted that anyone else was alive. "Maybe they did." He turned his attention back to the microphone, sending a new message.

Annie listened to the series of clicks, translating almost instantly now. All her old skills were coming back.

Vaughn stepped close to her. Despite his calm demeanor, Annie sensed the tension within him now. Vaughn was used to being in control of everything around him, and it was obvious that he knew he wasn't in control of their present situation.

"Tell him we can't keep talking," Vaughn instructed. "We have to save power."

Annie almost rebelled but caught herself in time. The radio conversation felt like a lifeline, a reminder that they weren't finished yet. And she was talking to Peter on the other end; talking and not arguing. It felt good, promising.

"He's right," McLaren said softly. "What does Peter say, Annie?"

Annie smiled, feeling better than she had in a long time. "They're coming to get us."

McLaren's encouraging smile turned into a pained grimace. He pressed his hand more tightly against his side and clamped his lips together.

Hold on, Annie thought as she looked at McLaren. *Just hold on a little longer.* She hoped he could because watching him die and knowing there was nothing she could do would be unbearable.

Chapter 12

Peter turned from the microphone, his mind already filling with ideas and plans. Not much of it was making sense, but he felt the driving need to get started.

Annie is up on the mountain.

He looked at the anxious faces gathered around him. The main question everybody in the command center had was how they were going to get the survivors down from the mountain.

"It's not gonna be just snow," Peter spoke up. The others stopped talking to listen to him. "It'll be rock. We'll need equipment. Drills. Winches. Jackhammers." He knew that from the description Annie had given of the blockage at the top of the ice cave.

Several of the older climbers glanced at one another with raised eyebrows.

Peter went on, not wanting to lose momentum. "I don't know how much of that stuff—"

A quiet, authoritative voice spoke up from the back of the command center. "And how do we get 'em up there, Mr. Garrett?"

Peter paused, thinking, feeling stupid and frustrated at the same time. There was no way to get heavy equipment

107

up onto K2. Helicopters couldn't get that high in the thin air, and there was no way climbers could pull up heavy equipment in time on their own. "Then we dig," he said. "With ice axes, shovels if we have to! We've got enough climbers here—"

Most of the crowd broke eye contact with him then, listening but not agreeing. They didn't respond in any way at all.

"What do you think we should do?" Peter shouted. "Leave 'em there?" He felt so mad and frustrated that he wanted to hit something, somebody. *Why aren't they listening?*

Annie is up on the mountain.

Skip Taylor stepped up beside Peter and took him by the arm. The big Australian pulled Peter into motion, ushering him toward the door. From the looks of most of the people, Peter realized they were glad he was going.

Outside the Vaughn command center, Skip rubbed a big-knuckled hand over his lower face and gave himself a moment for composure. All his life he'd been accused of speaking before he'd clearly thought things through. Seeing Peter exhausted and distraught, Skip knew that if he stepped on his toes the young man would probably try to deck him.

Just remember, mate, that's his sister up there. Skip spoke softly, but he spoke frankly. "Look, Peter, you can't ask people to work up there. You've never been that high. Just staying alive is a triumph."

Anger pinked Peter's face. "So we walk away?" He paused. "Forget about them?"

Skip patiently went on. "I figure they had one fuel can each. That means they can melt ice and rehydrate with water for a day. At twenty-six thousand, without it, their lungs will fill with fluid. Pulmonary edema. They'll die within another twelve. That gives us a window of thirty-six hours."

Even knowing the numbers and dangers, Peter wasn't

going to quit trying. "My father told me Montgomery Wick speed summited in twenty-four."

"We're not Montgomery Wick," Skip pointed out. "Even if we were, how long does that leave to get through the rock and ice filling that chasm?"

Peter didn't answer.

Don't hold back on him, mate, Skip told himself, hating how negative he was being. *He needs to hear it all, and he needs to know how impossible all of this is.* "We haven't even got the exact location! How much time is that gonna take?"

Pain filled Peter's eyes, and Skip almost couldn't stand the guilt that he'd helped put there.

When Peter spoke, his voice was low and firm. "I won't let Annie die."

"So tell me," Skip said, thinking he wasn't getting through to Peter at all, "what are you gonna do?"

Then, in the distance, the Pakistani guns launched another fusillade toward India. The harsh detonations rolled over them from the other side of Siachen Glacier.

Slowly, Peter turned toward the sound, and in his eyes Skip could see something stirring.

Peter followed Colonel Salim across the Pakistani Ranger outpost grounds. Once motivated, the colonel set a harsh pace and Peter had to hurry to keep up. But the brisk speed helped keep the urgent need clamoring inside him at bay. The rescue effort was up against the clock. Time didn't stop, didn't slow down, and didn't take a breath.

"Sergeant Asim," Colonel Salim barked.

The Pakistani sergeant guarding the small cinderblock building surrounded by sandbags saluted quickly, then reached out and opened the door. The colonel led the way into the small bunker.

Peter glanced around the interior of the bunker as Skip and Rasul filed in behind him. The only light in the room came from outside, leaving a lot of shadows. Wire racks

109

and shelves lined the walls and stood in the center of the room. Ammo crates and metal boxes stood neatly in line.

The colonel gave an order, and Sergeant Asim walked to a small crate at the end of one of the freestanding shelves in the center of the room. Gingerly, the sergeant knelt and removed a blanket from the shelf. Then he tugged the small crate from under the shelf so everyone could see the red-and-chrome canisters inside.

Colonel Salim turned toward Peter. "Nitroglycerin, Mr. Garrett. I wouldn't touch it with one of those English barge poles."

"The contractors use it to blast rock for the gun emplacements," the sergeant said in a low, reverent voice, as if concerned that speaking loudly might set off the nitro. "Low freezing point, apparently, and more powerful than Semtex."

Peter nodded. He'd seen nitro at work, but he'd never met anyone who was happy working with the explosive. He felt Skip looking at him, but he didn't look back. Rasul didn't look very happy about the thought of transporting the nitro aboard the helicopter. The nitro was the only chance Peter had been able to come up with for Annie.

"My responsibility for these materials ends at that door," Colonel Salim said. "I want to make that clear. This is your decision, Mr. Garrett. It has nothing to do with the Pakistani army." He shrugged. "Which is a legal way of saying I think it's madness."

Maybe, Peter thought, *but maybe madness is what it's going to take.*

"A magnificent madness, though," the colonel stated, smiling gently. "Good luck."

Peter nodded.

Cautiously, Skip stepped up to the canisters and crouched down to pick one up. It was hard to see them clearly in the gloom that filled the small building.

"Stop!" the sergeant commanded frantically.

Skip froze.

Peter looked down, following Sergeant Asim's pointing finger. The toe of Skip's boot rested in a puddle of greenish yellow ooze that must have leaked from one of the canisters. Sudden motion, Peter remembered from the colonel's warning, could set off nitro because it was so unstable. He swallowed hard. If Skip moved wrong, he could lose his foot, his leg, or even kill them all.

The room immediately went silent.

Slowly, Sergeant Asim knelt down and studied the boot. With his hands shaking only slightly, he held Skip's foot in place. "The boot," he said to Peter, who was closest.

Peter knelt, moving cautiously. He reached for Skip's boot and began untying the lace. Once he had the lace loosened enough, the big Australian lifted his foot out of the boot. Peter helped him keep his balance and move away from the spilled nitro.

Rasul came forward and pulled the boot from the nitro, then immediately headed for the door. Peter followed him, trailed by everyone else. The bunker was over two hundred yards from the rest of the camp, placed there so if it received a direct hit during an attack the exploding ammo wouldn't harm the Pakistani Rangers.

Rasul turned toward a snow-covered hill, motioning everyone else back. Peter ducked behind the sandbags with Skip, Colonel Salim, and Sergeant Asim. When he was certain everyone was safely back, Rasul threw the nitro-covered boot toward the hill, then dove to the ground himself.

The boot sailed through the air and hit the hill. The explosion threw off a wave of super-heated air that washed over Peter and left a crater in the earth. Peter stared at the damage and realized what he was about to do—what he was about to ask other people to do.

Back at base camp, Peter stood in front of the climbers he and Skip had assembled. Startled amazement registered on the features of most. He hadn't expected any less, and he didn't blame them. He only hoped enough were willing to try.

Malcolm Bench, looking as if he'd just gotten out of bed, was the first to speak. "Let me get this straight," he growled. "You wanna go up that hill with a can of nitro strapped to your back and hope it doesn't blow. Is that right?"

Peter wished there was a more tactful way to describe the scenario, but he wasn't willing to soft sell it. "Yes." Skip stood at his side, but Peter didn't know how much that helped. At face value, the idea was at least three steps on the other side of sane.

Arms crossed over his chest, Cyril Bench shook his head sadly. "One hundred thousand sperm, and you were the fastest?"

A few of the climbers laughed out loud before they could stop themselves. Peter ignored the comment. Cyril was playing to the audience, and the audience thought the idea was ludicrous.

"I've asked Skip," Peter said. "He's coming. I need four more. A speed ascent, climbing in pairs, one canister per team."

"People gotta share?" Malcolm said. "Won't everybody want their own bomb?"

There was more laughter this time but still no volunteers. Peter scanned the crowd, trying to find any friendly faces. He spotted Ed Viesturs at the back of the crowd. "Mr. Viesturs? You're the best climber here."

Viesturs met and held Peter's gaze for a moment. Then the climber looked up at K2. He shook his head. "Maybe you'll be remembered as a better man than me, but this is suicide."

"And if we just leave them there?" Peter asked challengingly. "What do you call that?"

"Reality," Viesturs replied. "You're willing to risk six lives to save three. How do you feel about that?"

"Exactly the way you do," Peter answered. "Your best

friend died on Everest, didn't he? Say he hadn't. What would you do if it was him up there?"

Viesturs remained silent.

Then a quiet voice spoke up from the back. "I'll go." Kareem stepped forward. "Ali is my cousin."

The other climbers looked at Kareem as if he was crazy, but some of them looked embarrassed as well.

"What about you, Malcolm?" Skip asked. "You and your brother have been up there."

The Bench brothers looked at each other, then turned back to Skip and answered together. "No."

"I mean," Malcolm asked, "who'd want to leave this place?"

Cyril nodded in agreement. "Excellent facilities—personal hygiene notwithstanding."

"Wonderful climate," Malcolm added. "Frostbite's almost cured."

"Stuff it," Cyril declared. "We'll wait till they put in the ski lift."

"Yeah," Malcolm said. "Terrible if we came to the Himalayas and actually had to do some climbing."

"It would take too much time away from working on the autobiography," Cyril pointed out, looking meaningfully at Viesturs.

"Or rustling up endorsements," Malcolm said.

Cyril turned around, and shouted at the other climbers. "What's wrong with you wankers?"

No one in the crowd made a reply.

Malcolm glanced at Peter. "We're in."

"Thank you," Peter said, feeling better. *It is crazy, but it can be done.* He was convinced of that. He had to be. "One more."

Dead silence filled the assembly area again. Peter looked around the crowd, feeling increasingly desperate. He wanted to shout at them, to make them believe the plan could work, just as he had to believe it could work.

Then Frank Williams stepped forward. Peter hadn't even known the corporate man was there.

"I'll write a check now to anyone who goes," Williams stated flatly. "Whether Elliot makes it or not, it'll be waiting for you when you get back. Five hundred thousand dollars."

The silence remained, filling the area at the bottom of the savage mountain. Then Cyril broke it. "Does that include the tip?"

Laughter broke the tension, but no other volunteer stepped forward.

Five, Peter thought. *If we can do it with six, surely we can do it with five.* It looked as if they were going to have to.

Annie listened to the radio clicks, converting them into a message inside her head. When Peter was finished, she signed off and turned to Vaughn and McLaren. The cold and the lack of oxygen were getting to them now. Both men were pale, and their lips had turned slightly blue from lack of oxygen. She knew she must look the same. A small headache had settled in behind her temples.

"Peter's been to the military," she told them. "They've got explosives. Says they're going to blast their way down to us."

McLaren stared at her, his face pasty in the light reflected from the ice walls. Despite the cold, his eyes burned with fever. "How are they going to find us? We're inside the mountain. We might as well be on Mars."

"I know," Annie replied. She'd been trying not to think about that. They all needed hope at the moment. "I guess he feels he's got to do something." Her voice broke a little at the end when she thought about how harshly she'd treated Peter the other night when he'd tried to warn her about the mountain. She'd thought he'd been afraid to climb, and that was why he was telling her that attempting an assault to a timetable was wrong. But the advice he'd given her, she now realized, was the same kind of advice their father would have given them.

Conceit had brought them to the mountain, to the spot they were in now. Annie glanced at Vaughn. The billionaire sat with his back to her and McLaren, but she knew he was listening. The conceit had been Vaughn's to begin with, but she'd fostered her own conceits as well.

Vaughn had emptied their packs while Annie was tending to McLaren and talking with Peter. All of their supplies were arrayed before him, carefully grouped and organized. They had a few fuel cans, a small stove they could use to melt snow for water, medical kits, two boxes of dex syringes, a handful of spare batteries for the radio, headlamps, and a coil of rope perhaps twenty feet long.

"We've got to lay down a schedule," Vaughn said authoritatively. "It's time that's going to kill us." He turned and glanced at them. "Edema sets in if we don't keep drinking."

Annie knew that. Once dehydration set in, their blood would thicken and increase the possibility of pulmonary edema. The increased pressure in the lungs would force fluid into the air sacs of the lungs, interfering with the oxygen and carbon dioxide exchange. If left untreated, a victim's lungs would literally fill up with fluid. Annie had seen cases of pulmonary edema but had never had it herself. The thought scared her.

"I figure three water bottles, half a cup every two hours," Vaughn said. "After that, we'll use the fuel cells to melt ice. Finally, we use the dex syringes." He paused, looking at them both as if assessing them the way he had the supplies.

Annie didn't like the look, but she understood it.

"We're going to get sick," Vaughn stated, "all of us. But it's a maintenance program. Maybe we can last."

Glancing at McLaren, Annie nodded silently. It *was* a plan, and she didn't have any better ideas.

Vaughn glanced at her. "Annie, we need to give them the last known grid reference we had, then let's conserve those batteries."

Annie nodded again, then transmitted the information. At the same time, though, the idea of Peter coming up the mountain now, with the storm possibly still lurking in the area, wasn't a comforting thought. But she didn't want to die.

Chapter 13

Base Camp, 16,700 feet

Peter stared at the army survey map of K2 that he and
Skip had spread across a large table they'd pulled into the
middle of one of the Snowline Adventures huts. Both of
them searched the large-scale topographical map for viable routes. Peter knew Skip had been up on the mountain several times, so the best advice would come from
him. The map, however, was detailed enough that an experienced climber could also get a feel for the mountain.

Outside the hut, business continued in base camp.
There was probably more talk than usual, but at least the
reporters were kept at bay by Skip's threats and the presence of the Bench brothers. If Peter had one more microphone thrown in his face while someone asked him about
Annie, he knew he was going to lose it.

Peter circled an area on the map with a felt-tip pen.
"Annie says they were three hundred feet above the Anvil,
heading down, east by southeast."

"The Shoulder is an ice field," Skip said, gazing at the
map.

Peter nodded. Both of them knew that an ice field
wasn't good. There was no real safety there, and anything
could happen. *Had happened*, he corrected himself.

Monument Valley, Utah: Disaster strikes the Garrett family

K2, the Himalayas: Two of Elliot Vaughn's helicopters land in base camp

Annie Garrett— her ascent of the Eiger was the fastest for a woman

Elliot Vaughn, billionaire businessman, is determined to summit K2

Tom McLaren, Annie, and Frank "Chainsaw" Williams listen to Vaughn's speech

Major Kamal Rasul—Peter Garrett's usual
aerial transport

Hanging
upside down,
Annie
traverses a
chasm

"This is base camp," Peter calls desperately, with Skip Taylor at his side. "Tom. Annie!"

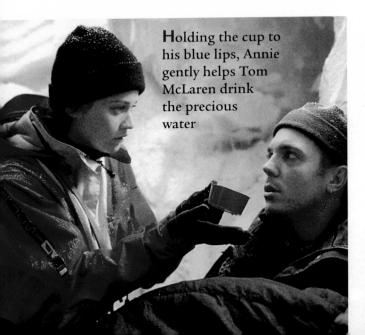

Holding the cup to his blue lips, Annie gently helps Tom McLaren drink the precious water

Palms pressed together, Montgomery Wick prays for inner peace

Peter and the rescue team set out

As Peter dangles over the three-thousand-foot drop, Wick yells, "Grab my hand!"

With the sureness born of experience, Wick ascends an ice wall

Barely hanging by her ice ax, Monique strains to support Cyril

Peter plunges down a few feet while rescuing Annie

Desperate, Vaughn swings his ice ax at Wick

Monique and Peter dig in, trying to haul up Vaughn and Wick

Back at base camp, Peter and Monique meet at Annie's bedside

"I've checked the climbing manifests," Skip said. "These are the supplies they've got."

Peter listened as Skip went through the list, and both of them knew it was best-case scenario. Annie and the others had everything on that list only if a pack hadn't been lost during the avalanche. "How long do they have?" he asked.

"We'll leave at dawn," Skip said.

Peter looked at the big Australian, not wanting to have to ask the question again.

"Twenty-two hours," Skip answered quietly, "if they're lucky."

The reply took Peter's breath away. *Less than a day? Annie would be dead in less than a day after they left?* He wanted to scream and barely managed to hang onto his composure.

"How high can we chopper in?" Peter asked.

"Twenty-one thousand, Rasul says." The pilot had volunteered his services. "Any higher, the air's too thin."

Peter made himself breathe. *Keep thinking. Think your way out of this. Dad always said a guy who can stay focused on a task could generally figure a way around it.* He looked at Skip. "Once Rasul drops us off, how fast can we get there?"

Skip tapped the map. "Negrotto Col's the only place he can land. From there, twenty-seven hours."

"Five hours short," Peter whispered, staring at the map again, seeking some answer they hadn't already discarded.

"And that's the best case," Skip said softly. "We need Montgomery Wick. He's the only one that's ever done it faster."

Peter looked up at Skip. "Will he come?"

"Four years ago a storm came out of nowhere. An American team got blown off the hill. Nine of 'em up there, including Wick's wife—she was the guide. Wick knew he couldn't help her, but he goes anyway, the only one that did. He lost all his toes to frostbite, but three blokes owe their lives to him. What do you reckon?"

Peter felt a little more hopeful. "Where is he?"

"On the mountain," Skip replied. "Up the Shoulder, I

117

guess. That's where he always goes. They never found his wife's body so he just keeps on looking."

That surprised Peter. Four years was a long time to hang onto something. Then he realized that Utah was three years ago and it still seemed like yesterday to him.

"The guy's insane," Skip said.

Peter smiled mirthlessly. "That's just what we need."

Skip nodded, smiling, too. "Strap on the nitro."

Despite the tension, Peter laughed. Who was he to call Montgomery Wick crazy? Skip laughed with him, and Peter realized perhaps everyone going on the rescue attempt was a little bit crazy. But it helped.

Sleepy, anxious, and not rested at all, Peter crossed the base campgrounds to the helipad, carrying his pack. Just before dawn he'd woken in the cot Skip had lent him, grabbed a semiwarm cup of coffee, and dressed. He'd felt guilty about even trying to sleep, but there had been no way Rasul could have flown them onto the mountain during the night.

The helicopter's rotors spun, gleaming in the first rays of dawn. Stacks of cargo sat on the snow around the aircraft, along with the chopper's storage bins, netting, and extra seats. They'd spent hours last night stripping out everything that wasn't necessary to keep the helicopter in the air, lightening the load.

Kareem had waited politely outside Skip's hut until he and Peter had stepped outside. The Bench brothers had hustled up carrying their own packs before they'd made half the distance to the helicopter.

When he got closer to the helicopter, Peter saw Monique Aubertine sitting in the stripped cargo area. She was dressed in hiking clothes and wore a heavy coat. She was smoking, seated almost comfortably beside the three nitro canisters.

Cyril stepped forward, grinning. "Now, that's a good idea—smoking next to the nitro." He paused. "Although,

118

Malcolm and I always thought you were really hot." He cracked up, laughing hard.

Pushing herself up, not even looking in Cyril's direction, Monique grabbed the lip over the cargo door and swung out of the helicopter. She dropped lithely to the ground, then wheeled without warning and punched Cyril on the chin, knocking him flat on his back.

Cyril looked up in total shock.

Malcolm stepped back out of Monique's range, laughing at his brother.

Monique rubbed her gloved fist and walked over to Peter.

"Why are you going?" Peter asked.

Monique met his gaze. "The money, of course." She glanced at Skip briefly, then back at Peter. "Skip hasn't paid anyone in months. Maybe you know a better way out of here."

"Can you climb?"

Monique turned to Skip, who had stepped away to start preparing the nitro canisters for takeoff. "Peter wants to know if I can climb."

The Australian shook his head sadly. "The worst I've ever seen. Couldn't climb a ladder."

Peter looked back at Monique. "That good, huh?"

"Yeah," Monique replied dryly. "But it was a very tall ladder."

That makes six, Peter told himself. *Three teams of two, and a bomb apiece.* He turned his attention to loading the canisters. He and Skip lifted them from the crate inside the helicopter's cargo area and passed them to Kareem and the Bench brothers, who wrapped them in blankets and rolled them tightly into backpacks. No one talked during the handling.

As soon as they were finished, Peter slid the cargo door closed and patted Rasul on the shoulder. The Pakistani major throttled up and the helicopter vibrated.

Peter sat with his back to Rasul's seat, waiting nervously. He held one of the nitro canister backpacks in his

119

arms, cushioning its movement. Skip and Cyril held the other two. If the nitro got jostled the wrong way, the rescue effort could be blown—literally—before it got off the ground. He tried not to think about it. *Hang on, Annie. I'm coming.*

Malcolm doubled over, his head between his knees.

"What are you doing?" Skip demanded tensely.

"Trying to kiss my ass good-bye," Malcolm replied.

In the next instant, the helicopter lifted from the ground, rocking slightly in the crosswinds. Peter glanced out the window, watching as they closed on K2.

Chilled and scared, Annie poured water into a cup for McLaren.

Vaughn was at the other end of the ice cave, chopping at the wall. Earlier, he'd suggested that the walls might be thin and actually cover other tunnels that led out of the mountain. He hadn't found one yet, but he kept trying. At the very least, he knew to tunnel up.

Annie admired the billionaire's ability to plan and persevere. He seemed not to know how to give up. The trait had probably served him well over the years.

Once she had the water measured out, she capped the water bottle and slipped an arm behind McLaren. Gently she eased him up and helped him drink, holding the cup to his blue lips. McLaren was barely holding his own with the pain now.

Annie glanced up, aware that Vaughn had stopped chopping at the ice wall and was watching her. *He's checking to make sure I measured the water out right,* she thought. That was one aspect of Vaughn that she didn't care for. Once a plan had been set into motion, there was no tolerance for error. Still, she knew there was value in being able to hold the line so strictly.

She helped McLaren lie back, cringing inside when she heard him gasp and wheeze, knowing that even though she was being careful that she was hurting him. "It's dawn," she told him, sharing what little hope she had. "If the weather's cleared, they'll be on their way."

"Yes," McLaren gasped, "I know." He met her gaze. "Has your brother climbed since Utah?"

Annie almost turned away. But she couldn't ignore the question for McLaren or for herself. It was something she needed to remember. "No."

"People say he lost his nerve."

Annie helped McLaren take another sip. It was work to get a full serving down him.

"Have you heard that?" McLaren persisted.

"Yeah," Annie admitted, "I've heard it." The truth was that she didn't know if Peter had lost his nerve or not.

"He'll need Wick," McLaren said.

Vaughn turned again to look at them, but Annie couldn't read the look. She remembered the confrontation at the barbecue. Despite Wick's protests that the climb might not be safe, she sensed that there was a lot more between Wick and Vaughn. She just had no idea what.

Aware of Annie's gaze, Vaughn took out his own water bottle. He dropped it, then reached for it. As he did, his helmet light lanced across the ice cave, landing on the mound of debris on the other side of the chasm.

The ice bridge gleamed when the light fell on it. Then the light fell on a piece of bright orange nylon.

Annie gently lowered McLaren and followed Vaughn to the chasm. Now she could see that the bright orange nylon was a backpack. She estimated that the chasm was fourteen or fifteen feet wide, too wide to jump across safely. But getting the pack might add to their supplies.

Vaughn knelt beside the ice bridge and tapped it gently with his ax. The edges cracked and broke easily, glittering in his helmet lamp beam as they tumbled into the black chasm.

Annie stared at the pack. It might as well have been a million miles away.

Chapter 14

Black Pyramid, 20,500 feet

"Om mani padme hum," Montgomery Wick prayed before the small, collapsible shrine in his tent. He pressed his palms together. "Om mani padme hum." He kept his eyes closed tightly, trying to will his emotions into the acceptance of the prayer.

The mantra was directed to Avalokitesvara, the goddess of mercy, the manifestation of the Buddha regarding compassion. The six syllables of the mantra purified the six poisonous negative emotions of pride, jealousy, desire, ignorance, greed, and anger.

"Om mani padme hum."

Since seeing Elliot Vaughn again three nights before, the old anger had burned in Wick, twisting his guts into knots. Myama had taught him so much about her faith, and he had been empty for so long. When she had been with him and his faith had been whole, he had known calm for the first time in his life.

Now that was gone, and he held Elliot Vaughn responsible.

The anger had driven fishhooks deeply into his mind and heart, pulling at pieces of him that could still be hurt in spite of him thinking them long dead. He'd left base camp before anything else had happened.

All he wanted was the peace he'd known when Myama had been with him.

"Om mani padme hum," he prayed. He reached for peace even though he knew it couldn't be fought for. A man had to be at rest within himself, and then the peace would come.

The prayer wheel spun beside him, catching the early morning breeze pushing in through the tent flaps. The ticking noises it made seemed to deepen and grow more frenetic.

"Om mani padme hum," Wick prayed. Then he recognized the stronger beating noise as belonging to a helicopter. His eyes opened and the anger stirred restlessly inside him. It hadn't gone away; it had only been lying in wait. He pushed up from the prayer cushion and went to the flaps.

The helicopter knifed through the sky and landed less than a hundred yards from the tent. The rotor wash pushed at the tent, shaking it.

Wick recognized Skip Taylor when the big Australian got out of the helicopter, but he didn't know the young man beside him. Turning his back to them, knowing only trouble brought men out this far, he started striking camp.

Whatever they had to say, Wick wasn't interested.

Peter grew frustrated talking to Montgomery Wick's back, but he didn't give up. He wasn't going to give up anything. However, the sun was continuing its journey across the sky, eating seconds that turned into minutes. And those minutes were precious. He laid out the whole avalanche story for Wick, thinking maybe he'd at least trigger a sympathetic response.

Wick hadn't paused a moment during Peter's story, continuing to dismantle the tent. But he paused when Peter finished, turning to him without expression.

"I'm not interested," Wick stated flatly, then he went back to folding the tent.

Peter glanced at Skip, not understanding at all. This man was nothing like the one Skip had described on the way up the mountain.

"Is it the rescue?" Peter asked. "You went on one before that everyone said was impossible. You were the only person who did. Three men owe their lives to you."

"Four years ago," Wick replied. "Now I climb just for myself."

Peter thought furiously, then took another tack. "My father was a climber. Royce Garrett." It was the first time Peter had said his father's name in three years. "He climbed with you once on Everest. He told me stories about you." Peter thought Wick might have hesitated when he heard his father's name, but he wasn't sure.

"I don't give a damn," Wick said. "I don't live my life so you can have someone to look up to."

Before he knew it, Peter took a step forward and his voice hardened. "My sister's dying up there, Mr. Wick. You can't just walk away."

Wick turned on him suddenly, and for a moment Peter thought the man was going to strike him. Wick's dark eyes blazed.

"Next time you lecture me," Wick grated, "get your facts right. It'll make it less embarrassing. Up there you're not dying, Mr. Garrett—you're already dead."

Barely controlling himself, Peter stared at the man. "What the hell happened to you?"

Wick turned and started to walk away.

Angry and frustrated, Peter didn't hold back. "Vaughn's people are offering five hundred thousand dollars to anyone who goes. Maybe that'll make a difference." For a moment Peter thought his words had fallen on deaf ears.

Then Wick stopped. But he didn't turn around. "Why would they do that?"

Before Peter could answer, Skip said, "Their boss is one of the people trapped on the mountain."

Slowly Wick turned to face Peter and Skip. Peter saw dark lights glittering in the man's eyes. "What's their supply situation?" Wick asked.

Peter stepped out of the conversation, letting Skip handle it. Somehow the big Australian had reached Wick. Part of Peter was angry that Wick would help Vaughn before he'd agree to help Annie, but he swallowed his anger. The good thing was that Wick was coming. At least, that's what Skip believed.

"They've got enough supplies to last for twenty-two hours," Skip said.

"Who's coordinating at the base?" Wick asked.

"The Vaughn team," Peter answered.

Wick shook his head. "That's your first mistake. I need someone down there with experience." He looked at Skip. "Taylor, you know more about the mountain than anyone."

"What are you talking about?" Peter demanded, feeling as if everything he'd set up was being destroyed. "Skip's one of the best climbers."

Wick wheeled on Peter, facing him squarely. "Before we get started, let's agree on one thing. This is not one of those climbing democracies. On a rescue mission we don't vote, we don't question, we don't argue. You listen and do exactly as I say. Understood?"

Peter fell silent, trying to figure out if having Wick involved was any better than his not being involved.

Wick turned to Skip and said, "The chopper will pick you up on the way back."

Skip looked at Peter, letting him understand it was his call. Peter studied Wick, knowing the man wasn't going to back off. He remembered what Skip had told him about Wick searching for his dead wife all over the mountain, and he remembered what his father had told him about the man. It was hard to reconcile the two images with the person that stood before him.

"Okay," Peter said quietly, but he wasn't convinced.

Montgomery Wick looked at the motley crew assembled in the helicopter cargo hold and didn't let any of the hesitation he felt show on his face.

Cyril and Malcolm Bench he knew from base camp, having heard stories even though he'd never talked to either of them. They were both stand-up guys and good climbers, but quirky and opinionated. It was better to get the testosterone out of the air early. Kareem, the porter, was a definite question mark because Wick didn't know if the guy could climb or not. The woman was another question mark. And Peter Garrett? Mentally, Wick shook his head. For all he knew Peter Garrett's nerve had ended up on the desert floor with Royce.

And this was the rescue crew.

Adding to that the fact that they'd be carrying unstable nitro strapped to their backs up a mountain, and it was one big cosmic joke. If it had been four years ago, Wick might have joined up and believed in what they were doing. Now he knew he was going because Vaughn was up on that mountain. There was only one way he was going to assuage the rage within him.

Wick raised his voice to be heard over the whirling rotors. "This is the way we split it. Malcolm, you'll climb with Kareem."

"No, I bloody won't," Malcolm responded instantly. "Let me tell you my rules, sport."

Wick bristled but quickly quelled his irritation. He wasn't here to argue, and the sooner they realized that, the better off they all would be.

"Don't eat at a place called Ma's," Malcolm said, "don't play cards with a man named Doc, and whatever else you may do, *never ever* climb with someone you don't know." He glanced at Cyril. "Bro and I go together."

Cyril smiled mischievously. "Frankly, I'd rather climb with the sheila."

Wick pinned Malcolm with his gaze, backing the bigger man down. "Thank you, Mr. Bench. Now let me tell you mine. I'm putting a strong climber with a weaker one. You'll go with Kareem."

Malcolm stared hard at Wick, but Wick returned the stare full measure. After a few seconds, Malcolm looked away.

Wick shifted his gaze to Peter. "Mr. Garrett, you'll be climbing with me." If the young man took any insult with the pairing, he didn't show it. "Cyril, guess what?"

Grinning, Cyril turned toward Monique and leered. "Come on, darling. Give us a kiss for luck."

Instead Monique shot him a devastatingly nasty look.

Wick ignored the byplay. With the personalities involved and the situation they were stepping into, there was going to be some tension that needed releasing. He turned his attention to the whole group again. "We'll take the west ridge. Cyril, up through the Mushroom. Malcolm, you climb Hockey Stick Gully. I've been up 'em all. The speed is roughly the same."

He spread out each team's map and started marking the route, working quickly and efficiently, lost in the rescue attempt—the climb—the way he used to be. It was almost like coming home, only there was never going to be a real home anymore.

At twenty-one thousand feet, the military helicopter was having real trouble keeping altitude. The air was too thin for the rotors to create much lift.

Peter sat in the cargo hold, arms and legs wrapped around one of the nitro canisters, watching through the windows as the crags of the mountain came closer. *One good bump,* he thought, swallowing hard.

Rasul sat silent and tense in the pilot's seat, keeping a firm grip on the yoke. The helicopter rose and fell in the uncertain air as if it were a ship at sea, slewing sideways at times.

Monique stared at the nitro canister in Peter's arms, then glanced at Peter. The look held just a moment too long before she looked away. Her face was white. Peter stared at Wick. The older man sat with his back against the cargo bulkhead, relaxed and waiting.

Peter caught sight of the tiny ledge that was their target on Negrotto Col. Although it looked much smaller from the wobbling helicopter, the area was nearly forty feet by sixty feet. Rasul didn't have room to put the helicopter down there safely in the buffeting winds. If the wind caught the aircraft wrong, it would smash the helicopter against the wall on the other side of the ledge.

Fighting the crosscurrents, Rasul gently guided the helicopter toward the ledge. Peter waited tensely. Then the helicopter vibrated slightly when the right skid made contact with the ledge.

Wick handed his pack to Malcolm and twisted the cargo door latch free. The wind caught the door and slammed it open, sucking the heat from the cargo area. Peter felt his exposed skin draw up at once.

Below them, the skid raked across the stone ledge.

"Move!" Rasul yelled back. "I can't hold it for long!"

Wick waved for Monique, helping her to the door. She moved with him, but the wild wind invading the helicopter cargo area pushed at her, making it hard to move forward even with Wick's help. She hesitated at the door.

From what Peter remembered of the maps, Monique was looking out over a three-thousand-foot drop. She took a deep breath, then nodded to Wick. He helped her step out onto the skid Rasul had managed to hang on the ledge.

As the wind battered her and shoved at the helicopter, she eased forward, having to fight the rotor wash coming from overhead as well. She went step by step, with Wick leaning out the cargo door to help her.

Skip Taylor watched through binoculars he'd found in Wick's campsite, scanning the assault on Negrotto Col.

That high up against K2, the helicopter looked a lot like a dragonfly. Both, he told himself bitterly, were about as fragile. One good smashup against the mountain, and helicopter parts and bodies would be raining down a good long way.

In disbelief, Skip saw Monique step through the cargo door out onto the skid. The wind whipped at her clothing, pulling at her while it rocked the helicopter. Skip's heart beat a little faster, and he felt guilty about not being there.

He felt guilty about Monique's presence there, too. He hadn't exactly turned out to be the knight in shining armor that she'd hoped he would be. *No*, he told himself, *that's unfair. She never expected a knight in shining armor. She was just looking for a guy who could hold his own. Somebody stable.* That person just wasn't him.

Barely breathing, not really even aware of the cold, Skip watched Monique slide along the helicopter skid, inching forward. She had more pure guts than any woman he'd ever known.

Monique clung to the side of the helicopter, rocking with the aircraft's sudden motion.

"C'mon, Rasul," Skip whispered hoarsely. "Just a couple of minutes, mate. Steady hand will do the job."

As he watched, Monique pushed off the side of the helicopter and jumped.

Chapter 15

K2, Negrotto Col, 21,000 feet

Monique Aubertine's stomach flip-flopped as she kicked free of the helicopter skid and threw herself at the ledge. For a moment she thought the winds had caught her just enough to push her off the ledge. Then her feet slammed into the frozen earth and barren stone hard enough to ache all the way up to her knees. She fell forward, catching herself on her hands.

Once she was certain of her footing, she stayed low until she was safely out of range of the slashing helicopter blades. She reached into her pack for a piton and her ice ax, glancing over her shoulder toward the helicopter. The landing skid popped against the ledge repeatedly, knocking debris into the waiting drop.

Peter started to go next, carrying one of the nitro canisters in his backpack. Wick stopped him with a hand against his chest.

Monique took a deep breath as she watched, realizing that if Peter misstepped and fell, the helicopter and all of them would be blown to bits. *I just want to get out of here and onto someplace new,* Monique reminded herself. *But I'm not ready for a harp and a halo yet.*

Wick signaled Malcolm forward. Just as Malcolm stood

in the door, Cyril pulled his brother's head toward him and kissed him on the cheek. Then Malcolm stood on the helicopter skid and started inching his way forward.

Monique turned her attention to the wall and set the piton. She drove the sharp end deeply into the rock, then snapped a carabiner to the piton and her safety harness, paying out line as she moved back toward the helicopter to help Malcolm.

Wick and Peter held Malcolm as the helicopter bucked as it struggled to stay aloft in the thin air. Malcolm's foot slipped, and he very nearly fell. Wick and Peter pulled him upright and started him forward again.

Setting her safety line so she couldn't be dragged over the side of the ledge, Monique reached for Malcolm's hand. Wildly, Malcolm reached for her, leaning forward till he had no choice but to keep going.

Brian Maki chewed gum as he shifted his attention from the Doppler radar readout and the live satellite feed showing the rescue team's landing attempt on Negrotto Col. The storm mass remained, dark and angry red as it swirled restlessly across the screen like a Portuguese jellyfish waving its barbed tentacles. At any moment the storm could break loose again, unleashing its destructive force.

Brian glanced at Frank Williams standing slightly to one side. The Vaughn CEO hadn't spoken to him since the encounter with Peter Garrett. According to Vaughn's and Williams's way of thinking, Maki had sold them down the river, placing someone else's needs above their own.

It didn't matter that Maki had been right and that Vaughn was now trapped in an ice cave up on the mountain. They'd accuse him of being weak, of turning against them and their agenda before things had turned bad.

To hell with them both, Maki thought. And although the Vaughn job was desirable and he'd miss it, there were plenty of other jobs out there.

On the satellite feed, Malcolm Bench took Monique

Aubertine's hand. She pulled him toward her, falling backward as she struggled to get him onto the ledge, and wrapping her other arm around him. They landed in the snow piled on the ledge. Malcolm rolled off her and helped her to her feet.

That's one gutsy lady, Maki thought. He turned his attention back to his crew, making sure they were staying on top of the situation and keeping alternate feeds ready in case the primaries went down.

Maybe his career at Vaughn's corporation was over, but Maki's job wasn't finished until those people were safely off the mountain.

If that was possible.

Once Kareem was on the ledge, Monique guided him to the line she had secured to the piton. Kareem pulled himself along the line and snapped his own harness to the piton. Malcolm's line was there already.

When Kareem looked back at Monique, she waved him over to the side and mimed hammering another piton home in the wall because she knew she wouldn't be heard over the loud rotor wash. Malcolm had hurriedly approached the helicopter, ready to help the others.

Kareem nodded his understanding, then gingerly shucked off the backpack carrying the nitro canister. He took a short moment to bank snow around the pack so the canister couldn't fall over, then took out a piton and found a place on the wall nearly ten feet distant from Monique's piton.

Monique let out a tense breath when Malcolm grabbed Cyril's hand.

The brothers stumbled across the uneven ground when Cyril touched down and almost fell. The nitro in Cyril's pack rocked uncertainly, and Monique wondered if the straps held the canister securely enough. Then the brothers hugged, both balanced and ready. Malcolm guided Cyril along the safety line.

The helicopter jumped again like a fish hitting the end of a line, bouncing up a couple feet before crashing back down. Somehow, Rasul managed to keep the skid on the ledge. The banshee screech of metal on rock filled the air, temporarily erasing the sound of the straining engine.

Wick checked the nitro canister on Peter's back, making sure the straps securing it were still tight. Satisfied, he motioned Peter toward the door.

Monique watched Peter grab the cargo doorframe. Skip had told her about Peter last night, after Peter had gone to sleep. Her heart had gone out to Peter when she'd learned about Utah, but she knew she'd already been interested in him the first day she'd seen him. There'd been something about the eyes. She'd never seen any eyes so blue or so haunted.

And that, she told herself angrily, *is how you end up in trouble.* She'd thought Skip was different, and he was. Skip Taylor was stronger and more individualistic than any man she'd been interested in before. But the big Australian lived in barely controlled chaos. Monique needed, or wanted, something different.

Peter Garrett might be interesting, but Monique planned on getting out of Pakistan, away from the mountain. With a half-million dollars in her pocket, there were any number of places she could go. If she lived.

The Bench brothers secured the second nitro canister on the ground. Malcolm started securing the other packs so they wouldn't be blown off the ledge by the rotor wash. Cyril pounded another piton into the wall.

Between the brothers, Monique realized, they'd have a million dollars. There was no telling what they would do with it, but whatever it ultimately was, she was certain people would talk about it for years.

Metal shrilled suddenly, and the helicopter tilted steeply to the left. Peter was caught with one foot down toward the landing skid, unprepared for the sudden shift.

Off balance, he flailed instinctively, releasing his hold on the doorframe and falling backward.

Monique yelled a warning, but she knew it couldn't be heard over the roar of the whirling rotor blades.

Moving incredibly fast, Wick grabbed Peter's jacket and held on. Although Peter was bigger than Wick, the older man was powerful enough to halt Peter's fall. The canister stopped only inches above the cargo hold floor. Slowly, maintaining his one-handed grip, Wick pulled Peter upright once more.

The two men stared at each other, both gasping for their breaths and relieved. Peter nodded his thanks and stepped toward the landing skid again.

An alarm from inside the helicopter blared shrilly, echoing across the face of the mountain.

"Get the hell out!" Rasul bellowed. "We're going to burn! Go! Go!"

There's not enough oxygen up here, Monique realized. *The fuel/air mix is off, running the engine hot.* That's why helicopters weren't used at this altitude or higher. If an engine conked out at this altitude, a helicopter dropped like a rock.

Rasul fought the helicopter, increasing and decreasing the throttle, trying to find a happy medium. The aircraft bounced along the ledge like a one-winged duck trying to take flight.

Peter and Wick stepped out onto the landing skid together. The shifting air currents hammered them, pulling at their clothing as if trying to rake them from the skids.

Monique moved forward, quickly reaching the end of her safety line. The climbing harness snugged up across her thighs and shoulders, holding her back as she extended her hand toward Peter, who was closer.

The helicopter alarm screamed louder, drowning out all other sounds in an ululating reverb against the mountainside.

Rasul shouted from the cockpit. "Brace your—"

Monique watched in silent horror as the helicopter sud-

134

denly dropped ten feet. Peter almost fell from the skid but managed to throw himself along the length of it, one leg dangling over the side as he grimly held on. Wick caught a railing beside the cargo door and hung on, legs touching nothing at all as the helicopter shifted sideways.

The shimmer of steel overhead warned Monique of the descending helicopter rotor. The whirling blades now chopped through the space where her head and shoulders had been only a heartbeat before. She kept hunkering down, and the blades kept coming after her.

Oh, God! she screamed silently, scrambling to get away. But the blades kept coming.

Behind her, Cyril started forward, but Malcolm held him back. Kareem tried to go around to the side, but there wasn't enough room. The angle of the tilted rotor blades had already cut off any help from that direction.

Monique got lower, then headed to the right on her hands and knees. The rotor blades chopped into the frozen ground behind her, deeply enough to leave jagged cuts, but not so deeply that the blades shattered. Scarred ice showed in the wake of the blades.

Monique flattened herself against the cold ground, knowing the rotor was still coming down on top of her. She felt the wind from the blades slapping against her in waves, the strident bleat of the helicopter alarm warring with the sound of the aircraft's failing engine.

Fully aware of the hammering chop of the rotors beating the ground as they came toward her, Monique crawled toward the only open space she saw, where the ledge was narrower.

She didn't look back, afraid she would lose her nerve or stick her head up too high and have it taken off before she knew it. She crawled, ramming her elbows against the hard, frozen earth and digging in with her toes as though she was going up the side of a steep climb.

Before she knew it, she was lodged against the mountainside, all out of ledge. The rocky ground beneath her vibrated as the rotor blades continued digging into it, coming closer with each drumming beat. Frantic, mind screaming, she flipped over, wanting to see if she'd made her way clear.

The rotor blades flashed only inches from her face, getting closer more slowly now. Gasping, her breath almost torn away by the whipping blades, Monique pressed herself back against the hard rock behind her, seeking another inch of safety as the rotor inexorably closed on her.

Skip Taylor held the binoculars to his eyes and swore. He didn't know if Monique was alive or dead.

"C'mon, Rasul, get that damned bird back in the air where she belongs!" He adjusted the magnification, sweeping the cockpit and spotting the Pakistani major frantically working the controls.

The helicopter jerked like a live thing in the jaws of a trap, surging toward the dark sky overhead. Peter slid from the landing skid, barely able to maintain his hold with one arm while flailing with the other. He dangled over the three-thousand-foot fall.

Chapter 16

K2, Negrotto Col, 21,000 feet

Fire ripped through Peter's shoulder as he held onto the helicopter's landing skid. His mind jumped inside his skull, making sure the nitro canister was still in his pack, wondering if Monique was all right or if she'd been hit by the blades, trying desperately to grab the landing skid with his other hand before he fell.

Fear didn't touch him now. He focused on Annie, thinking about where she was and that she couldn't do anything to save herself. He looked up, feeling his grip weaken. With the helicopter jerking and the wind pulling at him, he couldn't hang on long.

He whipped his free hand forward. The metal skid brushed across his fingertips. When he tried again, he caught hold of the edge and started pulling himself up. No one would go after Annie if he failed. He concentrated on that, pushing himself further than he thought he could.

Slowly, he pulled himself up till he could throw a leg over the skid. The helicopter jerked again, almost tearing itself from the ledge and from Rasul's stubborn control. Peter held on but just barely. Then he saw Wick above him.

Wick had gotten his feet under him. He held onto the skid as well and reached down. "Grab my hand! Grab it!"

His voice sounded fierce and loud even above the struggling helicopter.

Peter tried to make his hand move but couldn't. His own body resisted him, locked into survival mode and just short of being paralyzed.

"C'mon," Wick demanded hoarsely, "do it!"

Swallowing hard, his breath almost torn away by the wind and rotor wash, Peter forced himself to let go of the skid with one hand. He reached for Wick's hand, arm wavering unsteadily.

The helicopter shifted again without warning, throwing Peter backward. The aircraft dropped another foot, and the blades came dangerously close to shattering on the ledge. Peter felt his grip sliding, unable to hold on any longer.

Wick lunged down from the skid and grabbed for him. Peter slid beneath the grab and thought he was gone, his stomach turning cold and hugging his spine. Then Wick's hand closed on the top of his pack. The material ripped but held together.

Peter stopped falling and immediately reached for the skid and pulled himself up. Wick was yelling at him and at Rasul, growling commands that could hardly be heard over the tearing winds.

Scrambling, pulling himself up by sheer arm strength, Peter chinned himself on the skid. He shook his head at Wick, letting the man know his strength was fading fast. Even together they weren't strong enough to get him up completely.

The nitro canister bumped against the skid, sounding muted and hollow.

Monique froze as the whirling rotor blades continued to come at her. She strained against the rock as if she could find a crack to slide into and somehow get away. The glittering arc of death was only inches from her throat now. If her chin had been there she might have gotten her jaw slashed off.

Through the blurred haze created by the whirling blades, she saw Wick extended, something obviously very heavy at the end of his arm. *Is he holding Peter?* Whatever it was, she was certain Wick wasn't going to be able to hold the burden long.

The blades came closer. Monique's breath died in her lungs as she strained backward. There was nowhere to go.

Still, it was unbelievable when the rotor blades got close enough to actually slash through her coat sleeve. Down feathers filled the air, whacking into her face. She almost jumped, and only the cold realization that if she moved she would lose her head kept her in place.

The next blow, she told herself, trying to mentally prepare herself, amazed at how calmly she seemed to be taking it. *The next touch of those blades. At least it will be quick.* She wanted to close her eyes, but she couldn't.

The helicopter suddenly shifted again, catching a favorable twist of the wind. It rose abruptly, and the blades retreated from her throat. The helicopter kept rising, coming above the ledge now.

Peter hung from the landing skid, and Wick somehow managed to hang onto the skid with one hand and help hold Peter with the other. Monique had never seen such iron determination.

The helicopter continued to rise, and Rasul even managed to get it to hover over the ledge again. Malcolm and Cyril sprinted toward the aircraft and seized Peter between them, guiding him down to the safety of the ledge. They carefully took the nitro canister from the pack before it fell out.

Kareem ran to Wick's side, reaching up for him. Wick looked exhausted, barely managing to take care of himself now. The helicopter scooted sideways, out over the drop again. Kareem halted at the edge.

Realizing Kareem and Wick were going to need help, Monique made herself move, getting to her feet and running as fast as she could on legs still shaking. She paid out her safety line behind her, letting it slide through her gloves. The cut on her coat still leaked feathers, and she knew she'd have to patch it soon.

Rasul managed to bring the helicopter to within a few feet again, but the way the aircraft was shuddering, it didn't look as though he'd be able to hold it there for long. Gathering himself, Wick looked at Kareem and Monique—and leaped.

As he watched the live satellite feed and saw Montgomery Wick leap from the helicopter, the ledge's edge still a few feet from the landing skid, Brian Maki's heart rose to the back of his throat. Wick seemed to hang in the air for a moment, then the woman and the other man had Wick, pulling him to safety.

A thundering cheer filled the Vaughn command post.

Maki looked around in astonishment at the number of people inside the hut. Normally he'd have been territorially protective about all the equipment, but he didn't feel that way now. The people on that mountain needed as many people pulling for them as possible.

Onscreen, the six rescue climbers retreated to the ice wall, away from the violent winds and crosscurrents created by the helicopter's rotor wash.

They were alive this far, Maki knew as he checked the progress of the violent storm hugging the mountain, but their situation could get only more dangerous the higher they went. He also knew that Elliot Vaughn wasn't going to be happy about Montgomery Wick being part of the rescue effort—much less leading it. Maki had discovered more about what had happened when Vaughn had tried to take K2 four years ago.

Montgomery Wick and Elliot Vaughn shared a lot of history, and none of it was pleasant.

The helicopter lifted off the Negrotto Col ledge, then lost altitude rapidly. Skip watched through the binoculars, knowing that Rasul was trying to get more oxygen to the engines quickly so they wouldn't overheat from struggling with a too-rich feed.

He couldn't see the rescue party up on the ledge, but he knew they were safe. He tracked Rasul's progress, worrying about the helicopter and the Pakistani major. Performing the drop-off had been hard on both man and machine.

The helicopter flew easily, though.

Skip trained the binoculars up the ridge once more, but he still couldn't see any signs of the team. He put the binoculars away and stood where Rasul could see him, anxious now to get back to base camp to start coordinating the rescue effort as much as he could.

Even with this success, all the rescue team had managed to do was perhaps assure themselves of a death at a much higher altitude.

Peter lay on the ground and panted, looking up at the gray sky. Having his eyes open or closed didn't matter; he kept seeing the three-thousand-foot drop. And he kept seeing Utah.

He breathed out, then let his lungs fill again naturally, working out the cramped muscles and the leftover shakes. He watched Wick stand easily to look the group over.

"Ten minutes," Wick said, loud enough to be heard over the howling wind. He marched over to where the Bench brothers had secured the nitro canisters. "Get a drink, get centered. Then let's be on our way."

Peter sat up slowly, feeling long unused muscles ache. He studied Wick as the man took out a needle and thread from his kit and started repairing the torn pack. *What is driving you, Wick?* Peter wondered. *Why did you make such a turn-around in your decision about this rescue after you discovered Vaughn was going to be up here?*

Wick worked silently and efficiently, intent upon his task.

Peter drank a little water. Now wasn't the time to ask

Wick about his ties to Vaughn, but it would be soon. Annie was up on that mountain as well.

Shivering slightly, the headache still pounding at her temples, Annie watched the small yellow flame dwindling in the tiny stove. It bumped the bottom of the pan above it, slowly melting the ice inside. The fuel can supplying the stove would be empty soon, just as their water reserves had emptied.

She tried not to think about that. *Peter is on his way.* But that wasn't exactly a restful line of thinking, either. He could die trying to get there.

Vaughn sat on the other side of the tiny stove. He sipped his own ration of water from a cup and watched as Annie poured McLaren's. The billionaire looked haggard and worn; he'd been chopping at walls with the ice ax since he'd gotten up that morning. He took care never to overexert himself, but he'd worked steadily, not content to sit back and wait.

Annie knelt and cradled McLaren's head in her arms, then helped him drink.

The expedition leader was doing even worse now than earlier. He felt hot to the touch and was burning up with fever. His eyes wandered restlessly, unable to focus for long. He drank slowly.

Just as Annie was about to take the cup away to let McLaren rest, he was wracked by a series of coughs, then threw up the water she was trying to get down him.

Once the sickness abated, he leaned back into Annie's arms weakly, not able to sit up by himself. He wheezed when he breathed.

Annie opened McLaren's parka and looked under his shirt and thermal undershirt. The skin over the expedition leader's abdomen was puffy with bruising, and the discoloration was the dark purple of plums. Something had broken loose inside him for there to be that much blood under the skin.

Looking up, Annie caught Vaughn's eyes.

The billionaire didn't say anything. He rose easily to his feet and picked up his ax, heading back to chop on more walls.

Annie made McLaren comfortable and wrapped him tight again to keep him warm. McLaren's eyes closed, and she didn't know if he'd passed out or gone to sleep. She trailed after Vaughn, angry at his single-mindedness. He'd seen what she had seen and had decided to say nothing about it.

Even though she was upset, she forced herself to remain calm. Vaughn wasn't a man someone approached with ultimatums. "Elliot."

"Yeah." Vaughn swung the ax, biting deeply into the wall and sending ice chips flying.

"You saw Tom's ribs."

"Yeah." Vaughn struck the ice again.

"With those injuries, it's no wonder Tom couldn't keep the water down. We've got to start him on dex now." Annie turned away, her mind already made up.

"No," Vaughn said quietly. But there was steel in his voice.

Annie spun around, reacting to the authority in his words, not liking it at all. She couldn't believe Vaughn would deny McLaren the dex after seeing how badly off he was.

"We stick to the program," Vaughn said before she could speak. "Another nine or ten hours and the water runs out. You and I are going to need the dex. Our lives depend on it."

"Tom will die without it."

Vaughn nodded, coldly and ruthlessly, and Annie got a sense of what it might be like to sit across a table from him during a business deal. "Tom will die anyway," he said. "He's not going anywhere, Annie. We've done our best. We can't waste resources on a lost cause."

Annie let her anger show in her voice without attacking Vaughn personally. "Trying to save someone's life is not a lost cause."

"There are no rules in nature. Only necessities." Vaughn made it sound like a textbook lesson for elementary school. A rule of thumb every adult should already know. "Why should three die if two can live?"

Don't challenge him, Annie warned herself. *He's not a guy you can directly challenge.* She knew that about Vaughn even though the way he was acting now surprised her. She'd suspected some of the ruthlessness in him from stories she'd read about his businesses, and with it she'd expected some degree of selfishness. Those traits generally showed up in good climbers as well.

"If that's what you think, Elliot," she made herself say calmly, "why don't you go tell him yourself?" She turned to the medical kit again, intending to get one of the dex syringes.

"Tom," Vaughn called gently. "Tom."

In disbelief, Annie turned around.

Vaughn had crossed the cave and was kneeling by McLaren's side.

McLaren tried in vain to sit up, groaning with the pain. He didn't look completely conscious.

Annie crossed over to them. "Don't listen to him, Tom!"

Vaughn turned on her suddenly, eyes narrowed. "He has a right to know," he growled at her.

Groggily, McLaren looked from one of them to the other.

He doesn't even know what's going on, Annie thought. *The pain has him out of it.*

"What?" McLaren asked.

Vaughn talked softly, as if he had to work hard to be understood. "You're a climber, Tom," he said with sincerity. "You know the reality. Even if they get us out of here, they'll be exhausted by the time they get here. They can't carry you down—not from this altitude. Annie wants to give you the dex. I understand that." He put a hand to his chest. "I do. The truth is that it's only delaying the inevitable. You know our supply situation."

McLaren looked at him, comprehension pushing away

144

some of the bleakness in his gaze. "Just lie here and die? That's what you're telling me?"

Vaughn leaned in more closely, as though he was having an intimate conversation with an old friend he trusted and admired. "I'm asking you to respect life, not waste it. I know if I was in your position—"

McLaren cut him off. "You're not in my"—he broke off for a coughing fit—"position!"

Lowering his voice again, his words soft in the cold, still ice cave, Vaughn said, "Annie's trying to save you, Tom." He paused for effect. "Understand, though—it's not just me. You'll be killing her, too."

Seeing the defeat in McLaren's eyes, Annie quickly stripped the plastic wrap from the dex syringe. Maybe McLaren would put himself above Vaughn's needs, but he wouldn't put himself before Annie's. The billionaire had been playing manipulation games for a long time, and he was one of the best at it she had seen. Everything he said, everything he did, had a kernel of truth, but it was presented twisted and bent and headed in whatever direction he wanted it to go.

Before Vaughn or McLaren could stop her, Annie administered the dex dosage through Tom's pants and into his leg. She exchanged glances with Vaughn, but the billionaire rocked back on his heels and didn't say a word.

Annie reached down and took McLaren's hand, feeling his cold fingers in hers. She sat beside him, keeping watch to make sure that he was safe, not looking at Vaughn.

Chapter 17

K2, Negrotto Col, 21,500 feet

Peter jammed himself to the wall. Together, he and Wick had climbed it. Wick had led the way, hammering pitons into the wall because there were no cracks to use cams on. Even though Peter felt they were going slowly, he was winded, sweaty, and tired from the continuous exertion.

A thousand-foot drop lay beneath them. The wall was so smooth and so sheer that snow didn't even stick to it, which was one of the main reasons Wick had chosen it.

Utah lingered in the back of Peter's mind, filled with the horrible screams of the young climbers as they'd plummeted to their deaths—and the final look he'd had into his father's eyes.

He blinked to clear the sweat from his vision, then shook the drenched hair from his face. He knew the movement translated itself to the safety rope between himself and Wick, and he knew the older climber was looking at him that very moment.

Peter didn't look up. Every time he saw Wick's flat gaze, he wanted to ask the man what he was doing there, what had made him come with the rescue effort. But he couldn't because he felt Wick would have questions of his own and Peter wouldn't measure up in Wick's estimation.

Wick had already proven he was a stronger, more able climber. Where Peter seemed to gain inches, Wick gained feet as tirelessly as a machine.

Annie is up on the mountain.

Peter tried to focus, to bring his thoughts from the past to the present, but they all seemed knotted up somehow. He glanced at the nitro canister hanging from the pack at his side. It was attached to a piton that had been hammered into the wall. Climbing with it on his back had been too much so they'd hauled it up the wall in increments.

The wind caught the pack, pushing it gently toward the wall. Peter placed a hand against the pack carefully, stopping it short of bumping into the wall.

"Haul bag!" Wick called down.

Peter blew out a breath, trying to relax. Every time they hauled the pack up was nerve-racking. *One good bump,* he told himself as he freed the bag from the piton and securely tied it to the line. *That's all it would take.*

He held the bag clear of the wall, allowing Wick to see that the pack and canister were ready. "Up rope!" Peter called.

Wick attached a jumar to the kernmantle rope. Once the ascending device was in place, he started ratcheting the pack up slowly and smoothly.

Peter ascended the sheer rock face by using the handholds and footholds Wick had found, made, or improved upon. A few places were so sheer Wick had been forced to hammer in pitons for safety's sake, but that had slowed their progress.

Peter matched his speed to the bag's, staying close enough that he could reach out and touch it. His muscles ached from fatigue and strain and the cold. Tonight would be harsh, and tomorrow would be even harder. He tried not to wonder if Annie would be alive then.

Rock grated above him, drawing his eye automatically. Wick stood on a ledge that was little more than eighteen or twenty inches deep. It was a place where a climber could do no more than catch his or her breath.

In a frozen moment of clarity, Peter saw the half-dozen rocks tumble free of the ledge, coming straight down toward the nitro canister in the pack.

"Rocks!" Wick yelled in warning.

Moving instinctively, knowing he had no margin for error, Peter reached out and shoved the canister pack away from the sheer wall, out of the path of the falling rock.

Peter kept an eye on the pack as the rock rained down on him painfully. Catching the pack before it hit the wall and triggered the nitro was the only chance he and Wick had. He saw that he hadn't pushed the pack as straight as he'd thought. As the pack arced back at the wall, it traced a gentle curve that was going to place it ten feet beyond his reach.

Forgetting the fear that had been dogging him since they'd begun the ascent, forgetting about Utah for the moment, Peter concentrated on the swinging bag. Wick had the belay on and locked above, and if he'd done it right, Peter knew it would hold his weight easily.

Releasing his hold on the wall, grabbing the safety line and trusting his climbing harness, Peter twisted and planted both feet against the stone wall and kicked, sending himself flying forward.

He swung out from the stone wall only a few inches, listening to the material of his coat drag along the cliff surface in a long, frenzied whisper of movement. The thousand feet beneath him didn't matter. Only the pack did.

He reached for the pack and caught it with his fingertips at the apex of his swing. He barely hung onto the pack as he swung back to the wall. Twisting, he turned so that his feet were pointed toward the wall, making contact and folding his legs quickly to cushion the stop while he pulled the pack into his chest.

When all motion stopped, he leaned back, supported by the safety harness. He looked up, his arms around the pack.

Wick stood above him on the ledge.

Peter couldn't read the older climber's expression, but it was hard to keep a small smile from his own face. He'd forgotten about falling, hadn't thought about Utah, and he'd done what he needed to do—what he'd *known* he could do.

He looked up, almost challenging Wick, but not saying anything about the falling rock. "Up rope."

Without a word, Wick hauled the pack up the rest of the way.

Peter matched the pack's speed easily now, and his movements were looser, more confident. He joined Wick on the ledge as the older climber hung the pack on one of the two pitons he'd hammered in.

Wick coiled the extra rope after Peter had clipped his safety harness to the piton. "You're crazy," the older climber said, shaking his head slightly. "Crazy as your old man."

Peter looked away, losing the daredevil feeling immediately. For a moment it had felt good to show Wick that he could still climb well, that he could climb the way his father had trained him. But that was gone the instant Wick opened his mouth. The shared history he had with the other man was gone, and Peter fully expected Wick to be as full of blame as many of the other climbers he'd encountered over the last three years.

Wick kept working, but his eyes were on Peter's. He spoke softly. "You did the right thing in Utah when you cut the rope. Any good climber would have done it. Royce would have done it himself if he could have."

Peter stood, stunned, not knowing what to say.

But Wick didn't wait for a response. He turned back to the wall and started climbing again.

Peter wanted to ask Wick to repeat himself, but he didn't have the nerve. No one had ever told him he'd done the right thing before. Many had said they understood, but Peter had known that was a lie. A person didn't know how something felt until he or she did it.

He looked up after Wick with new respect and appreci-

149

ation. But there was a lot about the man that needed an explanation.

Malcolm paced through the snow on top of Nikel Ridge, peering over the edge the way they'd come. They were twenty-two thousand feet up now.

We could have been a lot farther along, he growled to himself as he watched Kareem. Malcolm wished he were with his brother. When he was climbing with Cyril, nothing seemed impossible. He didn't like being separated from Cyril. It was as though half of him was missing. At least it wasn't the smarter, better-looking half, though.

He glared irritably at Kareem.

Patiently, Kareem took out a red prayer mat from the pack that carried the nitro. He spread it on the frozen ground, knelt on it, and faced east. Placing his hands together, he began to pray.

Vaguely, Malcolm remembered that Muslims had to pray something like a half-dozen times a day, which he figured had to get pretty annoying. He took out his water bottle and drank. Then he couldn't be quiet anymore. "We're on a bit of a deadline, mate. Can't we do this later?"

Kareem glanced at him, rocking back and forth and praying in an unending stream that Malcolm couldn't decipher at all.

"He's all right, is he, this Allah bloke?" Malcolm asked. "I mean, he won't strike you dead if you miss one prayer, will he?"

Kareem glanced meaningfully at the nitro-laden pack as he prayed.

Malcolm looked at the nitro. "All right. One prayer. Under the circumstances."

Kareem touched his forehead to the mat and continued praying.

"Do Muslims believe in hell, Kareem?" Malcolm asked.

The prayer continued uninterrupted, but Kareem did shoot him a look.

150

Malcolm scratched at his beard. "Say I don't believe in this Allah, and this nitro blows. Am I going to hell?"

Kareem continued praying, more forcefully and a little faster now.

"The born-agains say if I don't believe in Jesus, I'm going to hell. Jews say if I *do* believe in Jesus I'm going to hell. Catholics say if I don't believe in the Pope, I'm going to hell." Malcolm shrugged. "Any way you look at it, I'm going to fry."

Kareem finished praying and quietly put away the prayer mat. "Muslims are forbidden to stop praying once they begin. If they do, they must begin all over again."

"Oh." Malcolm passed the water over. "So what'd Allah say? We gonna die?"

"All men die, Malcolm," Kareem replied. "But Allah says it's what we do before we die that counts." He drank a little water and passed the bottle back. Reaching down, he shouldered the nitro pack and took off again.

Malcolm capped the water bottle and looked after the smaller man. Silently, Malcolm figured that being predisposed toward dying wasn't exactly what he wanted to hear from his new climbing partner.

Holding a warm cup of coffee and feeling a little guilty about it while talking to Montgomery Wick at the other end of the radio connection, Skip Taylor studied the Doppler radar screen. The storm still raged, not yet touching the mountain again, but it had disrupted the live satellite feed and cut off video contact with the rescue team.

Brian Maki had promised to have the satellite feed back up and running as soon as the meteorological conditions permitted. Frank Williams stood by as well, directing security at the command center like a bulldog. Only a few journalists were being let into the center now, and they were the ones predisposed to saying good things about Elliot Vaughn. There was some growing resentment in base camp toward the billionaire because most people believed their friends wouldn't be in danger now if it hadn't been for Vaughn's self-indulgence.

"Copy that, Wick," Skip said easily as he sat. "What's your exact position?" He glanced over at the large map on the wall, where he was coordinating all three teams, marking their progress and ETAs. So far, Malcolm and Kareem had five hundred feet on everyone else.

"The snow arête," Wick responded. "Four hundred feet above Negrotto Col."

Skip studied the map and the time of the last contact with Wick. He checked his watch and noted the time, a little surprised. Then he thumbed the transmit button. "What's wrong? Figured you'd be at the top of the arête by now."

Standing on a ledge fifty feet above Peter Garrett, Wick spoke with Skip as he stared down at the young climber. Peter was sweating gallons, and sometimes his grip wasn't as sure as it should have been. Still, Peter was impressive. For someone carrying the history that he was, for someone who had been away from climbing as long as he had, he was doing well.

And the save with the nitro pack had been impressive.

"So did I," Wick answered honestly. But he didn't blame Peter. There was only one person he blamed in his world these days. "What's the status at twenty-six thousand?" He'd made the choice not to call the trapped people Vaughn's team.

"As far as I can read, okay," Skip answered. "McLaren's serious. Internal injuries."

"And Vaughn?" Wick saw Peter look up at him then, his face filled with curiosity.

"No word," Skip said.

No word? Wick wondered if that was true. Whatever happened up there, he hoped that Vaughn didn't die before he arrived. "Keep me informed. Out." He switched off the radio and replaced it in his coat pocket.

Peter finished the climb to the ledge, pulling up to where Wick was. His breathing was hard, ragged.

Although time was working against them, Wick allowed the younger climber to rest for a while. Peter had earned it, and he was putting all of himself into the job.

"What is it between you and Vaughn?" Peter asked.

Silently, Wick turned to survey the wall again. He'd already picked out the first forty feet of handholds and toeholds, thinking that they wouldn't even have to use pitons for that stretch.

Peter waited for an answer.

All Wick said was, "You're too slow, Mr. Garrett. We have to move faster." He picked up the lead rope and prepared to start climbing again.

Peter stood, reaching up to catch Wick by the shoulder. He pulled hard enough to spin him around.

Wick barely resisted punching the younger climber as four years of anger and hurt almost spilled out of him. "It's no concern of yours."

"If it involves my sister that makes it my concern," Peter stated.

Wick eyed him levelly. "I made this rescue mission clear from the very start. There would be no arguments, no questions."

"Then turn around," Peter said in a low voice. "Go back. It's about trust, Wick. And if I don't have trust in you, I'd rather go it alone."

Wick glanced at his watch, checking the time. "Your sister will be dead in fourteen hours." That was the only ace he had and the only ace he needed. He handed the lead rope to Peter. "Good luck."

Peter didn't move to take the rope.

Without another word, Wick turned and began the ascent. Vaughn wasn't something he was prepared to talk about. There had been enough talk. The only thing that mattered now was finding Vaughn.

Chapter 18

K2, Ice Cave, 26,000 feet

Elliot Vaughn struck the ice wall with all his might, burying the ice ax and channeling the rage he felt. Sparks flew as the steel struck rock.

He was still seething inside about the lack of control he had over his present situation. The ability to reach out and take control—as well as the strength and nerve to do it no matter what the cost—had been the one thing that made him greater than any other man he'd ever met.

His breath plowed out into the still air of the ice cave in gray clouds. Annie worked at his side, but he ignored her. She was weak, he knew now, not as strong as he'd believed in the beginning. But he hadn't directed the WNN network executives to give her the assignment because of her climbing skills. She was a woman, and her being there for the summiting would have drawn women to the advertising for Majestic Airlines as well as spurring the media coverage.

He slammed the ax against the wall again, willing it to give in. Somewhere, there had to be a way out. He checked their progress. Surely they'd tunneled five or six feet. The walls couldn't be that thick. This couldn't be the only cave in the ice and the only way out. There had to be another way, and if anyone could find it, he was certain it would be him. Nothing had ever defeated him before. He swung the ax and chopped into the ice again, breaking chunks loose.

At his side, Annie stopped, seized by a sudden wracking cough that sounded deep and watery.

Vaughn stopped work and looked at her. The cough hadn't sounded normal by any means.

"It's all right," she said self-consciously. "Just some spindrift in my lungs."

Vaughn continued watching her. They hadn't talked since she'd given McLaren the dex, wasting one of the precious few resources they had to aid in their own survival. He glanced over his shoulder at McLaren.

McLaren had pushed himself up to one elbow and was watching Annie with feverish interest as well. McLaren knew the score, Vaughn realized. The expedition leader knew that Annie was the only chance he had at escape. Maybe Annie wouldn't leave his side if an opportunity presented itself, but Vaughn would in a heartbeat.

Annie stooped to pick up her ax, putting one hand against the ice wall to keep her balance. When she took her hand away, Vaughn spotted the pinkish bloodstain she'd coughed onto her hand.

Pulmonary edema, Vaughn realized. *She knew she had it and was hiding it.* A fresh wave of anger flooded him as he thought of the lie she'd been carrying out. He had a right to know. Then at the same moment he realized that she hadn't told him because she'd known he wouldn't care.

The radio blasted to life. But it wasn't Morse code this time; it was a man's voice, one that Vaughn thought he recognized. The man's identity filled him with chill dread, but Vaughn had never let fear stop him, either.

"Summit team," the man said over the radio, "this is rescue group Alpha. Come in, summit team."

Annie and McLaren both started for the radio, but Vaughn beat them both, snapping it up from his pack, where he'd left it. "This is summit team," Vaughn replied, thumbing the transmit button. "Come in, Alpha. This is summit team!"

Wick stood high on an outcrop over the south face of the mountain. There was still a lot of climbing to go, but looking down, he knew he and Peter had put a lot of it behind them. Peter was still thirty or forty feet below, coming up the static lines slowly. The guy was out of shape, but he had heart, and Wick admired that.

Static crackled from the radio again. Wick had heard the voice and had known he was getting closer to Vaughn. Emotions twisted and turned inside Wick, and they were hard for him to control. Even after the passage of four years, he was surprised at how strong they were.

Wick placed the radio against his ear, barely able to hear the thin voice at the other end. "Annie Garrett? Is that you?"

Annie heard the man's voice at the other end of the radio channel clearly this time, but obviously he couldn't hear them very well. The speaker wasn't Peter, and she immediately wondered about her brother's safety. *We'd have been told if something happened,* she told herself. But she wasn't sure if that was true.

"No," Vaughn replied, straining to hear the man. "It's Elliot Vaughn. Who's this?"

The long pause at the other end made Annie think that the connection had been broken for a moment. Then the man spoke again.

"Montgomery Wick."

Vaughn hesitated for a moment, and Annie thought the billionaire didn't want to speak to Wick. But that instant passed, and Vaughn sounded pleasant enough again as he pressed the transmit button. "How many of you are there?"

"Three teams," Wick answered. "Coming by different routes. I'm in charge."

The declaration almost sounded like a threat to Annie. She felt another painful cough building in her chest and struggled to hold it back. She couldn't let Vaughn know what she already suspected.

"I thought you only climbed solo, Wick," Vaughn said.

"Rescue missions are different."

Even though Vaughn was trying to appear casual about the conversation, Annie sensed that the billionaire was struggling to keep up a front. There was something about Montgomery Wick that bothered Vaughn.

"Where are you?" Vaughn asked.

"The west ridge. Twenty-three thousand."

Only that far? Annie glanced at McLaren and saw that he realized help wasn't as close as the radio contact had made them believe or hope. McLaren's feverish look and shivering touched her, making her wish there was something else she could do for him. She honestly didn't know how long he could hold out.

"You'll have to climb faster," Vaughn said, looking at Annie. "Tell Garrett his sister's got edema. That should speed him up."

No! Annie screamed inside her mind, not knowing how Vaughn knew. She wanted to curse the billionaire for telling Wick. If Wick told Peter, it would only make her brother take more risks to hurry than he was already doing. If they were that far behind in the rescue, it was because conditions were unsafe.

She slammed into Vaughn, grabbing for the radio. He didn't put up much of a fight to keep it from her. She fit the radio into her hand and swallowed another coughing jag. She thumbed the transmit button. "Wick! Wick!"

Only white noise issued over the radio. Wick had disconnected.

And Peter was going to know about her condition.

Standing on the ledge, Wick calmly put the radio back in his coat pocket. The wind slapped coldly into his face, stinging just enough to be noticeable. He thought about what Vaughn had said, about Annie Garrett having edema.

Wick believed it. Vaughn might make something up to get his way, but the truth would be much harsher and the billionaire knew it.

Peter climbed steadily below. The young climber had great skill, an uncanny feel for the ascent, but he was out of shape. And the way was difficult with all the wind trying to suck them from the wall.

Breathing out, the gray fog of his breath instantly shredded and disappearing, Wick considered his options. Edema. His wife had died from edema. Although he'd never found her body, he knew that had to have been the cause of her death. She'd been at high altitude when she'd disappeared. If she'd lived, she would have come back to him.

But whether to tell Peter about his sister, that was the question. Wick knew if he did Peter would struggle even harder to get up the mountain, and the young climber was already putting everything into it he had.

Wick closed the flap of his coat pocket, securing the radio. He wasn't going to tell. Peter didn't need the motivation and would know soon enough. Wick glanced up, laying out the course in his mind. In the meantime, they had a lot of mountain to climb.

Annie looked up from the silent radio in her hand. Vaughn had already returned to the tunnel they were carving. Even with help on the way, the billionaire wasn't about to give up rescuing himself.

Or maybe Vaughn's not convinced help is on the way, Annie thought. Whatever was between Vaughn and Wick obviously ran deep.

She glanced at McLaren. The expedition leader watched her with concern, measuring her. He evidently hadn't known about the edema.

Annie picked up her ax, intending to join Vaughn. Attacking the ice would give her something to do, and it would help her stay warm by burning sugar in her body. Then the cough returned with a vengeance, tearing at her lungs with tiny, ripping rat's claws. She grabbed a gauze pad from the medical kit and placed it over her mouth as she coughed.

Both men watched her. She couldn't stop coughing, and that made her angry as well as frustrated. Finally, the coughing spasm passed, but it had left bloody splotches on the gauze. She wadded it up and put it into the plastic bag she was using for waste.

Vaughn didn't say anything and returned to his assault on the wall. Ice chunks littered the ground at his feet. He took the time to kick them over the ledge and into the abyss that ran beside them.

McLaren watched Annie as she struggled to recover. She felt as if she was drowning in her own body, but she knew if she just kept calm for a few minutes longer her lungs would open a little more.

"She needs dex," McLaren called out to Vaughn. His voice was a weak whisper in the ice cave, barely audible over the echoing thwacks of Vaughn's ax.

"We don't have enough," Vaughn replied without turning around. "She'll have to wait." He planted his ax again, splintering ice.

"Annie," McLaren encouraged. "Get the dex."

Vaughn wheeled immediately, holding his ax across his chest. He took a step toward the medical kit, and there was no doubt in Annie's mind that he'd attempt to stop her if she tried to get the dex.

"I warned you," Vaughn said to Annie. "I said it would come to this."

She stayed in place, hating him for the selfish streak that was so obviously at his core. She didn't know how she hadn't seen it before.

Vaughn turned to McLaren. "You saddled up that pony. Now she can ride it."

"You're not sick!" McLaren protested.

"I will be if you two use it all," Vaughn replied. "We hold to schedule. It's our only chance."

"For you maybe," McLaren said.

"You know, Tom," Vaughn said in a surprisingly even voice, "intelligent people don't threaten me. Stupid people do."

"We wouldn't be here if it wasn't for you," McLaren accused.

Vaughn grinned coldly and mirthlessly at the prone man. He spoke quietly. "You were the leader, Tom."

McLaren tried to get up, rage finally adding some color to his face. But he didn't have the strength to get to his feet.

Annie crossed to McLaren's side and took his arm, guiding him back to a resting position. "No, Vaughn's right." She looked up at Vaughn, seeing some of the deep fear in him now that she hadn't been able to see before. "None of us are going to make it." She turned and looked at the half-buried pack on the other side of the ice cave. It still sat there, just out of reach across the ice bridge over the chasm. "You want to survive, get it."

Vaughn glanced at the pack on the other side of the bridge. He breath gusted out in gray plumes. But he made no move toward the bridge.

"Yeah," Annie said sarcastically. "That's what I thought."

Monique sank her boot crampons through the deep snow covering the Pulpit Ice Field, seeking out the stony ground below. With the snow layer so deep, the gentle incline was more treacherous than it should have been. Her body ached from the rigors she'd been putting it through, but at twenty-three thousand five hundred feet, she and Cyril still had another twenty-five hundred to go.

She spotted Cyril sixty or seventy feet ahead of her. Considering the all-nighters he and his brother pulled at base camp and the drinking binges they did, his stamina was surprisingly good. At first she'd believed she would have walked him into the ground. But he had to wait on her.

Cyril gently pulled the nitro pack from his back and placed it on the snow beside him. He took the water bottle from one of the pack's pockets, uncapped it, and drank. He turned his attention up the ice field for a moment.

Seeing how much farther we have to go, Monique realized. The slope was wearing on her, too. Leaning into the incline as well as the wind was getting old. Walking as they were, they presented bigger targets for the wind.

Cyril turned to put the water bottle back into the pack, but his foot slipped on a patch of ice under a thin layer of snow. He fell heavily, and his foot struck the nitro pack.

Immediately, the nitro pack took off down the slope as if it were on runners.

Taking two long strides, Cyril threw himself at the pack, trying desperately to grab the nitro canister. He landed on the powdery snow, sending a gleaming, rainbow-streaked cloud of it flying into the air. Then he was sliding along the slope as well, gaining speed like an out-of-control bobsled.

Chapter 19

K2, Pulpit Ice Field, 23,500 feet

Cold horror slammed into Monique as she watched the nitro pack and Cyril skidding down the slope. She couldn't tell if they were going to hit her or not. She braced herself, digging her crampons deeply into the snow but aware that an impact by Cyril would probably knock her loose as well.

And an impact with the nitro pack that was too sudden and too hard would obliterate her, Cyril, and a good chunk of the ice field.

Incredibly, Cyril managed to catch up to the nitro pack and grab one of the straps. He tried to dig his boot toes in but all he left behind were two shallow trenches in the deep snow. A look of sheer terror filled his face.

"Use your ax!" Monique called. "Your ax!"

The ice ax bounced crazily at Cyril's side, taking great hopping skips, secured to his belt by a wrist loop. He grabbed for the ax, trying to free it.

Monique dug her own ice ax into the snow and went prone, her other hand extended to reach for Cyril. Between holding onto the nitro pack and the ice ax, he didn't have any hands left to grab back. She missed him by inches, watching in fear-filled frustration as Cyril skidded for the dropoff less than fifty yards away.

162

Squirming, Cyril managed to twist his body and slam the ice ax into the snow. The sudden drag brought him up short, yanking him over onto his face as he held on. Then his full weight hit the end of his arm and pulled the ice ax free again. Although slowed for a moment, he picked up speed immediately.

No! Monique screamed, watching as Cyril neared the drop-off. The only thing down that side was the Siachen Glacier nearly a quarter-mile below. If he went over the edge, he was dead.

Somehow, Cyril managed to bring the ice ax up and chop down for a last-ditch effort, pounding the keen edge deeply into the snow. It slowed him, but it didn't stop him from going over the drop-off's edge.

Annie stood at the edge of the crevasse and breathed out, trying to focus and be calm. The lingering cough in her chest kept her from breathing as deeply as she wanted, making her fear another coughing spasm. She concentrated on the pack on the other side of the crevasse, trying hard not to think about the long fall that would occur if things went wrong.

She'd stripped off her coat, safety harness, and climbing gear. Now she stood freezing in the cold that permeated the ice cave, as light as she could be. She kept the single, short piece of rope they had and tied it around her belt.

Then she thrust the other end of the rope at Vaughn. She didn't care for the man and didn't trust him completely, but she knew she could trust him in this. Whatever the pack contained, Vaughn could benefit from it. And if she went over the ice bridge, Vaughn wouldn't have to risk his own neck.

Wordlessly, Vaughn tied the rope around his own waist, belaying her.

Watching him do that made Annie feel a little more confident. If Vaughn hadn't truly believed he could hold her, she knew he wouldn't have committed himself so completely to the task.

Behind Vaughn, McLaren watched from a seated position, concern etched deeply into his pale face.

Annie breathed out again, concentrating on the pack and the bridge, trying not to see the drop that was waiting for her if it didn't hold. She stepped out gingerly onto the bridge, then gradually added weight. The bridge held.

Carefully, she slid her foot forward and took another step, both feet on the bridge now, as well as all her weight. She concentrated on the next step and pretended not to notice the trembling in her knees.

Two more steps farther on, she saw the large stone under the ice chunk. Snow had disguised it until now, not letting her see the danger it presented. The stone rested under the ice like a fulcrum. As she neared it, she felt the ice beneath her start to tilt, swinging dizzyingly as the weight changed from one side of the rock below to the other.

Annie felt herself fall, and Vaughn tightened his grip on the rope linking them. McLaren screamed out a warning hoarsely. But a few inches into the drop, the rocks held.

Annie took a measured breath that wouldn't aggravate the sickness in her lungs and continued toward the pack.

Cyril's ice ax stood out only slightly above the edge of the drop-off. Nothing of him or the pack was visible, but Monique knew from the way the ice ax clung to the edge that there was considerable weight at the other end of it.

Monique flipped her ice ax over and used it to glissade down the slope. She controlled the sliding descent down the Pulpit Ice Field with expertise, bringing herself to within inches of the dropoff. Cautiously, knowing that the edge of the dropoff was serac—a fragile shelf of frozen snow that had formed as the sun had melted some of the snow and the wind had cooled it again—she peered over the edge.

She could see Cyril's ice ax more clearly, but there was

no sign of the man. However, the nitro canister hadn't gone off either, and there had been plenty of time for it to hit bottom. The ice ax wiggled a little, sliding in the serac.

"Hang on," Monique said as calmly as she could. "It's gonna be okay. Just hang on." She checked her belt but found no rope and cursed vehemently beneath her breath. She'd lost the rope when she'd first tried to catch Cyril and hadn't noticed. Now it was too late to go back for it.

The ice ax shifted again, sliding three inches closer to the drop-off and cutting into it deeply.

"The ax is coming through!" Cyril bellowed from below.

"I see it!" Monique yelled back. "I see it!" She leaned back up the slope, spreading her weight, then put a foot on the serac. The thin ice cracked immediately but held. Whipping her ice ax through the air, she drove it deeply through the snow layer into the stony ground underneath. *Please let it hold!*

Cautiously, expecting at any second to feel the serac crumble beneath her, Monique wrapped the loop of her ax around her wrist and took another step toward Cyril. She knelt, stretching her fingers toward his ax. She still couldn't see him, but the ice ax sank another inch.

Monique strained, fingertips curling around the ice ax. She thought she felt the serac shift beneath her, but she couldn't be certain. She tightened her grip.

The serac beneath Monique gave way without warning, sending her plunging straight down. She spotted Cyril now, hanging by one hand from his ice ax, the nitro pack dangling from his other hand.

They both held on, slamming into the sheer wall beneath the dropoff edge. Monique's grip on her ax slipped, but the loop around her wrist caught and held with bruising force.

Although she didn't want to, Monique gazed down, watching the spray of serac fragments tumbling to the Siachen Glacier far below. She didn't know how she'd managed to hold on while supporting her weight and Cyril's, but she knew she couldn't do it for long.

Annie continued crossing the ice bridge slowly. The ice chunk shifted repeatedly, and the coughing spasm threatened her lungs. She knew if she gave into the spasm it would might be the death of her.

Halfway across the bridge, debris shifted from underneath, sliding into the crevasse, plunging down to disappear in the darkness below. She never even heard the rocks and ice hit bottom.

Before she knew it, she was at the end of the belaying rope. Almost half of the ice bridge remained to go. She glanced back at Vaughn.

The billionaire shook his head, letting her know she had all the slack.

You can do this, Annie told herself. *You have to do this. If you get the chance to talk to Peter later, it'll be better if you tell him you're okay, that Vaughn overreacted, and not cough up a lung while you're doing it.* Tentatively, she untied the rope at her waist, trying not to think that there was now nothing to keep her from dropping all the way if she fell.

Her stomach churning as adrenaline flooded her system and pinged off her nerves, Monique glanced up fearfully and checked her ice ax. It was embedded near the edge of the drop-off, but for the moment it was holding. The wind caught her and Cyril, rocking them slightly, reminding her that remaining suspended there wasn't an option.

She examined the cliff face and spotted a rock jutting out to their right. It held definite possibilities. But it was so far out of reach.

Her ice ax suddenly slipped, cutting through the snow and dropping them nearly a foot. Her shoulders burned with the strain of holding herself and Cyril. For a moment she thought they were dead and waited for the freefall sensation to kick in as they fell toward the Siachen Glacier at terminal velocity.

Cyril's grip slipped for a moment, then he caught hold again.

Monique looked back at the rock jutting from the cliff face. "The rock to your right. Do you see it?"

Cyril looked. "I see it." His voice was tight.

"I'm going to swing you over there," Monique said, starting to shift her body. She hoped she could do it before her grip failed.

Cautiously, fighting back the urge to cough because she didn't know for sure when the spasm would ease, Annie kept moving across the ice bridge. Perspiration stained her face and hands, chill drops that seemed to burn her skin.

When she stepped across the fulcrum, she felt the ice chunk begin to shift. She'd been expecting that and bent her knees slightly, lowering her center of gravity and spreading her weight across the ice chunk as much as she could.

She went three more steps, then threw herself forward, landing on the rock shelf beside the partially covered pack. She reached for it with trembling hands, wondering what—if anything—would still be inside and salvageable.

Raw pain flamed across Monique's shoulders and back as she swung Cyril. She pushed against the cliff face with her feet, arcing their bodies. If she hadn't had Cyril and the nitro canister to support as well, she might have been able to pull herself back up.

Cyril's body arced out, farther and farther each time. She knew the strain on him had to be getting unbearable as well. He bent his arm holding the nitro pack strap, pulling the strap down into the crook of his elbow to leave his hand free.

On the fourth swing, Cyril's fingertips brushed the outcropping. Snow and scree scattered in the wake of his hand as he swung away from it again.

C'mon! Monique told herself. *It's the only chance we have!* She started her next swing.

Without bothering to check the contents of the pack, Annie slung it over her shoulder and turned back toward the ice chunk bridging the crevasse. She'd looked at it only long enough to confirm that it was Ali's pack.

She started across the ice chunk before she had time to contemplate it too long. There was only one way back across. She slid her feet along quickly, keeping her weight distributed.

Not quite halfway there, almost within reach of the belaying rope she'd dropped, the coughing spasm came on her. She dropped to a prone position automatically as the ice chunk started to shiver. Debris showered from beneath the ice bridge as she continued coughing, her whole body shaking with the force. She was too weak to go on, but from the way the ice chunk was shifting, she knew she couldn't stay there.

She put a hand over her mouth in an effort to get control of the spasm. All she succeeded in doing was bloodying her palm.

Knowing she had nothing left in her, Monique swung a final time, pushing Cyril toward the outcropping. At the apex of the arc, as if sensing that Monique couldn't hang on any longer, Cyril let go of his ax and leaped for the outcropping. Caught unaware, Monique watched her pack tumble from her shoulder.

Fear balled up in Monique's stomach as she swung away from Cyril. Out of control for just a moment, she turned away from him, not able to see if he'd reached the outcropping. She kicked her legs and felt her arm shaking. She dropped Cyril's ax and grabbed the handle of her own ice axe with both hands. She worked hard to turn around.

Cyril clung uncertainly to the rocky outcropping, try

ing frantically to hang on and get his boots lodged to help take some of the weight. His right hand slipped and he flailed wildly. Before he could get his balance back, the nitro pack strap slipped from his arm.

Gravity pulled the canister down, tumbling end over end.

Monique watched, remembering how unstable and how explosive the nitro was. Even at the distance she didn't know if she was going to be safe from the concussion of the explosion. As she watched, Cyril started free climbing up the side of the cliff face, scrambling madly, pulling himself up two and three feet at a time.

Glancing down, Monique spotted a splinter of rock sticking up at an angle from the cliff face below like a branch jutting up from a tree trunk. Once there she'd have nowhere to go and would be totally dependent on Cyril to get her up. The concussion from the nitro might also rip her from the wall if she stayed where she was. Both moves were gambles.

She took a deep breath and let go the ice ax, falling at once. She bumped up against the rough cliff face once, bruising her cheek and rattling her senses. She almost caught the rock splinter too late, but she managed to wrap her arms around it and hang on.

The nitro continued to fall.

Miraculously, the ice bridge held till Annie's coughing fit passed. Blood gleamed darkly on the ice chunk where she'd coughed. Her lungs burned and felt rubbery.

Weakly, she pushed herself to her knees, making sure to keep her weight distributed. The ice chunk wobbled, but it didn't fall. She didn't think it would take much to dislodge it, though, and she tried not to consider that.

On her hands and knees, she pushed herself forward, no longer trusting herself to stand on her weakened legs. She glanced ahead, realizing she had only another four feet to go before she'd be within reach of the belay rope that Vaughn held.

* * *

Sunlight flashed on the falling nitro canister as it fell.

Heart beating frantically, Monique jammed herself into the small fissure behind the rock splinter, digging in with her fingers and boot toes to get in as far as she could. She had lost sight of Cyril and didn't know if he'd made the top.

She glanced down only a second or two before the nitro hit the ground. A massive flash of white, snow that had been blown in all directions, rose up. Then the mountain trembled, almost throwing Monique from the fissure. Small rocks and snow rained down over her.

The sound of the blast deafened her a moment later when it finally traveled up to her. She glanced down even as the sound rolled over her and was horrified to see a white cloud of destructive fury rolling up the side of the cliff at her. She knew it was going to reach her even before she could scream.

It enveloped her, peppering her with stinging debris and broken ice, turning her whole world into a white maelstrom. *Hold on!* she told herself as she clung to the rock splinter.

170

Chapter 20

K2, Ice Cave, 26,000 feet

K2 shuddered.

A moment later Annie heard the horrendous explosion. *Peter,* she thought, remembering the nitro he'd told her about. She glanced at Vaughn and McLaren, knowing they'd heard it, too.

Then more debris began to give way from under the ice chunk. Annie felt it writhing beneath her, shifting as the debris tumbled into the crevasse and disappeared. Rocks, snow, and ice tumbled from the ceiling overhead as the deafening roar filled the ice cave.

The roar grew in intensity as it channeled through the crevasse. The ice chunk shook, becoming more unstable. Then the fulcrum dropped from under the center of the ice bridge, and the ice chunk started a slow, long fall into the crevasse.

Annie pushed herself to her feet as adrenaline kicked her system into hyperdrive. She threw herself forward while the ice chunk dropped, clutching at the rope. She didn't even realize she had it for sure until she slammed into the side of the crevasse and stopped falling.

Above her Vaughn yelled, "Get up here, Annie! The

ground is slick!" He struggled to stay away from the edge of the chasm.

Weak from the edema, Annie turned and kicked her feet into the crevasse wall. She started pulling herself up the rope, Ali's pack heavy over her shoulder.

Fear turned the blood cold in Malcolm Bench's veins. He and Kareem stood atop a ledge looking back at K2, but he couldn't tell what direction the explosion came from. Was it Peter and Wick? Or—

He couldn't finish the thought. It was just too wrong. Cyril couldn't be—

Malcolm turned to Kareem, snatching the radio from his hand. The explosion still echoed all around them, rolling, finally fading. Malcolm looked at the radio, frustrated with it, suddenly not knowing how it worked. He used to know how it worked, didn't he? He glanced at Kareem in angry, helpless frustration. "How do you work this—"

Kareem reached out wordlessly and clicked it on.

Malcolm glanced wildly around the frozen mountain and screamed into the radio.

"Cyril?" Malcolm's voice boomed from the radio Peter held. "Are you there? *Cyril!*"

Peter stared at the white powder exploding upward from the overhang at the bottom end of Pulpit Ice Field. Monique and Cyril were supposed to be there by now. And the detonation that had taken place had definitely not been a natural event.

Peter glanced at Wick, who looked back at him expressionlessly. Dreading what he had to say but knowing he had to tell Malcolm, Peter lifted the radio to his mouth. "Malcolm! This is Peter. It's not us."

Malcolm swallowed, looking toward the Pulpit Ice Field. But from the angle he was at, he couldn't see anything. If it wasn't Peter and Wick, it had to be Cyril and Monique.

He thumbed the transmit button again and screamed hoarsely. "Cyril! You answer me right now! Do you hear me?"

Only his voice echoed over the snow-covered slopes.

Dazed, her face bleeding from small lacerations and her bruised cheek throbbing, Monique stared up at the ledge above her, searching. There were no nearby handholds, no easy way to the top.

And it was too far even to think about going down by herself.

She looked up again. "Cyril! Cyril! Are you there?" Only the wind answered her, hardly making any noise at all above the ringing in her ears. "Damn it, Cyril! Answer me!"

Something long and snakelike dropped over the cliff's edge, whipping down at her. Monique drew back instinctively before she noticed that the snakelike object was a rope. She grabbed it, wanting to make sure it was real, then looked up.

Cyril was leaning over the cliff's edge, grinning down at her. "Nag, nag, nag. Always nagging."

Monique didn't know whether to laugh, cry, or throw up. "You're sick." She put some of her weight on the rope, testing it to be certain it would hold her. At first she thought the low, rumbling noise was a figment of her imagination, part of the ringing in her ears from the explosion. Then she realized the cliff was vibrating.

She glanced up at Cyril, able to see him plainly now that he stood at the slope's edge. He was caught flat-footed by the avalanche that rolled down Pulpit Ice Field. The spray of whirling white hit him in midscream, drowning it out in the turbulent rumble of force as it shot over the edge and carried him along as though he'd been shot from a cannon.

Monique abandoned the rope and jammed herself into the fissure again just before tons of snow and rock poured down the side of the cliff like a waterfall. She watched Cyril for a short instant before his body was lost in the mad whirl of snow.

The falling debris broke off most of the rock splinter she'd taken shelter behind. The vibration from the impact shot through her feet and up her legs, almost causing her to lose her balance.

Long seconds later the avalanche hammered the Siachen Glacier and the K2 foothills. There was no sign of Cyril.

Breathing hard, Monique glanced up at the hopeless expanse of bare rock that stretched toward the mountaintop. There wouldn't be any help coming. The other teams were already on a rescue mission. Probably they believed she was dead. *After that explosion and the avalanche,* she thought, *I'd believe I was dead if I was them.*

They were all on borrowed time on the mountain, and the clock was moving.

Monique was on her own.

"Cyril! Do you hear me? Click once if you hear me!"

Peter listened to the raw emotion in Malcolm's voice as it was transmitted over the radio. It was almost more than he could bear. Peter knew he'd come looking to save his sister, and now Malcolm had lost his brother.

Glancing up at Wick, Peter said, "I'm going back. They could still be alive." He turned, not wanting to argue with the resistance he could already see in the older climber's eyes.

"Mr. Garrett!" Wick called strongly.

Peter headed for the slope. The man was going to have to stop him to keep him from going.

"Your sister has pulmonary edema," Wick stated.

Peter managed one more step before he stopped and turned around.

"We don't have the time," Wick said.

Peter listened to the older climber's words, wanting them to sound bloodthirsty or callous, anything that he could fight against or fault Wick for. But his declaration was only a statement of fact.

"Monique and Cyril are question marks," Wick said in a softer voice. "Your sister is not."

Still, Peter knew Wick wasn't completely innocent in keeping to the agenda. The older climber had his own reasons for seeking out Vaughn. *I wonder,* Peter thought angrily, *if Vaughn wasn't up there with Annie if you'd be in such a hurry to get to them. Or would you go back to see about rescuing Monique and Cyril?*

He stood there for a moment more, knowing he wasn't going to be able to convince Wick to do anything other than what he wanted to do. Then silently, Peter headed toward the top of the mountain. Annie was up there, maybe dying. Taking hours to conduct a rescue operation before they got to her would only insure her death and probably be fruitless as well. After that explosion and the avalanche, there probably wasn't enough of either Cyril or Monique to find.

Malcolm stared at the silent radio in his big hand. No matter how much he willed it to operate, no matter how much he wanted Cyril to radio him to tell him this was part of some big joke, the radio remained silent.

Kareem waited nearby, not saying a thing.

Looking back up at the mountain, in the general direction of where he'd thought Cyril to be, Malcolm thumbed the transmit button once more. "I'm sorry, bro. We have to go." Then he turned the radio off, stored it in his coat pocket, and started walking again, away from Cyril.

Malcolm was empty inside, and that emptiness was what convinced him of Cyril's death more than anything did. As long as Cyril had been alive, he'd always felt him. There was no feeling now. He went forward because he knew there was no going back.

Monique stood on the shattered remnants of the rocky splinter, swaying in the cold wind that whipped against the cliff face. She refused to admit that there wasn't a way out of her situation. The thought of staying there till she died of hypothermia, altitude edema, dehydration, or starvation scared her. She knew she'd rather jump from the cliff face than die a slow, agonizing death.

When the wind changed directions again, she spotted the rope Cyril had thrown down. The kernmantle dynamic line dangled only yards away.

Only yards, Monique thought bitterly. *I need it here!*

She forced herself to breathe deeply and become calm. Staying on the cliff face like a scared little girl wasn't a viable option.

Long minutes passed before she spotted the small crack in the wall. There wasn't a foothold or a toehold within reach, but the crack held promise. She took a small cam from her belt, judging it to be about the right size to fit into the crack.

Balancing herself against the cliff wall, Monique stretched as far as she could toward the crack. Her calf muscles burned from the strain as she stretched toward the crack. Stubbornly, the crack remained just out of reach.

Is it deep enough to hold a cam? she wondered. From her angle she couldn't tell. She held the cam in her fist, thumb ready to trigger the spring-loaded action so it would lock and hold.

Finally, she had to give up. Her back and legs shook from the maintained effort. She flattened herself against the cliff wall, trying to rest, but the changing winds kept battering her, kept making her shift her weight so she didn't fall. Staying there wasn't restful either. Her thighs trembled, threatening collapse. She knew only minutes remained during which she could hold that position.

She took a deep breath, focusing herself, making the fear go away. She wanted to leave K2, and she wanted to leave Skip. She wanted control of her life again, to be able to make decisions on her own. She was tired of feeling trapped and ineffective.

All you have to do is take that first step, Monique reminded herself. *And don't look down.*

Before she could lose her nerve, she leaped toward the crack in the wall, not even thinking about missing because there were absolutely zero decisions to make after that one. She had her arm stretched out, the cam locked between her fingers. She aimed deliberately—*don't miss!*—shoving the cam toward the crack—*please!*—working it into the crack—*hold! Please hold!*—and snapping the cam so the springs flexed.

Metal grated against stone. It sounded like the cam was pulling free.

Monique wanted to scream but couldn't. Her breath locked in her lungs. She fell to the end of her arm and slammed back into the cliff face, grating skin from her brow and cheek.

Her shoulder screamed in pain. Desperate, knowing she couldn't hold onto the cam for long, she turned and glanced toward the rope. It was still several feet away, waving in the wind, tantalizingly close, but not within reach.

However, a projection she hadn't been able to see earlier was now within reach. Beyond it was another projection, and below them both was a narrow ledge no more than two inches wide.

She reached for the projection and got a hand on it, but it was too uneven to grab properly. Panic gnawed at the back of her mind now, chewing quickly and sharply, stripping away the thin amount of control she maintained. She pulled herself toward the projection, then felt the cam loosen in the crack. Her hand slid from the projection, putting her full weight back on the cam. The camming device skated again, pulling loose even as she hung on it.

177

Chapter 21

Monique turned and rolled outward from the cam, spinning so her back pressed up against the cliff wall, reaching out for the projection she hadn't been able to hold earlier. Her left hand caught the projection and she supported her weight with both her arms. Thankfully, the cam stopped skating, holding her weight.

She turned slowly and stared at the kernmantle line. It was moving three feet away in the breeze, sweeping sideways along the cliff face like a rat's tail. A nylon loop hung from the line almost at eye level, offering her two or three inches' more grace.

She stretched her foot down, intending to rest it on the small ledge. But the ledge crumbled almost as soon as she put weight on it, the pieces skittering down the mountainside and into freefall. She pushed herself back up.

Her arms trembled as she faced out from the mountain. Her strength faded quickly. She concentrated on the rope, timing it. As the line started toward her again, she kicked against the cliff and pushed up with her arms, launching herself across four feet of space.

Her leap ran out of steam early, and she knew she was going to end up short. Then the nylon loop fluttered against her fingertips. She caught the loop, wrapping her fingers in it just before she fell.

Her fingers caught in the loop, and she stopped falling. Now blinding pain filled her forefinger just before she slammed into the cliff. Crying out, she looked up and saw the end of her gloved forefinger turned almost at right angles to her finger. She had no doubt that the finger underneath matched the glove.

She dangled limply from the rope, but the pain threatened to sweep her senses away.

Elliot Vaughn stood and watched as Annie Garrett emptied the pack she'd recovered. The billionaire shifted his gaze to McLaren, seeing the desperate hope in the man's eyes.

After she'd made it back across the crevasse, Annie hadn't offered to share anything that she'd found in the pack, but Vaughn didn't worry about that at the moment. She carefully took out the well-worn copy of the Koran and a few photographs.

Then she removed a box with three more dex syringes from the bottom of the pack.

Vaughn's interest was piqued when he saw the dex. He tried to hide his response, but he knew Annie saw through him. If they'd been doing business together, she never would have seen anything about him but what he wanted to show her. That was how it had been until they'd ended up in the ice cave.

Even then, Vaughn thought, *she hasn't seen everything I'm capable of. She only thinks she has.*

Annie watched him as she stripped the wrapping from one of the syringes. If he said anything now, she'd only argue.

And we're way past arguing, Vaughn told himself. He watched as she gave the dex to McLaren. *Damn waste. And both of them should know it.* He curled up with the anger inside him. The anger was hungry and fetid, like a half-

179

starved wolf with its leg in a bear trap. But he tempered it with the control he'd perfected over the years.

Stripping another syringe, Annie gave herself a dose of dex. She looked at him as if daring him to say something.

Vaughn pushed himself to his feet and took up his ax. *That was just a battle. We've yet to see who is going to win the war. And Tom, old buddy, you've become more of a liability than ever, sucking up dex like that. There's no reason to be wasting dex on you anymore.*

Vaughn surveyed the tunnel he was making. It was curving up now, and he was beginning to think the work was getting easier. One way or another, whatever it took, he was getting out of this mountain alive. He drew the ice ax back and smashed it home, driving it deep.

Peter dumped snow into the pan atop the tiny stove from the equipment pack. The snow melted slowly over the low flame, but once it did he could refill the water bottles.

Wick stood high on a steep slope, setting the first belay they were going to use to go higher. He still hadn't spoken, and Peter's attention centered on the older climber. Whatever drove Wick had to be some kind of personal demon. Peter knew all about those. But he had no idea what Wick's was. Something worried at the back of Peter's mind, but he couldn't quite get hold of it.

A soft scrape reached Peter's ears, and he turned automatically. The trail he and Wick had blazed stood out clean and fresh, so the figure that followed in their wake had no questions about which direction they'd gone.

Monique, he realized when the figure got closer. He pushed himself to his feet, feeling muscles ache all over his body, and trotted toward her. When he reached her, she was barely making it on her own, obviously in shock and in pain.

Wick looked down from his belaying station but didn't join them. If he was surprised, he didn't show it.

Monique talked as Peter guided her back to the tiny stove, telling him what had happened on Pulpit Ice Field, surprisingly unemotional. But Peter could see the hurt in her eyes. Maybe she wouldn't talk about what she felt about what had happened now, but a time would come when she would need to.

Peter noticed the way she favored her hand. "Are you hurt?"

Monique hesitated for just a moment, then shook her head. "It'd be pretty stupid to tell you I wasn't, wouldn't it?"

"Yeah." Peter held out his hand. "Can I see it?"

There was another momentary hesitation, then Monique stuck her hand out. "My finger's dislocated."

Gently Peter slipped off her glove. Judging from the difficulty he had in removing it, the dislocation was a bad one.

Monique groaned and bit her lip.

When he had the glove off, he saw the forefinger was dislocated at the knuckle. *At least it didn't tear off,* he told himself, *but it must hurt like hell.*

"You've got to straighten it," Monique said.

Peter felt her hand trembling in his. He nodded and examined the rest of her hand, the joints and tendons, making sure there wasn't any other damage he might make worse by trying to help. She had bloody scratches all over her face as well.

Monique waited nervously.

"It's going to be all right," Peter said. "Just look at me." He held her hand and looked in her eyes.

"Don't lie to me, Peter," Monique said. "I'm a nurse."

He shrugged. "Where were you going?"

She stared at him, confused. "What are you talking about? Just get on with it."

"You took the money," Peter accused, "to get out of here. Where were you going?"

She held his eyes, curious now. "Anywhere."

"Tell me!" Peter demanded, striving to make her angry or defensive or anything that wouldn't let her think about what he was going to have to do to straighten her finger.

Monique almost lost it, then she smiled.

Smart, Peter thought, but he hadn't given up on distracting her.

"Paris," Monique answered. "I did two years of pre-med. I wanted to finish it."

"Any career worth this?"

"Two years on Everest. Three years going broke at K2. I hate it. Skip makes the Pakistanis look well organized. Into the bargain, he's a sexist—"

Peter interrupted her, ready to make his move. "And how long were you together?"

Shock showed on her face, but she was angry enough to answer. "Two years. Not that it's any of your business."

Peter twisted her finger back into place, not hesitating. Speed and force were the only mercies he had to give her at the moment. He felt the end of her finger slide back into place.

Monique screamed but only once. Then she leaned into him, and he held her as she gasped in pain. He soothed her as much as he was able, feeling her shake in his embrace, but he watched Wick high up on the slope still working single-mindedly on the belay.

Malcolm swung the ice ax hard, smashing his way up the steep slope, trying to burn out the sense of loss and hurt and betrayal that filled him. Cyril should have climbed with him. Wick was wrong about that. If Cyril and he had climbed together, Cyril would be alive now.

Angrily, Malcolm lifted the ax and brought it down again, testing the crust and ground in front of him, not wanting to step into a crust-covered crevasse, but not caring too much if he did, either. Breaking through the crust was hard work that left him winded and weary. They were almost at twenty-five thousand now, and the air was getting seriously thin.

Kareem walked ahead of him as if he could walk forever.

Suddenly, without warning, the pain inside Malcolm got to be too much. He and Cyril had come on the rescue effort as much as for a lark as for rescuing the climbers trapped up there. The million dollars they'd been promised together wasn't even real.

Climbing the mountain had been just a lark—just for laughs and for stories to tell the women who showed up at base camp.

Only now Cyril was dead, and there was no one to laugh with and no one to fight over the women with.

It was too much.

Malcolm dropped to his knees and fell to his hands in the snow. Tears blurred his vision, and he knew Cyril would have made fun of him for crying.

Kareem took Malcolm's arm, startling him. Malcolm kept his face turned away from the other man. He gripped Kareem's hand when it was offered.

"I think you should go back," Kareem suggested gently.

Malcolm nodded as if he agreed.

Kareem released his hand and went forward again, following the trail he'd already broken.

Watching Kareem for only a moment, Malcolm shoved himself to his feet. He stood for just a moment, then took off after Kareem.

You can't leave this undone, mate, he told himself gruffly. *No matter how much this hurts. This was the last thing you and Cyril were gonna do together, and it's bloody well gonna get done.* He stumbled after Kareem, watching the sun come out of the clouds ahead of them.

Colonel Salim sat at his desk in his office and checked the clock on the office wall. It was almost three o'clock, almost time to fire the 80mm guns again. He stood up, automatically adjusted the polo mallet on the wall behind him, and glanced at the pictures of his family, whom he hadn't seen in months. It was too harsh to bring any of them up into the mountains even for short visits. He was thankful he would be getting another break in a few weeks—unless the Indians foolishly decided to attack.

He walked around the desk and took a cup of tea from the service his orderly had brought in earlier. Now that it had cooled properly, he could enjoy it.

He took the tea with him to the window and stood staring across the compound. The artillery crews were already in position, which was good because they knew he appreciated—and checked for—punctuality. Maybe Siachen Glacier wasn't a desirable posting, but it was his, and while it was his it would run like a Swiss clock.

He gazed up at K2 briefly, wondering how Peter Garrett was faring. So far the news Rasul had transmitted back from K2 base camp had not been promising. They'd already lost at least one canister and probably the team that was carrying it.

The explosion had even reached the outpost, echoing in the mountains for a short time.

Thinking about the nitro brought his attention to the bunker where the engineering corps had stored the explosive. The nitro was abominable stuff, and he was glad to be rid of it. As he watched, the sun broke through the clouds, racing across the outpost, covering the bunker and coming straight for his—

Ka-boom!

Before the colonel even had time to register the explosion, he was thrown across the room. He rolled across his desk and smashed up against the wall behind. The superheated air filled the office through the huge hole in the wall where he'd been standing.

It was a wonder he hadn't been killed outright, but the wall had been strong enough to resist most of the destructive force.

Colonel Salim got to his feet with difficulty, feeling dazed. He was bleeding from a dozen different cuts, but none of them appeared to be life threatening. He walked to the damaged wall as his aide burst through the door. The colonel waved at the man to stay back.

At the huge hole, Colonel Salim stared at the outpost.

The artillery hadn't fired. But there was now a huge crater where the bunker that had housed the nitro had been. He turned to his aide.

"Get Major Rasul for me," the colonel ordered. "Hurry!" It appeared that Peter Garrett and his rescue party were carrying the seeds of their own destruction.

Skip Taylor bolted from the Vaughn command center, racing for the helipad. Rasul was in the pilot's seat, talking rapidly in Urdu. When he saw Skip, the major ripped his headset off and handed it over. "Colonel Salim."

Skip took the headset and pulled it on. "Skip Taylor."

"Bad news, I'm afraid," the colonel said. "The nitro your young friend is carrying appears to be even more dangerous than he believes. In the opinion of my munitions officer, the nitro has gotten even more unstable as it has aged, and is now reactive with sunlight."

Skip shook his head, trying to make sense of the information. "What are you saying, Colonel?"

"If those canisters are exposed to sunlight for any length of time, so that they warm up quickly, they're going to explode."

Skip changed the frequency immediately, cutting the colonel off. Peter and Wick had the only radio that was kept on at all times. The big Australian thumbed the transmit button. "Peter! Wick!"

"I'm here, Skip," Peter called back almost immediately, then he was lost in a blast of static.

"Come in, Peter!" Skip bellowed, stepping from the helicopter and looking up the mountain. "Peter! The nitro reacts to sunlight! Come in! The nitro—"

185

Chapter 22

K2, Lower Ice Field, 24,300 feet

Peter dropped the radio and sprinted toward Wick, who was nearly fifty feet in front of Monique and him. Monique had heard Skip's message as well and ran through the snow with him, but his longer stride put her behind. Pain ripped through Peter as he ran, and the altitude made his breath harsh and ragged.

When the sunlight had stabbed down over them only seconds ago, he'd been grateful, thinking it was an omen or a blessing. Now he was terrified of it. He ran harder, finally getting his arms and legs working together, driving his boots hard through the deep snow so he could lift his knees clear of the waist-high snow.

"Get the pack!" he shouted to Wick. "Get it out of the sun! It's gonna blow!"

Wick turned slowly, the nitro pack on his back. Clearly, he hadn't heard.

"The pack, Wick!" Peter shouted. "The sun!"

Realization that something was wrong with the pack galvanized Wick into motion. He shucked it off his back and looked at it.

Even at the distance, Peter could see that the top of the canister glowed bright white. *How much time do we have?*

Annie— If anything happened to him, who would be there for Annie?

Coming abreast of Wick, Peter dove and scooped up a double handful of snow, heaving it onto the canister's glowing white top. The snow hissed as it melted. Then he and Wick each grabbed a side and started walking very quickly toward a narrow gully no more than thirty feet away. If either one of them tripped— Peter didn't finish the thought.

Peter told Wick Skip's message as he frantically dug in the snow and tried to cool the canister down. Wick joined him immediately, and soon they had the canister covered. Both of them watched it, then noticed when the canister top started to resume its original coloration.

Monique joined them at a run, the radio close to her mouth. "Emergency, Malcolm! Come in, Malcolm!"

Peter looked up at her, but only static came from the radio. "It's not their call time!" Wick had set up the staggered call times for the other two teams to conserve batteries.

"Respond, Malcolm," Monique continued, "please! Come in! Come in, Malcolm!"

Peter glanced at Wick. "You take the shoulder! I'll try the ridge!" He held his hand out for the radio and Monique passed it over. Then he turned and ran, noticing that Wick had already gone.

Peter free climbed the huge ice block that led up to the Shoulder, hoping that his field of view would be as wide as he believed. Monique came after him, climbing quickly although slowed by her injured finger.

Breath burning the back of his throat in ragged gasps, Peter pulled himself onto the ice block. He pushed himself to his feet and raced onto the snowfield covering the Shoulder, scanning the horizon quickly. The sunlight seemed to be everywhere now.

Then, in the distance, Peter spotted Malcolm and Kareem. He cupped his hands around his mouth, hoping his voice would carry over the distance. *"Kareem!"*

They were walking in full sunlight.

Peter saw the pack was in the sunlight as well. He shouted again, and Monique joined in. Just when he had almost given up, Kareem stopped and looked in their direction. Peter waved the radio.

Kareem reached into his pocket and took his radio out.

Peter saw Kareem speak into the radio, but all he heard was a burst of static. He thumbed his own transmit button. "The sun! Get the pack out of the sun!" He kept repeating himself, willing the communication frequency to work.

"Repeat, please," Kareem called, and the words were plain.

Frustrated but hopeful, Peter tried his message again. "Get the pack out of the sun! It's going to explode!"

Peter's message came through clearly at last, but it wasn't anything like what Malcolm was expecting. Kareem was already running for the shade of a nearby snow tower when what Peter had said finally clicked.

He cursed, sprinting after Kareem, catching up quickly. In the shade now, both of them heaved snow onto the canister.

Malcolm saw the glowing white top of the canister as he heaped snow and ice onto it. The canister rested on an incline only a few feet into the shade. He hoped it was enough.

"I think we've stopped it," Kareem gasped, placing his hand on his knees and trying to breathe deeply.

"Good," Malcolm wheezed, "because I've about had it, mate." He rested on his knees for a moment, then got up and staggered away. He took his water bottle from his belt and uncapped it, then noticed that Kareem stood right behind him. Instead of drinking first, Malcolm handed the water bottle over. Maybe Kareem wasn't Cyril, but the man had stuck by him, and that meant a lot.

Kareem took the water bottle appreciatively and drank deeply. Then he passed it back.

Malcolm took the bottle and drank. Out of the corner of his eye, he noticed the liquid spill. The liquid was greenish yellow, moving sluggishly across the snow and ice, but stretching forth a dozen fingers toward the sunlight.

A warning started to form on Malcolm's lips as the first of the fingers reached from the shadow and stabbed into the bright sunlight. The liquid glittered, then the world disappeared in a fiery rush.

Heart still hammering from the near miss, Monique sat on the frozen ground next to the last nitro pack. She pulled out her tobacco tin and papers. Rolling a smoke with a bum finger was hard, but she was determined to make do.

Then a wall of incredible force hit her, ripping the paper from her fingertips and knocking her over. She glanced around frantically as the sound of the explosion filled the air.

Peter! she remembered as she went down. She glanced up at the ice block they'd climbed. Peter had waited up there for just a moment before starting down. As she glanced up, she saw him propelled over the side of the ice block and drop out of sight.

Snow and rock debris from the blast site came crashing down out of the air, dangerously close to the nitro canister only a few feet away.

Monique dove for the canister.

Disoriented from the blast, Peter landed hard but in deep snow. The impact drove the wind from his lungs, but he didn't think anything had been broken. Then he realized that Malcolm and Kareem had been at ground zero of the blast. He wanted to scream, and if there'd been any air in his lungs, he might have.

Rocks and ice chunks rained from the sky, thudding painfully into his body. Knowing he was going to be a patchwork of bruises in the morning, he glanced around and spotted a nearby rocky overhang that offered some protection. He crawled for it quickly, throwing himself forward, sliding across the snow like a seal.

Then he remembered the nitro pack he and Wick had left unprotected.

Skip Taylor watched the white mushroom of exploding snow erupt from K2, kicking up high into the sunny sky. He cursed vehemently, thinking about all the climbers up on the mountain now and trying not to feel guilty that he wasn't among them.

One explosion, not two, he told himself silently. That had to mean something. There still had to be a chance that they weren't all dead.

Then the sound of the explosion finally reached them, drumming over base camp like hoofbeats.

As soon as the mountain shook a second time, Elliot Vaughn stopped digging and dropped to the ground, realizing there had been another explosion. *Only one explosive left,* he thought desperately as he covered his head with his arms. Annie dropped to the ground beside him.

Icicles broke from the cavern roof and shattered across the ledge. A few of them hit him. The ones that missed vanished into the darkness of the crevasse. The echoes of the detonation lasted longer this time, stronger.

They were closer, Vaughn realized, uncovering his head and looking up.

"Please, God," Annie whispered beside him, "no."

Vaughn shook his head. Peter Garrett had come onto this mountain because he was worried about his sister; now she was worried about him because he was there. He thought she'd have been better off worrying that the one team that must have been left continued to be more efficient at carrying their explosives than the two that had been scratched.

A coughing spasm suddenly welled up in Vaughn's lungs. He put a hand to his mouth to cover it, feeling as though his head would explode. His lungs felt like water balloons now, and he didn't think it was just the thin air anymore.

Slowly and out of Annie's sight, Vaughn opened his hand and studied the blood-mist pattern that had formed on his palm. He wiped it off in the snow, then mixed it in so it couldn't be seen.

He glanced at Annie and McLaren, who were still watching the ceiling with concern. *Okay, folks,* he thought coldly. *The democracy is over. From here on out, things are going to be done my way. And sacrifices are going to be made.*

Wrapping her arms around the nitro canister, Monique held it tight and prayed that nothing would hit it hard enough to set the explosive off. Rocks and ice chunks hammered against her, promising lots of bruises later. But nothing touched the nitro canister.

Okay, she told herself. *It's okay. You can get up now.*

But she stayed hunkered down over the nitro canister for a slow count to twenty. When she looked up, she saw that the blast had broken a lot of serac free from the surrounding terrain. It almost looked as though the explosion had shaped another land.

Then she noticed the dead woman in front of her.

The dead woman wore climbing clothes and rested on her knees against the back wall of a shallow cave in front of Monique. She was obviously Indian and about middle-aged. Evidently a thick layer of serac had covered the cave, broken loose by the explosion that had killed Malcolm and Kareem.

Hypnotized by the sight of the dead woman and still in shock from the loss of three of the rescue party members, Monique unwound herself from the nitro canister and walked over to the dead woman. Hesitantly, thinking wildly that somehow the woman wasn't dead at all—only sleeping—Monique reached for her.

"Don't touch her," a harsh, grating voice growled.

Startled, Monique turned and saw Wick behind her.

Wick stood there for only a moment, then he crossed over to the dead woman and knelt beside her. His own face looked frozen as he reached for the corpse, taking her gently into his arms.

That's his wife! Monique realized suddenly. She'd heard the stories about Montgomery Wick and his missing wife from Skip and many others at base camp. She just hadn't put everything together. Now it made sense why Wick had changed his mind so suddenly about being part of the rescue effort after he'd found out Vaughn was one of the trapped climbers.

Wick sat and looked at the dead woman for a long time. Then, tenderly, he opened the collar of her parka, breaking free the ice layer that covered it, and lifted the gold chain from around the woman's neck. He unfastened the chain, revealing the ring hanging from it.

It's her wedding band. She didn't wear it while she was climbing. Monique watched quietly out of respect.

Wick put the chain and ring inside his coat pocket, then turned his attention back to the dead woman. He went through her clothing carefully, searching for something, but Monique had no clue what it might be.

Footsteps crunched on the snow. Monique looked up and saw Peter standing there, his eyes boring into Wick's back. He looked disheveled from the explosion and held a box in his hand.

"Is this what you're looking for?" Peter asked.

Chapter 23

K2, Lower Ice Field, 24,300 feet

Montgomery Wick turned, his anger and pain almost getting the better of him when he heard the challenging note in Peter Garrett's hoarse voice. He looked at the young man, noticing Myama's dex box in his hand. There was no question in Wick's mind that the dex box belonged to Myama. She'd made it herself because she didn't want to trust the syringes to just any container.

"Where did you get that?" Wick asked, striding over to Peter. He snatched the box from the younger climber's hand and opened it to reveal the emptiness inside.

"In a cave only forty or fifty yards from here," Peter answered. His blue eyes held Wick's. "Four years ago an American team got blown off the mountain. Your wife was the guide."

Wick could see that Peter had already pieced events together. But it was none of his business. It was between Wick and Vaughn. Wick looked back at Myama, remembering all the good times they'd shared, the quiet moments they'd had, and the few plans they'd made for their future.

"What happened?" Peter went on. "Did she take shelter with Vaughn?"

Leave it alone, Wick thought, not looking back at him. *Just leave it the hell alone and let me handle this. It's been a long time in coming.* Tenderly he stored Myama's box in his pack.

"Twenty-four, thirty-six hours," Peter went on. "I figure she died of edema. That wouldn't have happened if she'd had dex with her."

Wick swallowed his anger, staying focused. Peter Garrett wasn't the enemy.

"What did Vaughn do, Wick?" Peter asked. "Use the dex for himself? Is that what you think?"

Wick brushed past Peter. There were a number of things he had to do. He wasn't about to leave Myama here any longer.

"Answer me, dammit!" Peter shouted. "Is it?"

Wick couldn't hold back his anger anymore. The writing was on the wall, and Peter couldn't see it. Wick turned suddenly. "Of course he did!"

Peter held his gaze, then spoke in a gentler voice. "How long have you known?"

"I've always known. They interviewed Vaughn after he came down from the mountain. He said the dex got swept away. That was a lie. She always carried it on her."

"You let it go four years, Wick?" Peter asked in disbelief.

"The mountain owned Vaughn," Wick replied, not certain if Peter would understand that concept. "I knew he would come back."

"And now you're going to kill him."

"My wife died of—" Wick's voice broke, and he hated the weakness in him. "My wife. Do you know what edema does to your body?" He continued on, wanting Peter to hear it, wanting to get it out. All those years he'd held it in and now he didn't have to anymore. "Your lungs fill with water. It strips the skin from your throat. You drown in your own bodily fluids."

Peter shook his head slowly. "I can't let you do it, Wick."

Wick eyed the younger man harshly. "Do you know where we are, Mr. Garrett? Above twenty-four thousand, you're at the vertical limit. You're already dying." He pointed to Peter. "Look at you. You can barely stand, put one foot in front of the other. You think you can rescue your sister without me, go right ahead."

Peter didn't have anything to say to that.

Without another word, Wick turned and walked away.

Peter lay in his sleeping bag inside his small tent. It wasn't much warmer inside the tent than it was outside, but at least the nylon walls knocked off the wind.

Despite how badly he'd wanted to press on, there was no way to do it through the night. Their helmet lamps would have given out quickly, and the mountain terrain would have been too difficult to see. The only choice they'd had in the end was to get up at dawn.

They'd lined up the three tents close to a gully to take advantage of some of the natural shielding. None of them were talking, and probably, Peter felt, none of them were resting.

Monique had gone quietly to her tent, and Wick had set about burying his wife. Peter had offered to help, but Wick had declined forcefully enough that he didn't consider asking again.

The older climber labored out in the wind. He chanted as he worked, and though Peter didn't understand the words being said, he felt the pain of loss resonate in them.

"Om tare tuttare ture svaha," Wick chanted over and over.

Peter didn't know how long the digging and the chanting had gone on. He lay on his back restlessly, his mind full of the losses of that day, and of Utah. Wick's words had made him feel somewhat better, but Annie didn't think the same way as their father and Wick. And without Annie's support, Peter didn't think he'd get around what had happened.

He wished he could talk to Annie, and tried not to think that it might be for only one last time.

Wick worked hard in the frozen ground, scooping out a shallow grave with a trenching tool from his pack. He continued chanting.

"Om tare tuttare ture svaha." It was the Green Tara Mantra, the Deliverance Mother. She was born from the left eye of Avalokitesvara and from his compassionate tears. She had the ability to fulfill dreams and lead thinking persons across the sea of samsara.

Once the grave was deep enough, Wick picked up his wife's body. He'd covered her in a blanket because it was all he had. He knew Myama wouldn't mind. She'd never been one to complain about hardship.

Wick couldn't help wondering, though, how she'd felt when she found out Vaughn had taken all her dex and condemned her to a harsh death. Still, knowing her as he had, Wick was certain she'd embraced her faith and died with dignity.

Tenderly he laid her body in the grave, then began covering her.

"Om tare tuttare ture svaha," he chanted. But he told himself, *Tomorrow, Elliot Vaughn. We'll see each other tomorrow.*

Annie sat up with her back against a wall of the ice cave. She couldn't sleep. Her lungs were filled with fluid, and she was coughing all the time now. Every coughing spasm made her chest feel as though it was in a vise and over-filled at the same time. Blood came up with every forcible expulsion of breath now.

McLaren lay nearby so she could keep an eye on him. She didn't trust Vaughn around him, and she wanted to be close to him in case he needed her. McLaren was on his back, face coated with a fever-induced sheen of perspiration.

Vaughn slept on the other side of the ice cave. He stirred a little but didn't wake.

Feeling warm liquid at her mouth after a coughing spasm, Annie wiped at her lips. The gauze came away crimson with her blood. She was scared, more scared than she'd ever been anywhere except Utah.

But she knew what she had to do. It was the only thing that made sense. She picked up the radio at her side and thumbed the transmit button. She'd spoken briefly with Peter earlier while Wick and Monique had been around. McLaren and Vaughn had been awake as well. They hadn't gotten to talk by themselves, and there were still things that needed saying.

She knew he would be awake wherever they were camped and listening to the radio in case she needed him.

"Peter. Come in, Peter."

Wide awake and heart hammering now, Peter reached for the radio. "Annie? Annie, what's wrong?"

"Where are you?" she asked.

"Five hours away," Peter promised. *Come dawn, we're only five hours away. I promise.* A moment passed, and he thought he'd lost the connection.

"Go back, Peter," she said hoarsely.

Peter swallowed hard. He'd never heard Annie beaten before. She hadn't sounded this bad even after Utah. Losing their father had hurt her, but it hadn't broken her. She'd seemed to become stronger because of it. "Annie—"

"Don't risk it," she insisted. "There's no point. We won't be here. At least Tom and I won't."

"What have you got left?"

"An hour, two at the most."

Peter fell silent, hurting badly.

Annie listened to her brother's silence and knew that he was feeling lost. Maybe she was wrong about the hour or two they had left, but she needed Peter to believe that. Anything to turn him back before he got himself killed.

"Peter?" she asked, her voice cracking, thinking maybe she'd lost him. "Peter?"

"I'm here, Annie."

She took a deep, shuddering breath. "I've been thinking." She laughed a little then because it was obvious that was all she had to do while waiting to be rescued.

197

"There's not much else to do here. I've been thinking about Dad."

In his tent, Peter couldn't reply. Every time their father came up in their conversations, they ended in arguments. He listened to his sister's ragged breathing, telling himself everything was going to be all right.

"We made a mistake," Annie said, her words echoing inside the tent. "We shouldn't have had a grave for Dad. We should have brought his ashes here together."

Tears filled Peter's eyes, and he didn't trust himself to speak. That was the first time she'd talked of them as *together* in three years.

"Remember how he talked?" she went on. "This is where he was happiest. He was a climber, Peter. I think every real climber would want to stay on this mountain."

Is that what you're trying to tell me, Annie? That you want to stay here? Peter shook his head, knowing he wasn't going to let that happen.

Annie felt hot tears run down her cheeks, but she worked hard to keep an emotional quaver from her voice. "What do you think?"

"Maybe we'll come back one day," he said. "The two of us. For Royce."

Annie smiled in spite of her tears. "I would have liked that." She wished Peter would understand that she was saying good-bye the best way she knew how.

"I'm coming for you, Annie."

She heard some of his old strength in his words then, the way he'd been before Utah. She didn't want that from him now. She just wanted him to listen. "No. No." She wiped the tears from her face with a coat sleeve, feeling the chill of the nylon. "Promise me! I don't want you to die, not for nothing."

"I don't care—" Peter said.

Annie cut him off. "Don't put me through it! You understand? Coming up here now, it's for nothing!"

There was no reply.

Annie keyed the transmit button again. "Good night, Peter." She hesitated. "I love you." Then she switched the radio off, not able to talk to him anymore. The tears took her then, and she held herself in the darkness of the ice cave.

Peter sat looking at the dead radio, knowing Annie had switched hers off or was ignoring his calls. *I love you.* That wasn't forgiveness; that was something much better.

And he wasn't going to leave her there to die. He couldn't do that.

Tucked into the sleeping bag in her own tent, Monique quietly switched off the radio. Tears ran down her cheeks.

At first she'd felt guilty about listening to Annie Garrett's call to her brother. But now she was glad she had. She knew from Peter's voice what he was going to try to do, and now that she knew, she also knew that she wasn't going to let him do it alone.

Elliot Vaughn came awake in the ice cave. Only the sounds of the labored breathing from Annie, McLaren, and himself filled the area. Cautiously, he sat there a moment, wanting to make sure both of the others were in deep slumber. He coughed suddenly, bowing with the wracking explosion.

When the fit passed and neither of the other two awakened, Vaughn stood and crossed over to McLaren, where the medical kit lay on the ground. Quietly, he opened the lid and took out one of the dex syringes. He stripped the bubble pack off the syringe and gave himself the shot in the arm.

He'd used dex before with good results. Four years ago, it had been the only thing that had helped him remain healthy enough to walk off the mountain. Knowing he had the medicine in his system working for him made him feel a little better. It was purely a psychological edge, but he knew the worth of such things. A psychological edge could be used as armor or as a weapon.

Hunkered down, Vaughn gazed at McLaren, listening to him suck in one slow, bubbling breath after another. *Man, why don't you just give it up and die?* Vaughn thought. Every sucking breath made him hate McLaren just a little more.

With the shape McLaren was in, Vaughn knew the expedition leader was a lost cause. McLaren was just a dead man using up everyone else's clock.

He was also using up everyone else's dex.

Vaughn had no doubt that Annie would wake in the morning or slightly before and give another dose of dex to McLaren. It would be further wasted effort and take away from the supplies Vaughn needed to live.

McLaren was a liability, and the only thing keeping Annie Garrett from being a liability as well was the fact that her brother was still out there. If she was dead, or her brother suspected she was dead because she couldn't talk on the radio anymore, Peter Garrett might well turn around and head back to base camp. After all, Vaughn smiled coldly, he was the reason his sister was in danger. Probably wasn't any love lost there.

And Montgomery Wick? Well, Wick might crawl to the top of the mountain just to watch Vaughn die. No, the billionaire decided, there were just entirely too many problems with the situation at the moment to make it a good deal.

Vaughn lifted the empty syringe, barely able to see it in the early morning light starting to filter in through the cavern roof. He pulled the plunger back, filling the syringe with air.

Moving quickly, he crouched over McLaren and clapped a hand over the man's mouth, shutting off the painful sucking noise of his breathing.

Chapter 24

K2, Ice Cave, 26,000 feet

To Vaughn's surprise, McLaren still had some fight in him.

Vaughn leaned forward, putting most of his weight on the arm holding McLaren's mouth shut. McLaren's eyes popped open, feverish and near dead. But the man simply wouldn't give up.

Vaughn adjusted his grip on the air-filled syringe, preparing to stab it into McLaren's neck. McLaren reached up with both hands and caught Vaughn's wrist, somehow finding the strength to hold it back. The billionaire glanced over his shoulder, making sure Annie was still asleep. Vaughn was sure he could overpower one or the other, but not both.

Shifting, Vaughn brought a knee up and planted it in the center of McLaren's badly bruised ribs, feeling the shattered bones grate. McLaren tried to scream, growing steadily weaker as the lack of oxygen, the pain, and the struggle took their toll.

Gradually, Vaughn moved the air-filled syringe closer to McLaren's neck. The billionaire felt no remorse at what he was about to do, only frustration that he wasn't able to do it more quickly.

Finally he stabbed the needle deep into McLaren's neck. Vaughn pressed the plunger, shooting an air bubble into a vein. Vaughn dropped the needle and placed his hand against his victim's forehead, shoving him back, willing him to die. Once the air bubble hit McLaren's heart, the man would die of an embolism. Vaughn had heard it was painless.

That wasn't entirely true, Vaughn found out. When the air bubble entered McLaren's heart, the man jerked, almost breaking free of Vaughn's grip. His eyes flared open wide, the whites turning more bloodshot by the second. For a moment Vaughn was afraid that McLaren was going to break free, that he was going to manage one last cry for help.

Suddenly McLaren just stopped. Then he slumped to the ground like a puppet whose strings had been cut. His eyes remained open, staring up at the darkness at the top of the cavern.

Vaughn waited, keeping his hands in place on McLaren's head and mouth in case it was some kind of trick. The billionaire wasn't one to take even death at face value. He would have faked his own death under the circumstances in an effort to fool someone trying to kill him.

A minute passed by Vaughn's watch, then two. Finally, the billionaire removed his hands, ignoring the fact that they shook from his own weakness and exertion. His own breath slid out into the ice cave in gray puffs, but nothing came from McLaren.

Satisfied that the man was dead, Vaughn went back to his own sleeping bag and lay down. He was racked by a series of wet coughs, but he didn't worry about that. The dex was working in him now, and what was left of the medicine would be used to keep him alive. And possibly Annie Garrett awhile longer.

Once the coughing spasm subsided, Vaughn closed his eyes and slept only a few feet from McLaren's cooling corpse.

Montgomery Wick rose slightly before dawn, wakened by the internal clock that had served him in the military and on the mountain. He'd slept well the night before, curled up with peaceful dreams of past times with Myama instead of the nightmares that had sometimes raged in his sleep.

Peter and Monique hadn't disturbed him the night before, for which he was both thankful and surprised. Peter had a lot of grit in him, a lot of the strength and power that Wick remembered from Royce Garrett.

After putting on a pair of dry socks, Wick pulled on his climbing boots. He laced them up tight, listening for movement in either of the other two tents. Sunlight was starting to penetrate the tent. Monique and Peter would notice.

Suspicion filled Wick as he pulled on his coat and went outside. He noticed two sets of footprints already half-covered by the swirling snow. He didn't figure either set was much more than an hour or hour and a half old. The tracks the three of them had made coming to the campsite had already vanished during the night.

Wick strode over to Peter's tent and opened the flap. The tent was empty.

Wick turned and gazed at the two sets of tracks in wonder. *Well, I'll be damned.* The kid had guts. Wick had to give him that.

Peter smashed through the frozen crust of snow covering the ridge ahead of him. He was at the top of the couloir, a steep snow- and ice-covered gully that led toward the summit.

Perspiration covered him under his clothes. His muscles ached and quivered, but he forced himself to go on.

Don't give up on me, Annie, he thought desperately as he gazed out over the snow-covered terrain. He didn't know how he'd find her after he got to her last known grid location, but maybe she could direct him and Monique by radio.

He glanced back and saw Monique climbing the couloir after him. She seemed to be moving more easily than he was. Only his longer stride kept her from catching him. They'd broken camp early that morning, before the first red fingers of dawn had bloodied the sky.

Peter knew Wick would be angry when he found out they'd gone on without him. But it was better to deal with Wick's anger than allowing him to try to kill Vaughn. Peter knew he couldn't be part of that. He had already been part of one man's death.

He took his water bottle from his hip and drank, letting Monique almost catch up to him. Then he went on, smashing through the snow.

I'm coming, Annie. Just hold on.

Annie came awake groggily, her eyes bleary as she looked around in the dim light of the ice cave. She felt surprised to have made it through the night, not knowing whether to be happy or disappointed. Or perhaps even scared. *Death has to be harder to accept when you see it coming,* she thought.

Her arms and legs felt frozen. She shivered, feeling the coughing spasm flex in her lungs. Swallowing hard, feeling the dryness in the back of her throat, tasting the coppery flavor of blood on her breath, she held her breath for a moment in an effort to prevent the coughing attack.

She stubbornly held her breath till spots swam in her vision and she felt as if she was on the verge of passing out. Then she gave in to the wracking, coughing wheeze. Blood flew from her mouth now, and she didn't try to block it with her hands, heaving it instead onto the frozen ground. Her head felt as if it would explode.

Feeling washed out and weak, Annie heard Vaughn still chipping at the ice with his ax. He worked methodically, nowhere near as fast as the day before, but seemingly as tireless as a metronome.

Then she noticed Tom McLaren lying only a few feet away. He was so quiet and still. Cold dread knotting along her spine, Annie crawled over to him. *No, Tom!* she screamed inside her head. *No! I made it through! It's not fair! Peter's almost here!*

McLaren's eyes were open, staring at the ceiling. He'd gotten so cold that his eyes had frozen, glassy as marbles, beet red around the irises as if he'd had a heart attack. Spindrift covered his skin and eyes like confectionery sugar. He looked like something out of a taxidermist's shop.

Hesitantly, still needing to confirm what her eyes already told her, Annie put her fingers against the side of McLaren's neck. The flesh was hard and solid, all resiliency gone. *He's been dead for hours.* He'd passed away while she was sleeping. Guilt hit her and she crumpled over, too worn out and too dehydrated to cry.

Behind her, Vaughn's ax continued to chop into the ice. If the billionaire knew McLaren had died, he didn't care.

Something on the ground beside McLaren's body gleamed in the dim light, catching Annie's eye. Hand shaking from sickness as well as emotion, she reached for the object, shoving her fingers under McLaren's shoulder to get it. She hooked her fingers around the object and pulled it out.

The dex syringe rested in her shaking hand.

She gazed at it, knowing McLaren hadn't had the strength to get to the medical kit and wouldn't have used the dex without telling her. *But how did it get over here?* She wiped her eyes with the back of her hand to clear them. Looking more closely at McLaren's face, she saw bruising on his cheeks and splits on his lips that hadn't been there yesterday.

Annie looked back at the empty syringe, listening to Vaughn hammering faster in the background now. She studied McLaren's dead eyes, looking at the exploded veins around the irises that had turned his eyes deep red. A heart attack could cause that kind of damage, but so could an aneurysm. There was no reason for the syringe to be under McLaren—unless it had been accidentally dropped and forgotten about.

An air bubble, Annie suddenly realized, looking at the

205

way the syringe needle was bent. *Tom didn't die; he was murdered.* She turned and stared at Vaughn, feeling the hate she had for him well up inside her.

Pushing herself up while checking on Vaughn to make sure he wasn't watching her, Annie retreated to her pack. She searched through the contents quickly, finally coming up with a heavy gauge piton. She fisted it and left the pack behind as she crept up on Vaughn.

The billionaire had cut his way through the ice wall and gone past a boulder behind it. There had been a tunnel or a chasm on the other side, but now it was filled with scree. He worked diligently, looking up at the ceiling above his tunnel area. Scree had dislodged from there, leaving a hollow space.

Annie stood behind him quietly, both hands wrapped around the piton. Even sick as he was, Vaughn was bigger and stronger than she was. She knew she might have only one chance to take him down, but she wasn't about to leave herself at risk with him anymore. McLaren was dead; she'd already waited too long.

Vaughn buried the ice ax to the hilt in the scree. Before he could draw it back, Annie swung, coming straight off the shoulder the way she swung a bat in softball games.

Something must have warned Vaughn that she was there because he turned a moment before the piton hit him. The heavy gauge spike split the skin over Vaughn's cheek and thick blood ran down his jaw. He raised a hand to defend himself, but Annie hit him again before he could stop her.

Vaughn stumbled backward, lifting both hands in front of his face. "What the hell are you doing?" he screamed.

Annie didn't have the strength to answer him as well as continue her assault. She drew the piton back again, her breath rasping against the back of her throat. She found it hard to swallow the dry spittle in her mouth. She wheezed and the wind whistled from her lungs.

Vaughn sidestepped her next swing and caught her full in the face with a balled fist.

In pain and shock, Annie fell backward. She tried to get

up at once as Vaughn closed in on her. He was staggered, though, and unable to walk very fast or straight. When he reached down for her, she swung the piton backhanded like a tennis racket, catching him on the chin.

Vaughn reeled back. Head spinning, lungs burning, Annie pushed to her feet and followed him. The piton felt heavy in her hand, almost too heavy to lift again, but she did. She swung too slowly the next time. Vaughn raised an arm to block the weapon and screamed when it hit him. He slapped her with his other hand, driving her back, then hit her in the stomach.

Annie gasped as the air left her lungs. Her bloody breath sprayed Vaughn's face, making him look even more savage. Spots swam in her vision, pinwheeling and exploding as she struggled to stay on her feet. She drew the piton back again, wanting to break his skull open with it. McLaren had been defenseless.

Annie swung and missed, tripping over her own feet and falling forward. Vaughn tried to push her off him when she landed against his chest, but he lacked the strength. She fought to bring the piton up, aware that he was reaching for the ice ax embedded in the scree behind him. She pushed against him and punched him in the face with her empty hand, feeling her fist skate across the blood on his jaw.

When he yanked the ice ax from the pile of scree he'd been working at, a sudden deluge came down. It poured over them, pounding them down and pushing them apart.

Ali's corpse sifted out of the streaming scree, sliding over Annie until his dead face was only inches away from hers. Gasping for breath, Annie shoved the dead man away from her, barely controlling the panic that filled her, squinting against the harsh sunlight that—

Harsh sunlight? Transfixed, Annie glanced up at the top of the pile of scree. Maybe a ton of it had cascaded from the chasm mouth overhead, spilling across the ledge and them, most of it tumbling into the crevasse on that side of the ledge.

But there at the top of the chasm was a fist-size hole open to the outside world. Visible through that hole was a clear blue sky.

Remembering Vaughn, Annie scrabbled for the piton she'd lost when Ali's body had struck her. She curled her fingers around it, feeling only a small degree of protection.

Vaughn lay on his side, his hand over his mouth as a coughing spasm overcame him. His eyes were on the hole in the ice thirty feet overhead.

Annie pushed herself to her feet, wanting to take advantage of him while he was incapacitated. But she couldn't. It was one thing to hurt him when he was able to defend himself, when she was certain she was going to be the next one Vaughn killed, but another to attack him now.

She gazed at the hole in the ice in wonder. Peter was out there somewhere. Or he would be soon. She glanced back at Vaughn, who was looking at her with wary wolf's eyes.

208

Chapter 25

K2, Couloir, 22,400 feet

Monique fought her way up the couloir, pulling on the rope Peter had thrown down to her. He'd had to fight his way up with an ice ax in each hand. Once he'd gotten to the top, he'd taken maybe a half-dozen breaths, then waved her up.

She didn't know how Peter kept going the way he did. He was pulling all of his weight and half of hers. He kept pulling, leaning back to get all of his weight into play. His breath came out in long streams, rapidly.

When Monique finally reached the top, her whole body ached and she couldn't get enough air into her lungs. Peter swayed in the harsh wind as he worked to untie the line from his waist. She tried to untie hers as well but was hampered by her injured finger. Finally Peter had to do it for her.

When he had coiled the line, he slung it over one shoulder, then turned and headed up the mountain again.

"You should rest for five minutes," Monique gasped.

Peter shook his head, his blue eyes haunted. "Those may be five minutes Annie doesn't have."

On the verge of exhaustion, wanting to give up, Monique watched him walk away for just a moment, then fell in behind him. She leaned into the wind, trudging through the path he'd made in the snow.

Monique had never seen a man do what Peter was doing. She'd heard stories, especially in the base camps of Everest and K2, but she'd never seen it. Whether Peter saved his sister or not, Monique knew she'd never forget this as long as she lived—however long that was.

Annie cut her nylon pack into inch-wide strips, running the knife from top to bottom to get the longest strips possible. She watched Vaughn working on one of the other packs, the sharp knife glittering in his hand. He watched her, too, but one of his eyes was partially swollen shut from one of the blows she'd given him.

He doesn't trust me not to try to kill him when he turns his back, she thought, glorying in the fact that she'd put fear in his eyes. But she was just as afraid of him. She knew he was a killer, and he knew she would tell. She owed it to Tom McLaren's family to tell them how he'd really died.

Vaughn worked steadily, cutting the strips and laying them aside. Between them were a distress flare, four tent poles, a length of twine, and a plastic Ziploc bag. They were the components of the plan they'd come up with together.

Once the sunlight had lanced down into the ice cave, there had been no more fight in either of them. They couldn't depend on Peter to find them in time without marking the area for him somehow. And each couldn't do that alone. For the moment, as obscene as it seemed to Annie, they needed each other. Neither of them was at full strength.

She also knew Vaughn couldn't afford to let her live to talk. Even if McLaren's body couldn't be taken from K2 by the rescue team and used as evidence against Vaughn, her story would hurt him, maybe cripple his companies. It was possible that his lawyers and public relations people might be able to put a better spin on the events, but Annie also knew the damage would have been done.

Vaughn pushed himself forward into a kneeling position. He laid two of the flexible tent poles end to end, then overlapped them a foot and started tying them together with the nylon strips. If they were lucky, four poles lashed together in such a manner would be long enough to extend through the hole in the ice cave roof.

The question is, Annie thought as she finished cutting strips from the pack, *when will Vaughn try to kill me?* A sudden rumbling deep in her chest was the only warning she got before the wracking cough tried to shred her lungs. She doubled over with the pain and the shuddering cough, hammers banging at her temples. She coughed again and again, dripping blood onto the frozen ice in front of her. When she finished, her eyes felt inflamed and the warmth of her own blood trickled down her chin.

Vaughn watched her with bright interest but quickly looked away when she caught him looking.

I'm not going to die that easy, you bastard, she thought. *I'm going to live to see you suffer.* She turned her attention to the remaining two tent poles, lashing them together as Vaughn had.

As she finished, Vaughn experienced a coughing spasm that bent him over and left him trembling. Blood dribbled from the billionaire's mouth, joining the blood already dried and matted in his beard. He stared at her, one eye nearly swollen shut, and shook his head, letting her know he wasn't going to die.

She pushed the tent poles over to him and turned her attention to the small pan on the tiny butane stove. The fuel can beneath it was almost empty. The weak yellow flame barely touched the bottom of the pan. The snow in the pan had hardly started to melt.

Three colored marker pens they'd hoped to use for dye rested on the snow in the pan. Annie stared at them in helpless frustration. The distress flare they had was for use at night, and shooting it into the air without knowing where Peter and the rescue team were would have been stupid. They had only the one chance. She'd come up with the idea of mixing the marker pen fluid with water and making a crude dye bomb.

"Ready?" Vaughn croaked, holding up the four lashed-together tent poles. In his weakened condition he was barely able to control the pole. That was why he and Annie needed each other.

"I can't get the markers to melt," Annie replied hoarsely. "They're frozen."

"Boil the water!" Vaughn ordered irritably.

Annie pointed at the dying flame on the fuel can. "With what?"

Desperate, Vaughn held his knife tightly in one hand as he stumbled toward Annie. Annie backed away, lifting her own knife, but watched as he went past her to stand by McLaren's body.

The billionaire dropped to his knees and pulled McLaren's arm from inside the sleeping bag. The corpse's limbs were stiff. The knife gleamed as Vaughn sliced the wrist, but the blood—still warm enough to be liquid—poured out of the cut vein.

For a moment Annie thought she was going to be sick. Bile popped sour bubbles at the back of her mangled throat, burning intensely. *He'd already planned to use Tom's blood,* she realized.

Vaughn took the Ziploc bag and filled it with McLaren's blood. When he was satisfied, he dropped the dead man's arm and got up. "I need the flare."

As quickly as her trembling fingers allowed, Annie tied the twin to the ring-pull detonator on the other end of the distress flare. When she was sure it wouldn't come off, she dropped the flare into the bag of blood Vaughn carried.

He sealed the plastic bag and crossed over to the tent poles. He tried to tie the bag to the end of the lashed-together tent poles, but finally had to rest a few minutes before he could do it.

Annie watched and waited, shivering. She hid the knife she'd used in her coat pocket.

"Let's do it," Vaughn croaked.

Annie got to her feet and stumbled over to the wall adjacent to the hole above them. She climbed up the side of the wall as far as she could, managing almost half the distance before she could go no farther.

Vaughn hauled the tent poles up gradually, keeping the end with the blood bag and flare up. There was only one flare, so they'd only have one chance to get it right. Vaughn lifted the pole toward Annie. She guided the pole toward the hole, adding her strength and control to Vaughn's. She also paid out the twine attached to the flare.

"Left!" she said. "Left! More!" The blood bag skirted the edge of the hole. Then it caught on a small rocky projection above Annie. They hadn't been able to air-seal the bag due to the string attached to the flare. Blood spilled from the bag and splattered her face as she looked up. She shuddered and almost lost her hold on the wall. Then a coughing spasm cramped her lungs, demanding release. She stopped breathing for a moment till it passed.

Vaughn kept heaving the tent poles toward the hole, not succeeding in pushing it through.

"Push!" Annie ordered. "Harder! Before it breaks!"

Vaughn did push harder, and she knew he was giving it everything he had.

Blood continued to drip from the bag. Annie thought perhaps they'd already lost a quarter of the bag's contents. She guided the pole to the hole, and Vaughn finally shoved it through.

Daylight shone on the blood, turning it bright crimson.

"Hold it there," Annie said.

"Hurry it up," Vaughn gasped.

Cautiously, she took up the slack in the twine, then yanked it hard enough to detonate the flare. Trapped as it was inside the bag of blood, the flare exploded, throwing crimson in all directions around the hole.

Barely hanging onto consciousness, the cough spasm returning with a vengeance now, Annie climbed down the wall. She couldn't stand when she reached bottom, having to drop to her hands and knees and pant. She glanced across at Vaughn, who was still looking at her but was just as exhausted.

Now there was only the waiting to see who lived and who died. Hand inside pocket, Annie kept a tight grip on her knife.

Peter fought the wind with iron determination born of fear. Since they'd left the tents, he hadn't stopped anywhere to rest. He hadn't allowed himself. Time was too valuable. He felt sorry for Monique, who was still managing to keep up with him, but he was impressed with her endurance.

He leaned into the whipping winds, using his hands to crawl to the top of the rise. Once there, he stared in disbelief. According to the topographical map of the area, there shouldn't have been a chasm before him.

Monique came to stand beside him.

The chasm was thousands of feet deep from the looks of it. The bottom disappeared in the whirling maelstrom of spindrift and shifting snow. It spanned at least twenty feet, and it was too long to go around.

If the other side of the chasm had been lower than the one they were on now, Peter thought he might have had a chance of jumping across. But it was a good ten or twelve feet higher. He'd have to be a pole-vaulter to get across. Or maybe he only had to be crazy.

"I'm sorry, Peter," Monique said gently. "You tried. I've never seen anyone try so hard."

Peter shook off her words and the feeling of helplessness. Then he shook off his pack. He ignored Monique, concentrating on what he had to do. Turning, he held an ice ax in each hand and paced off fifty feet along the ridgeline, hoping that was enough distance.

Once he was there, he turned to face the chasm. He

214

sucked in air greedily, trying to charge his system with as much oxygen as he could get. He curled his fists around the hafts of the ice axes, concentrating on the other side of the chasm.

"Peter," Monique called, understanding what he was about to do, "don't do this. There's another way. We can go down, find another way around."

Not in time, Peter thought. He gripped the ice axes by the haft near the heads. Then he started sprinting, digging his crampons into the snow and ice as hard as he could, aware that one misstep too close to the chasm's edge would spell disaster. His heart pumped, and he thought only of Annie. He wasn't going to be too late; he wouldn't allow that to happen.

"Nooooo!" Monique shrieked. "Peter, nooooo!"

Then he was past her, his arms and legs moving with machinelike precision. His body was a piston, driving him forward, exploding with the last bit of energy he had. The chasm's edge was ten feet away, then five.

He gathered himself and leaped, throwing himself outward without hesitation. Make it or miss it, he'd left nothing behind when he pushed off the chasm edge. He knew he was going to be short. There was no way he wasn't going to be short. The distance was too great.

At the apex of his leap, just as he started going down, he slid his hands down the ice ax hafts and raised them together over his head. Even though he was dropping now, his forward momentum hadn't completely died. But it was going to be close.

"Peettteeeerrrrrr!" Monique yelled.

Peter bent his body backward like a bow, then exploded forward just before he hit the icy wall on the other side of the chasm. Both ice axes smashed into the frozen ice and stone, biting deeply. Peter slammed into the wall, wondering if he'd stay conscious or strong enough to grip the ice ax hafts or if the ax blades were going to stay set.

Death waited below.

But he'd cheated it. Bracing his crampons against the wall, he tugged one of the axes free and slammed it home two feet above the other one. Then he did the same with the other ax, dragging himself up to the ridge.

Long minutes later he stood on the other side of the chasm, breathing hard but feeling more alive than he had in years. Annie wasn't far away now; he could feel it.

Monique tied a line around her own ice ax, then whirled it overhead and tossed it across the chasm. Peter retrieved the ax and tied the rope around his waist. He stomped his feet down hard, digging the crampons in, then nodded at Monique.

"On belay?" she asked.

"Belay on," he responded, then took her weight as she swung across the chasm and started climbing.

Annie sat with her back to the wall opposite Vaughn. They stared at each other, panting, breaking into horrendous fits of coughing that left bloody flecks on the snow before them.

McLaren's and Ali's corpses lay between them, grim reminders of all the hate that had built up between them.

Fatigue from the exertion and the sickness dragged at Annie's eyelids, and a warm lassitude was filling her limbs. She just wanted to go to sleep. But if she did, she knew she was dead. If the edema didn't fill her lungs and drown her, she knew Vaughn would throw her into the chasm. She held the knife naked in her fist.

And they waited because they'd done all that they could do—except die.

Chapter 26

K2, the Shoulder, 26,000 feet

On the other side of the chasm, the wind and spindrift picked up again in steady flurries. Peter led the way, anxiety making him want to walk more quickly. They were on the ridge above the Shoulder now, looking down over the area where Annie had disappeared.

Peter strained his eyes, staring across the smooth snowfield. Everything looked the same, and that scared him. This was the last known grid reference Annie had given, but there was no sign of her.

Then, in the distance, he saw a smattering of red on the snow around a small hole, like a gunshot wound.

Annie! Peter thought, his throat tight and his pulse suddenly racing. He started down the ridge, the nitro pack bumping gently against his back. *Please, God, don't let me be too late.*

Annie slumped over in the ice cave. They were out of water and dex. Fluid was steadily building up in her lungs, drowning her. The back of her throat burned fiercely. She tried to keep her eyes open, and she tried to keep them on Vaughn.

So far, he'd shown no signs of getting up, or even having the strength to get up. He sat with his arms folded across his knees, his forehead resting on his arms. She knew he was conserving his strength, waiting for what he considered to be the right moment to strike.

Maybe he thinks he can kill Peter, too, Annie thought suddenly. She wanted to cry. Peter was coming into more danger than he expected.

Annie forced herself to sit up a little straighter. She had to live at least long enough to make sure Peter was safe. Vaughn noticed her movement, watching her with a predator's intensity.

Then something pinged overhead.

Glancing up at the hole in the roof of the ice cavern, Annie caught sight of a piton skittering down the wall like a runaway sled. It stopped only a few feet from her.

Head spinning, Annie reached for the piton, noticing the paper bound around it. She unfurled the paper and read the single word printed on it: "BANG!"

Carefully Peter poured the greenish yellow nitro from the canister into a hole he'd chopped in the ground not far from the one splattered with red dye.

He checked the amount in the hole, then added just a bit more. From the two explosions they'd witnessed so far, he knew the nitro was exceedingly powerful. He capped the canister and reached into his pack for one of the Type 6 detonators Colonel Salim had sent along with the nitro. Gently, he eased the detonator into the nitro and set the timer for thirty seconds.

He gazed back at the hole before starting the timer. Annie had to be in there, and she had to be alive. He glanced at the fissure again, telling himself that the place he'd chosen for the nitro was the best. If things happened as they were supposed to, the explosion would rip the ice crust off the top of the ice cave and reveal any other treacherous chasm that had been covered over.

It was amazing, Peter thought, how big the word *if* suddenly was.

He hadn't gotten to talk to Annie, either. Going close to the hole in the ice hadn't seemed like a good idea until he knew what he was dealing with. If he fell through at another spot, he'd be just as stuck as they were. He breathed a quick prayer and said a word to his father, hoping he was watching over them.

Peter tripped the detonator and the digital readout started counting down. He and Monique grabbed the sides of the nitro canister and hustled it off. If things didn't work out as well as he'd hoped, he could try again. They went as fast as they could go safely toward a circle of boulders they'd chosen to act as their bunker.

Struck by another coughing spasm, Annie hunkered down in the ice cave as far from the ice hole as she could. It was an obvious target for an explosive.

Vaughn sat beside her. She held onto her knife and told herself that Vaughn wouldn't dare attack her in a manner that wouldn't be consistent with an accident.

She really tried to believe that, but she felt his eyes on her, his hot breath across the back of her neck.

Then the sound of the explosion rang throughout the ice cave and it seemed as though the world crashed down on them.

Snow, rocks, and debris blew high into the air as Peter watched, painting a tall plume that looked terrifying. The nitro had been even worse than his expectations. Before the debris had even started to fall, he was on his feet, sprinting toward the huge open area where the small hole in the ice had once been.

As much debris as had shot into the air, Peter was certain that at least that much had dropped down. *Annie, be okay!* He stopped at the edge of the fissure that had been revealed by the explosive and fearfully peered down.

Nothing but a snow-covered and debris-strewn ledge beside a deep chasm was below.

Peter turned cold inside as he looked down. *Were they blown off?* Frantically, he started readying his gear as Monique ran up to join him.

Then a hand broke through the debris pushing up.

Not Annie! Peter thought, realizing the hand belonged to a man.

In the next moment, Elliot Vaughn climbed out. The billionaire was blood-streaked and battered, hardly resembling the man Peter had first seen a few days ago. He looked dazed, then turned and started digging through the snow and debris rapidly. He uncovered another body, this one lying facedown.

Peter recognized Annie's coat immediately. A strangled cry died in his throat, and his chest ached.

Vaughn grinned to himself as he scraped snow and ice and debris from Annie. He felt certain she was dead. There was no movement and no sign of breathing. *And I get to be remembered as a hero for trying to save her.* It was all too rich, too much of a joke.

He'd been canny and he'd been lucky in his life, and he'd take lucky any day. The only thing that had ever really beaten him was K2, and one day he'd beat it, too.

He grabbed hold of Annie and rolled her over, ready to hear the anguished shouts from her brother.

Then she opened her eyes. Her look told him everything. She was going to be too mean to die, and she was going to stand up to him. A coughing spasm shook her in his arms. She couldn't speak, but she didn't have to.

Vaughn glared back at her. *That's fine,* he thought. *It's a long way down this mountain. We'll see who makes it back this time.*

Shudders ran through the ice cave without warning, shaking icicles and debris loose. Vaughn looked around, suddenly realizing he hadn't even made it out of the ice tomb yet.

The whole area's unstable, Peter realized as he felt the ground quake beneath his feet. The explosion might have ripped the top off the ice cave, but it had evidently set off some internal problems that were tearing at the chasm below.

Farther back from the ridge, Monique drove her ice ax into the frozen ground and looped a rope around herself. She threw the belaying line to Peter. "Go," she said, setting herself. "Belay on."

Taking the rope, Peter heaved the end down to Vaughn and Annie. "Annie first."

Feeling the ledge quake and quiver beneath him, Vaughn quickly tied the rope to Annie's harness, intentionally leaving the knot a little loose. With a little luck, a terrible tragedy would occur as they hauled her up.

He stepped back and signaled Peter to start hauling. When the rope grew taut, he stood under her, helping lift her up. The farther up she was if the knot gave way, the more certain her death.

Icicles and debris continued falling into the chasm. More shivers ran through the ledge.

Peter peered down into the ice cave and hauled on the rope. Annie wasn't moving, wasn't able to help herself. She was deadweight at the end of the rope. Every foot he gained on the rope pulling hand-over-hand was passed back to Monique. She continued to belay the line.

Not wanting to bump Annie against the wall on her way up, Peter took another step closer to the ridgeline, trying to haul faster and safer, wanting to make sure she was fine. Without warning, the ridge beneath his feet crumbled.

Peter fell, plunging down a few feet before he was able to turn and lock onto the ridge with both hands and one foot. But his grip wasn't secure. The ice was hard to get traction on, and Annie's weight kept dragging him down. The rope pulled hard at him, cutting into him.

Monique struggled to hold the belay. Behind her, the ice ax moved in the frozen ground, threatening to come loose.

Peter's leg slipped, leaving him hanging onto the ridge with his hands, which were giving way quickly. He glanced over his shoulder and saw Annie swinging wildly below. Half the time she was over the chasm, and if she dropped there, Peter knew there would be no saving her.

He struggled to hang onto the edge. He pressed his toes into the wall below, looking for holds. Glancing at Monique and hoping that she could hold them long enough for him to get some kind of purchase, he saw that the belaying rope was sliding through her hands.

The rope had ripped through the glove on her injured hand and drops of blood spattered the snow between her feet. Peter knew the pain had to be incredible, but she wasn't letting go.

Then the ice ax popped up from the frozen ground. Monique was yanked from her feet, forced to take a couple of running steps toward him, dragged by Annie's weight.

A man moved behind Monique, traveling quickly. Peter recognized Wick as the older climber slammed a boot on top of the ice ax, driving it deeply into the shaking ground. Wick leaned down and caught hold of the rope, taking most of the tension.

"We'll secure her down there," Wick told Peter. "You get up here."

Winded, Peter hauled himself to the ridge and started trying to get to his feet. When he managed it, he helped Wick lower Annie safely back to the ledge.

Wick plucked the ice ax from the ground and slammed

it home again, this time deeper. He walked past Peter, making for the ridge.

"No," Peter said. "I'll go down there."

Wick shook his head, glaring over the side of the ridge with his steely gaze. "No. This is something I've got to do."

"Wick," Peter called. "I can't let you hurt him."

Wick made no reply. He picked up the rope that was still tied to Annie and rappeled down.

Staggering slightly from fatigue and overexertion, Peter peered down into the cave. One of the walls had shattered completely, opening even wider the chasm beside the ledge Annie was on. The trembling didn't feel as if it was going to stop any time soon.

Wick slid down the rope to the ledge where Annie Garrett stood against the wall and landed gently. He ignored the vibrations and shifts taking place underfoot and walked right up to Vaughn. Wick's anger and pain burned deep inside of him. Images of Myama and snatches of conversation kept running through his mind.

Elliot Vaughn had taken all of that away.

Wick watched as Vaughn reached behind him. Vaughn pulled out an ice ax and swung it with all his strength and all the speed he had.

Moving easily, more than a match for the sick billionaire, Wick caught Vaughn's wrist, stopping the ax. He pushed Vaughn back across the shaking ledge, aware of Peter's and the women's eyes on him. Wick liked the young man, not enough to care what Peter thought of him, but enough that he didn't want to add to his confused guilt.

Vaughn tried to fight Wick, but the older man pushed Vaughn backward, out over the precipice, past his balance point, until the only thing preventing the billionaire from taking the long fall was Wick himself.

Still holding onto Vaughn's arm, Wick popped the billionaire in the nose with his elbow, then twisted the wrist he had hold of. The ice ax slipped from Vaughn's fingers as he yelled in pain and fear.

Wick held Vaughn there, letting him feel what it was like to be powerless to prevent his own death, to look at it and see it coming. Then Wick moved quickly, snapping a carabiner to Vaughn's safety harness and pulling him back from the ledge.

Maybe Vaughn had taken Myama away from him, Wick decided, but he couldn't let the man take the legacy she'd left him as well. Knowing Myama had remade Wick and filled all the hollow spots in his life. He couldn't—wouldn't—desecrate that.

Wick ran the belay line from Annie's harness to his, then tied Vaughn on.

Backed by two ice axes working the belay line, Peter stood with Monique at the ridge above the ice cave. Another tremor broke more ice and snow free inside the cave as well as around them, making him feel more anxious. The chasm at the bottom of the ice cave was like a hungry maw, swallowing everything around it.

Wick stood halfway up the wall, acting as an additional belay as they lifted Annie from the ledge. He guided her, keeping her from bumping her head against the wall.

Another tremor struck, and this time part of the wall next to Wick sheared off, dropping into the chasm.

"Pull," Peter said to Monique. His breath rasped in his throat, and his arm, chest, and shoulder muscles burned from the strain of lifting Annie. At least Wick and Vaughn would be able to help themselves somewhat.

He gazed at Annie's pale face, noting the blood and the fevered eyes. *God, what if I've gotten here just in time to be too late?* He didn't want to think about that, but the possibility kept crossing his mind. He hauled harder on the rope, pushing his arms out far so she wouldn't get grated against the cliff.

Peter smiled encouragingly at her, wishing he had something to say.

Below, Wick stayed on the wall and Vaughn paced restlessly along the ledge. Pieces of it had broken off now, so that it was less than half its original size.

As Annie's head came level with the ridge and Peter got ready to grab her, an electrifying crack sounded from below. He looked down just in time to see the entire ledge beneath Vaughn crumble away.

Vaughn fell—and when his safety line yanked taut, he peeled Wick off the wall as if he was nothing.

Terrified, Peter watched as the safety line between Wick and Annie snapped tight, too. Then she was gone, yanked almost from his arms and suddenly falling back toward the chasm.

"Belay!" Peter screamed at Monique, setting himself for the shot. When it came, he thought his arms were going to be ripped from their sockets. He was aware of Monique at his side, straining as much as he was. Somehow, they held.

Pulled partly over the ridge, Peter glanced down, seeing that Annie hadn't fallen far. She was still within arm's reach, but she dangled over the chasm with Wick and Vaughn.

Peter looked at her, feeling gravity pull her away from him, not knowing if he and Monique could hold three people, much less draw them back to any kind of safety. He wanted to scream out his frustration. He'd been so close to saving Annie.

The rope popped at her waist, then he spotted the knot unraveling. If she fell, she would take Wick and Vaughn with her. Only her line clipped her to Monique and Peter.

Moving quickly, Peter released the rope with one hand, maintaining his grip on the belay line with Monique. "Give me your hand!" Peter yelled. "The knot's coming loose!"

Annie glanced down, watching the knot untie itself.

"Give me your hand!" he bellowed again, reaching for it.

After only a moment, Annie reached for him. He grasped her hand just as the rope separated from her harness.

Peter felt the increased strain of supporting three people pull all along his arms and shoulders. He didn't know how he was going to get them all back up. His boots slid despite the crampons, leaving deep scars in the frozen ground.

Monique slipped as well, coming closer to the ridgeline. Suddenly, the two ice axes pulled out of the ground.

Peter dropped to the ground, lying on his chest, his hand tight around his sister's. She had no strength to help him. He struggled to hang on, then noticed her lips moving.

"Let go," she said.

"No!" Peter yelled, tightening his grip on her hand. She wasn't going to be lost to him—not now. He held tight, his whole body shaking, feeling the mountain still shifting beneath him enough to send debris falling into the chasm. There had to be a way to save this, to save them.

He glanced down and caught Wick's eye. Farther down in the chasm, Vaughn was screaming, wanting help, wanting up. But Wick's dark eyes were cool and calm, accepting. He reached into his pocket and took out his clasp knife.

"Nooo!" Vaughn screamed.

Peter tried to dig in, tried to hold the line, but he knew he couldn't. He was going to fail. He kept his eyes on Wick's, hypnotized by the calmness there. He knew what Wick was thinking: Better three should live than five should die.

Then, while Vaughn was still screaming, threatening, and pleading, Wick grabbed the line above his head. He looked up at Peter, chanting, "Om mani padme hum." The clasp knife flashed once and the rope was severed.

Vaughn and Wick dropped at once. Vaughn screamed all the way down, but Wick never made a sound.

Freed of the extra weight, Peter was able to cling to the wall better. He watched Monique fall backward, digging her crampons into the ground and pulling, gaining only inches at first, then feet.

Still holding onto Annie's hand with his own, Peter found handholds and toeholds that he used to push himself up the wall. He got to his knees on the ridgeline, bringing Annie up with him.

Tears were in her eyes now, as well as a look of disbelief. She was barely able to stand on her own when he got her to the top, but he hugged her tightly, holding her to him, unable to quit thinking how close he'd come to losing her. Not just a moment ago, but after Utah, too.

But that wouldn't happen again. There was nothing left to get between them.

that made sense. She picked up the radio at her side and

Epilogue

Base Camp, 16,700 feet

Peter stood in the doorway of Annie's hospital room at base camp. His sister lay quietly under the sheets. Medical equipment beeped and hummed beside her. They'd come down from the mountain two days ago, picked up by Skip and Rasul in the helicopter at twenty thousand plus.

On the way down from the mountain, Annie had collapsed. Somehow, Peter had found the strength to haul her down from the Death Zone into air that could support the helicopter. Annie hadn't regained consciousness in that whole time.

Peter had undergone treatment for exhaustion, hypothermia, and a light case of AMS. He'd slept a lot on a pallet near Annie's bed and in a chair out in the hallway. He kept waiting for her to wake up, trying very hard not to be afraid that she wouldn't. Or that if she did, she wouldn't be the Annie he knew.

Monique, dressed in nurse's scrubs and wearing a splint on her injured hand, finished checking Annie's vitals and turned around to find Peter standing there. She came over, smiling.

"How is she?" Peter whispered.

"Amazing," Monique admitted. "Talk about a will to live."

Peter looked into Monique's eyes, trying to figure out what he saw in them and if he should be scared of it. Before he had an answer, Monique took his hand, then leaned forward and kissed him on the cheek. She smiled and left, and he watched her go.

When he turned back around, Annie was awake and grinning at him. Then, very softly, she started to sing a song, teasing him about being in love.

She was singing! Peter's heart pumped, and he knew he had a goofy grin on his face. It had been so long since he'd heard Annie sing. Even with the hoarse raspiness lingering in her voice, it was the most wonderful thing he'd heard in three years.

He crossed over to her bed and held her hand. "That's not a song. No way that's a song. You're making it up."

Annie shook her head. "Definitely a song. A good song. A *winning* song by the sound of it."

Peter laughed and she joined him. A huge, cold knot seemed to dissolve from his chest.

Annie looked at him, suddenly serious. "That was a hell of a thing, Peter. Anybody else would have given up."

Peter shook his head, smiling. "No, not everybody."

She nodded, understanding. "He would have been proud of you." She swallowed to ease her throat. "Angry, but really proud." Her eyelids fluttered tiredly.

That was fine, Peter thought. That was just fine. "Get some sleep," he told her. He waited till her eyes closed, then turned and left the room. There was still a piece of unfinished business he'd been meaning to take care of.

Later, after Annie had drifted off to sleep and the sun had turned the western skies scarlet and gold, Peter walked over to the K2 memorial. He looked at all the plaques commemorating those who had died on K2.

Then he added those that he wanted to remember, that he thought others should remember. He'd scavenged pictures and arranged to have the plaques made. Carefully, he set them out, putting them among the others.

Ali and Kareem. Tom McLaren. Malcolm and Cyril Bench. And Peter placed a picture of Montgomery Wick next to his wife, Myama.

Gone but not forgotten, Peter thought as he looked at the pictures. *Never forgotten. Mountains may break men, but they make legends. And legends live forever.*

About the Author

Mel Odom lives in Moore, Oklahoma, with his wife and five children. In addition to such movie tie-ins as *Vertical Limit* and *Blade,* he's written novels for Buffy the Vampire Slayer, Angel, Sabrina the Teenage Witch, and Young Hercules series. He's written dozens of novels, including a recent fantasy trilogy for Wizards of the Coast called *Threat from the Sea.* His e-mail address is denimbyte@aol.com, and he welcomes e-mail.

About the Screenwriters

Producer and screenwriter Robert King has worked as a writer, producer, and director for film and television. He has written such films as *Red Corner,* the Chinese courtroom thriller starring Richard Gere; *Speechless,* the political romantic comedy starring Michael Keaton and Oscar-winner Geena Davis; and the detective comedy *Clean Slate* starring Dana Carvey.

Additionally, King has written and directed two telefilms for ABC's *Wonderful World of Disney: Principal Takes a Holiday,* starring Kevin Nealon, and *Angels in the Infield,* starring David Alan Grier and *Seinfeld*'s Patrick Warburton.

Next year King is set to direct his first feature, *The Question,* a comedy about a Hollywood executive going through a crisis of faith who moves to a mission in Mexico. He has also written *Small World,* a comedy to be directed by Jon Pasquin for Fox next year.

Screenwriter Terry Hayes has worked as a writer and producer for both film and television in the U.S. and Australia. As a screenwriter, Hayes has worked on such notable films as *The Road Warrior, Mad Max: Beyond Thunderdome,* and *Payback,* all starring Mel Gibson. Among his other credits, Hayes was the writer and producer of the feature film *Dead Calm,* starring Nicole Kidman and Sam Neill, and *Flirting,* which garnered the 1990 Australian Film Institute Best Film Award and starred Thandie Newton and Nicole Kidman.